STEALING BREATH

Joanne Brothwell

www.crescentmoonpress.com

Stealing Breath
Joanne Brothwell

ISBN: 978-1-937254-33-9
E-ISBN: 978-1-937254-34-6

Cover Art: Liliana Sanchez
Editor: Nancy S. Brandt
Layout/Typesetting: jimandzetta.com

Crescent Moon Press
1385 Highway 35
Box 269
Middletown, NJ 07748

Crescent Moon Press electronic publication/print publication: March 2012 www.crescentmoonpress.com

For Darren, Elizabeth and Alec,
for overlooking my disappearing act.

CHAPTER ONE

I awoke to rustling outside my tent. The crunching of footsteps on gravel, twigs and branches snapping. Was that a voice? I lay motionless inside my sleeping bag, heart pounding, listening.

"Help." A disembodied whisper. Was it right outside? I strained to hear but the throbbing pulse in my head drowned everything else out. I sat up. The atmosphere within the domed tent was wet, ripe with morning breath. The tip of my nose was cold as an icicle.

"Help." The murmur came a second time, more audible than the last. I was sure it was a child's voice. My heart skipped a beat. Could it be the voice of the eight year-old, Jessica Crow, who had gone missing from the neighboring Indian Reservation three days ago?

I thought of the drive out to the campgrounds when my friends, Amber, Kate, and I had been listening to the radio report on the status of the missing girl from the Wakina Reservation.

Poor Amber. Once again, she'd cried at the reminder of her third cousin, Jessica, lost and alone in the forest. Everyone in the community, including Amber, had been searching for her night and day but had found nothing. I'd practically dragged Amber along camping, telling her she needed a night off from her worries. It was a hard sell, but she'd finally agreed.

I glanced at where Kate and Amber should have been laying, but their sleeping bags and pillows were missing.

The last I'd seen them had been around the bonfire at two in the morning. They could have ended up crashing just about anywhere, and I wasn't about to go peeking into random tents to find them.

Having fallen asleep in my jeans and a long-sleeved shirt, I slipped on my jacket and shoes, pulled the ponytail holder off my wrist and wrapped my hair into a tight bun. I swallowed hard and took a deep breath. Then, unzipping the door flap of the dome tent, I stuck just my head out.

Nothing was out of place. Empty cooler bottles atop the picnic table, charred wood in the fire-pit, and the car we came in. Every campsite around us was nearly silent. The sounds of late-night make-out sessions, pounding music, and yelling were replaced by the occasional snore.

Using my empathy, I focused on trying to pick up on the emotions of any lucid person around, hoping I would hone in on Jessica's emotions. Normally, the waking feelings of others hit me like a gale force wind, without my even trying. In fact, it had always felt like a bit of a curse that I was a walking sponge for other people's pain. But right now, all I felt was...nothing.

The voice had seemed right outside the tent. Could I have imagined it?

I slipped out. A low, white fog blanketed the earth, enveloping the world in silence. The temperature hovered around freezing, way too cold for camping. And last night's vodka was no longer taking the edge off. I shivered.

After checking around the cars and circling the campsite, I started down the road. Inside the forest, the eerie glow of early morning and the cool fog blanched the world a ghostly white. The moist nip in the air sharpened the scent of pine needles that littered the camp ground. I continued down the road for about ten feet until it led to the mouth of a hiking trail.

Now that I was half-frozen and shivering, the May long weekend at the campgrounds of Greater Slave Lake, North Dakota, seemed like a very stupid idea, even if it was the annual spring kick-off party.

"Help!" the diminutive voice called out again, this time, louder.

The memory of Jessica's face flashed through my mind when I'd met her last summer; honey-brown eyes and springy hair that always stuck up around her head with static, and her sweet smile, part baby teeth intermixed with adult teeth. She was such a sweet, innocent child. If she had survived this long, she could be dangerously close to death from cold. My heart battered against my chest wall, and I fought off the urge to start running, directionless, into the bush to find her.

The voice had originated from further within the tree-line, I was sure of it. Closer now, yet still far away. I entered the trail and headed straight.

"Jessica?" I called out. No response but the echo of my own voice from the trees around me.

The trail was straight and narrow for well over a hundred feet, the trees like two solid walls of green on either side of me. Then the trail began to snake back and forth until it forked into several side-trails. I stopped to listen.

A dry crackle emerged from the trail to my right, and I immediately followed the sound. This far into the forest it was darker, the only light filtered through evergreens and fog. I looked back. The vapor had closed in behind me, obscuring the pathway like a curtain of white. Shivering transformed into shaking.

Despite running these trails in the early morning numerous times, today it looked different. I cursed under my breath and shoved my hands into my pockets.

"Hello?" I called, my voice immediately diminishing,

muffled by the woods. Other than the odd bird chirp and frog croak, the forest was quiet. If the voice really had been Jessica, she would need help and most likely immediate medical attention. I forced myself forward.

The trail wound to and fro, the brush dense, the fog almost material as it clung to the spruce needles. The path grew thin and sparse, barely enough room to place one foot in front of the other, with the way the underbrush encroached on the trail. I stumbled on twigs and logs as branches clawed my cheeks and pulled my hair. I began to trip, reaching out for something to hang onto. I fell, my hand forced into a thorny bush.

Damn it! I stood up and peered at my scraped hand, blood beading out of paper-cut sized scrapes. I'd been out here for at least ten minutes, but still, I heard nothing but the crunch of my feet snapping the twigs underfoot and my breath echoing through my own head. Ready to turn around and head back to my tent, the high-pitched voice rang out once again.

"Help."

Like a fire was lit beneath my feet, I continued to push my way through. I wanted to help her so badly, my stomach twisted at the thought of it.

I focused once again on trying to pick up on the child's feelings. Once again, I felt nothing. Why wasn't my empathy working? Normally, a child's emotions would have registered inside of me, loud and clear. Terror of being lost in the woods would have felt like a steel knife through my chest. But I felt nothing from her. Not even a twinge.

I turned back, cutting through bush diagonally to connect back to the main trail. From here, everything looked different, the landmarks off, the terrain less familiar somehow. I tried to pick up speed, but the thick brush and poor visibility prevented it.

"Help!" The voice rang out, loud and clear as day; a

child's high-pitched tenor. It was closer. Much closer. I turned again, toward the source of the sound, this time, just to my left. I'd come this far, there was no point in turning back now. I had to find her. If I could just find Jessica, I would worry about retracing my steps later. Soon, it would be lighter out and I'd have a better sense of direction anyway.

Making a mental note of landmarks at my exact location, I glanced around. Fallen tree, three rocks, huge anthill.

"Where are you?" My voice echoed off of something that remained out of sight.

"Help!" Now the disembodied voice sounded slightly to my right, just a little further into the forest once again. It made no sense. Why was she moving around like this? Or more importantly, how was she moving back and forth without me seeing her?

My body felt as tense as an over-tightened drum.

"Where are you? Say something." I waited, but when I heard no response, I continued on through the trees. "I can't help you if you don't—"

Suddenly, the trail stopped and the trees abruptly ended, opening into a clearing.

I froze.

An abandoned house, large and foreboding, loomed directly in front of me. Foliage had grown in around it, making the former yard so thick with gnarled brush and trees it was nearly impassable. Years of sun, wind and rain beating down on the wood had faded it to a dilapidated gray. Waist-high quack-grass nearly obscured the wraparound deck

The windows had been broken, most of them now gaping holes. The openings gave the house a ghostly look, like a face. The way the front of the house was configured created the appearance of a mouth shaped into a soundless, shrieking O.

~ ☾ ~

I inched toward it, blood pounding in my head. Would the girl be inside? Could she have been hiding, surviving for the past eight days?

The decking on the porch was rotten, and in several places holes had broken through. I eased my weight onto the disintegrating wood. It creaked and groaned, but held. I stepped gingerly to the door and listened.

A light rustling sound emerged from within; enough evidence for me. I pushed the door open and stepped in.

Inside, the only light came from the minimal glow of the window openings. Temporarily blinded, my eyes strained to adjust to the dark. Eventually the outline of the room came into focus, revealing chaos and destruction.

Parties had destroyed the interior. Beer bottles littered the floor, and the once elegant oak hardwood was now charred black as if there was once a fire. Graffiti covered almost every square inch of the four outer walls, the array of brilliant green, bright fuchsia and electric blue magnifying the fact that the interior walls had been kicked in and now the wooden studs were the only remaining evidence that there had been inner walls at all.

A low creak sounded overhead. I glanced at the long staircase that snaked through the middle of the room. I took a deep breath and placed my foot on the bottom step. The stairs groaned under my weight.

A high-pitched, feeble whimper resounded from above.

She's here! I took off up the staircase, two steps at a time.

The top step gave way, and my right leg slipped part-way through. I lost footing and fell forward on my elbows. Heat blasted through my arms as I clawed at the floor, fingertips raking at the splintered hardwood. My nail beds burned in pain as gel nails bent backward and broke right at the quick. I cried out.

With the weight of my torso offsetting my legs, I inched ahead, dragging my lower leg from the broken step. The wood bit at my calf as if it were a giant mouth, the teeth jagged and razor-sharp, and splinters piercing my skin.

I held my breath as edges of fragmented wood scraped from my calf to my ankle. I managed to turn over onto my back and sit up. My favorite jeans were torn near the bottom, and blood speckled the fabric like crimson polka dots. I pulled back my ripped jeans to examine the injuries. The scrape was a good two inches long, but not very deep. The blood welled from a few points where the tiny splinters were embedded; the cuts weren't very serious, considering the amount of pain they caused. I felt around in my pockets for some tissue, but there was nothing, so I opted to wipe the blood onto the sleeve of my jacket and stood up.

"Help!" The voice called again. But this time, it sounded different, with a strange tone to it. Now it was lower and more...sing-song?

"Help me..." A raspy voice hung in the air. The child-like pitch was completely gone.

I looked in every direction. My ears flooded with the pounding of my heart. Oh, God. Could I have been wrong all along? It hadn't been my imagination, I was sure of that. But who was it?

Out of the corner of my eye, I caught a movement. My breath caught in my throat.

A translucent figure, bipedal and barely human in shape, hovered directly in front of me. It began moving toward me, floating. Acid-yellow eyes glowed like a predatory cat, growing more vivid the closer it came.

Every muscle in my body screamed at me to run, but somehow, I couldn't move.

The form shimmered and undulated, like scorching

heat off pavement. It drifted toward me right through the frame of the walls. My chest tightened as a scream lodged in my throat. I backed up, moving away from this creature until I ran into a wall board. The figure closed in. I cringed, inching sideways, back toward the staircase.

A horrible energy emitted from it, making my hair stand on end the closer it got. I glanced around for a way out. The broken staircase was the only option, but before I could move, cold pulses of static began to flow over my skin, followed by tightening and pressure that tugged at my body, like being caught in an airless vacuum.

Grasping the banister, I stepped toward the stairs, my gaze fixed on this creature, and sank down, my foot wiggling wildly, trying to locate an intact board below the broken top step as the thing glided even closer.

Finally, with my right leg bent at nearly a ninety-degree angle, my toe met the resistance of a step. I placed my weight on it while holding onto the railing for dear life in case the step gave out. I inched backward down the stairs, my heart thrashing in my chest.

I focused my empathy on picking up its feelings, opening my mind to receive.

Like pond scum had just been poured into my mind and body, its feelings slithered into me. Slimy, dark, and putrid. My mouth suddenly tasted like I'd swallowed a gallon of ditch water. Dizziness swept over me and I struggled to remain upright.

It backed up a few feet, its acid eyes fixated, staring. I concentrated, focusing my mind on that ugly feeling. The creature's emotions began to tighten up inside me, like my mind alone was forcing them to be identified. Suddenly, they hit me clear as day.

Pain. Grief-stricken pain.

The creature hurled itself at me, its force knocking me

backward down the staircase. I half stumbled, half skidded down the steps with the creature hot on my back. Grasping at the railing I tried desperately to keep myself upright.

I reached the bottom, my knees almost buckling under me, my calf throbbing.

Unbelievably, it was directly in front of me, its bilious eyes mere inches from mine. I tried to scream, but my voice was cut off instantly, my vision blurring. What was happening? The thought shattered apart in my mind when my body felt like it had begun to expand, as if from the inside out.

Like every bone in my body was about to burst, a pressure formed within me, an ever-expanding force, as if I was being filled with volatile gasses. White-hot pain tore through my body as the sound of my ligaments stretching creaked through my head. I forced myself to stay lucid.

"No!" I screamed.

I focused my concentration on its emotions, its pain, and tried to hone in on it even more. They felt ragged and raw, like a festering wound.

Going on instinct alone, I pulled at those feelings, those dark, horrible feelings, and imagined forcing them back into the creature. I willed the foreign emotions out; and like holding a formless, invisible ball, I hurled them out of me.

The creature immediately began to waver, its form vacillating like it was made of tiny, shimmering waves. The pressure in my body lifted and then stopped with the sensation of a wet pop. The creature launched itself backward violently, trying to get away from me.

Elbows throbbing, calf riddled with pin-prick pains, I forced myself to step forward. The transparent body was huddled in the corner at the bottom of the staircase, flickering in and out like a strobe light. It began to

~ ☾ ~

cower, its filmy body folding in on itself as a low, guttural moan filled the house. Like an old soundless movie flickering in and out of focus, it began to shrink before my eyes.

Then it disappeared.

~ ☾ ~

CHAPTER TWO

I scrambled for the door in a half-run, half-limp, my calf silently screaming in agony as I bore weight on my leg. Heart thrashing against my breastbone, I glanced back, sputtering on the dust that floated like haze in the air.

There was nothing here, not even the slightest shred of evidence that anything had been in this house with me at all, despite the fact that two seconds ago, I was under attack. My mind whirred as I struggled to retain my grip on reality.

What was that thing? What the hell just happened? I shoved a blinding wave of panic to the back of my mind as I tried to refocus on my task at hand; to get out of here and back to the campsite.

Grasping the frame, I pulled the door open. The morning sun broke through the branches in streams of yellow light, birds singing, squirrels chirping. I burst out as fast as I could.

As I side-stepped the broken sections of the stairs, my footing slipped. I fell, landing on the spongy wood, directly on my butt and left hip.

"Ow!" I yelled.

"Hello?" A low voice called out, somewhere close. My heart seemed to jump into my throat.

I forced myself back up as a cold sweat beaded on my brow. I pressed forward, back to the trail, into the trees, and ran directly into a man.

"Hey! Are you okay?" he asked as I bounced off his chest.

~ ☾ ~

I looked up. Brow furrowed, eyes wide, the guy stood gawking down at me. His head was canted forward so that black-brown hair flopped over his forehead.

"What happened?"

At first, relief flooded my system. Finally, I wasn't alone.

Before I could say a word, my stomach heaved. I covered my mouth with my hand, but it was too late. Bending over, I threw up. Vomit splashed all over my trail tennis shoes, and from the side, I saw the man step backward to avoid the splatter. The taste of last night's peach vodka coolers ignited another round of retching.

Head spinning, I straightened up, and stumbled sideways. I grabbed hold of a branch as he simultaneously reached out to steady me.

"Hey! Are you okay?" Looking at me with eyes an electric shade of blue, he stepped forward and reached out with his other hand as I skittered backward, off balance. With his help, I righted myself before I fell again.

I stared at him. He looked to be well over six feet tall, and judging by his supple skin, he was probably around my age, maybe twenty-one. "I can't..." Panic had me tongue tied, and I continued hobbling forward, instinctively needing to put space between me and that house.

"What happened?" he asked again, following along beside me, hands flexed as if he was ready to catch me at any moment.

My legs started to wobble at the thought of those acid-yellow eyes, the way that creature had floated right through the wallboards. How could I answer his question? What could I possibly say that wouldn't sound crazy?

I took a deep breath and tried to stop shaking. "I...I hurt myself," I said. My voice warbled from trembling.

~ ☾ ~

"My foot slipped through a floor board in there." I gestured with my thumb back toward the house. "It's just a scrape."

As much as I wanted desperately to tell him what had just happened, I knew there was no way he would believe me.

He looked at me, dark brows furrowed, accentuating their dramatic arch, his full lips slightly parted. "You don't look like it's nothing." His expression exuded concern, caring.

Tears burned my eyes and I bit down on my quivering lip. *Don't. Cry.*

"I'm fine," was all I could say. I wasn't about to admit out loud I'd been attacked by a glowing-eyed monster.

"Are you sure? You just threw up all over me," he said. His voice was soft, his gentle gaze fixed on me.

I gave him a furtive once-over. He looked normal enough, jeans, hiking shoes and a high-end, sporty black jacket. I focused on picking up his feelings, digging around, sending out feelers. But oddly, I couldn't feel a thing. Was pain and stress impeding my ability to sense his emotions?

"I was out for my morning run," I said, trying to maintain control over my voice. "I don't know why I went into that house." I attempted a smile but my face rebelled against it.

Just keep walking, Sarah. Keep walking. Get as far away from that house as possible.

"You're limping," he said. "It must hurt?"

"Yeah. Not only did my foot go through a step, but when I came out, I fell again," I said, continuing to hobble along, him following. He seemed pretty intent on staying with me, and as much as I hated to admit it, it was far better than being alone after what had just happened. "What brings you out so early? Do you live around here?"

~ ☾ ~

He shook his head. "No. I just bought this property. I came out to see if the ground is dry enough to get some heavy equipment in here to bulldoze that old house to the ground."

"You bought this land?" I winced every time my right leg hit the ground.

"I did." Now he gave me the once-over. "Listen. You're obviously hurt. Can I do anything to help?"

I sucked in a long breath and dug deep for my yoga calm. "I'm okay. Just a scrape." I took a step forward and involuntarily flinched. Luckily, I successfully stifled a gasp.

"Just a scrape." He dropped behind me and when I turned around, I realized he was checking my torn and bloodied pant leg. "Looks like more than a scrape to me. Maybe I should take a look at it?"

"No, thanks. I'm just going to keep on going to the campsite..."

I glanced back. The house was just barely within view, and my chest suddenly tightened at just the thought of that creature. I looked away, taking another step forward, closing my eyes as my calf and hip fought for the title of Most Destroyed Body Part.

I tried not to think about how he was watching me stagger along at a snail's pace.

"This is going to take you a while. We're at least a half-mile from the campsite. Can I offer you an elbow?"

As if on cue, my left hip seemed to lock up and my foot slid into a puddle of bush bog that smelled like a mix of cat urine and rotten turnip. "Ugh!"

He offered me his hand and I took it. As soon as we made contact, the sensation of a warm electrical current passed from his skin directly into mine and caused my heart to go into a strange arrhythmia.

He stepped forward and slid an arm under my shoulders so that immediately my weight was taken off

~ ☾ ~

my sore calf. I tried to step out of the bog puddle, but the mud was so thick it was like suction. With the force of our combined upward pull, the mud finally gave, releasing my shoe and sending muck flying everywhere, including onto his pant leg.

"Oh! Sorry about that," I said, taking a breath. "Thanks." I righted myself, choosing to place my weight on my dry foot. He slid his arm further down around my back and pulled my torso into him, the length of our bodies touching.

A languid euphoria stole over me, and I felt like I was floating. Blue and purple spots skittered across my vision, with hints of fuchsia at the corners. My head lolled to the side and the warmth spread within me. I strained to focus through the blur in my vision, my eyes unable to make the distinction between the purple and blue spots and the man.

A second later, his face came into sudden focus and I could see he was motionless, his mouth slightly open.

The moment was over, and he looked down at me once again, his eyes different—brighter, somehow, with shimmering flecks of silver and black, the skin of his cheeks flushed pink.

"What...just happened?" I said, closing my gaping mouth.

His eyes widened, pupils dilating as he peered down at me. "I don't...know?" He looked as confused as I felt. Then he cleared his throat. "What are you talking about?"

Could it be the stress of the situation that made me imagine that weird sensation? Perhaps I'd just had a dizzy spell from the pain or the trauma? I recalled the fainting spells I'd had three years ago, right around the time of high school graduation when my stress had been at an all-time high.

I looked away. "I felt funny for a second there."

~ ☾ ~

"You still look a little sick. Maybe you're dizzy from getting hurt and throwing up?" he said.

Most likely a fainting spell. *Great*. "I'm really not feeling well."

"Should we keep going?" he asked, his arm still snaked around me.

I took a deep breath. "Yes, please."

He took a step forward, his hold on me taking most of my weight. The solidness of his body was noticeable right through his clothes.

"I'm Evan, by the way. Evan Valente."

"I'm Sarah Ross."

After about thirty steps, he turned to me once again. "Do you usually run in this area so early in the morning?"

I nodded. "I do when I'm camping. I come here a lot in the summer. Why?"

"I was just surprised to see you. I hardly ever see people when I'm up this early, especially in the middle of the forest."

"What about you? Are you usually out at this time of day?" I asked.

"Not always. Just when I'm excited about something. Like buying this land." He chuckled. "I couldn't sleep."

I nodded, contemplating how much to tell him. "I thought I heard something. A voice, actually. I thought I heard a child's voice." I watched his face to gauge his reaction.

"A child's voice?" He scratched the dark stubble on his chiseled jaw.

"Yeah. I thought it might be that missing girl, Jessica Crow. Have you heard about her in the news?"

"Yes. You thought you heard her voice, so you went looking for her?"

"Stupid, right?"

He tightened his hold under my arms. "No, not

stupid." He paused. "Brave, not stupid." He smiled down at me with straight, pearly white teeth.

The throbbing of my hip seemed to lessen, and I began to grow used to the pain of my calf. I stopped.

"Thanks." I looked at the perfectly carved bone structure of his face, smooth skin, and silky hair and forced myself to look away. It was a face I could look at all day long and never grow bored. Could I trust him? Looks could be deceiving. I'd learned that the hard way.

I silently cursed my cheating ex-boyfriend, Tyler, who'd ruined me for trusting anyone with a Y chromosome.

The walk back through the forest was a test of mental and physical endurance, my calf slowly starting to get sore again and making me limp. Like a perfect gentleman, Evan helped me over every stick, twig, and rock, careful not to go too fast, always letting go of me when I could walk alone.

When we finally reached the road, I glanced around and spotted the location of our campsite to my left, about another hundred feet away.

"My truck is right over there." He pointed to a vehicle that was mere yards from us. "Can I help you get bandaged up? I have a first aid kit."

The thought of taking weight off of my aching hip and angry calf appealed to me in a way words couldn't describe. "Sure."

When we reached his black SUV, he pulled open the hatch and retrieved his emergency supplies. I glanced around at the luxurious trunk space. I'd never seen a vehicle like it before, especially not in Slave Lake, my small town. There was just something different about it, a little more chrome and a slightly more sophisticated shape than what I was used to. I took a peek at the make and model. It was a Mercedes.

His expression was focused and intense as he shoved

bandages and other items into his jacket pocket. Then he turned and hoisted me up onto the back of the cargo space and knelt before me. Pushing the pant leg up to my knee, he gently touched the skin around my cut. His fingertips felt soft and warm on my leg.

He frowned. “They’re not deep, but there are quite a few scratches. Let’s get them cleaned up.” Long, tapered fingers wrapped gauze around my calf and ankle, taking special care to avoid touching the sore spots.

“Okay, all cleaned up. That should hold you until you get it checked out by a doctor.” He lifted me off the SUV, placing me softly on the ground in front of him. His arms remained wrapped around me for longer than necessary, and for a second, I forgot to breathe. He dropped his arms to his sides.

I looked up at him and my face warmed. “Thanks Evan. I should get back.”

“Okay. Maybe I should walk you to the campsite?”

“Sure.”

I took a step forward and cursed under my breath when the burning sensation returned. He instantly placed an arm around me, offsetting my weight. With the way my entire body ached in response to moving again, I was more than grateful for his help.

Back at my campsite, I unzipped the gray tent door and was hit with the stench of sweat and vodka breath. Obviously Kate and Amber had both found their way back to the tent to sleep while I was out trying to stay alive.

“Guys. Wake up,” I whispered. “I need to go to the doctor.”

Kate’s eyes popped open, her mascara smudged and drool still slick on her cheek. She did not look like a happy camper. “Sarah...what?”

“I—” I searched my mind for something non-crazy to say, but nothing came to mind. “I hurt my leg.”

~ ☾ ~

Amber, who lay on the other side of the tent, sat upright in her sleeping bag. Her jet-black hair was matted into two huge cowlicks on either side of her head. "What do you mean 'you're hurt'?" she asked.

"I went out for a walk this morning." My nerves were still raw as my mind flashed back to those glowing eyes and that suctioning sensation within my body. "I heard a child's voice. I thought it was Jessica, and I went out looking for her."

"What?" Amber said. Her pain washed over me in a wave, like a sheet of thick, black molasses. I had to suck in a huge breath to maintain my composure.

"You left the campsite this morning to look for Jessica?" Kate asked.

My cheeks began to warm. "Yeah."

"What happened?" Amber asked. Her blood-shot eyes seemed to magnify the hazel color of her irises.

"I came to a dead end at an old broken-down, abandoned farmhouse. I...I got hurt."

Kate's expression turned from annoyance to concern. "How?"

"My foot broke through an old rotten step." I turned around and glanced at Evan, who stood outside our tent, listening. Amber and Kate leaned forward and looked out the tent flap to see who I was looking at. Their confused expressions mirrored one another.

"Guys, this is Evan." I gestured toward him and he nodded at them. "He helped me walk back."

"Hi, Evan," Kate said, and then turned her attention back to me. "Is it bad? Are you okay?" She blinked rapidly as she picked the sleep out of the corner of her eye.

"Not too bad. But I should probably have it looked at."

"Okay, let's go." Amber climbed out of her sleeping bag and began shoving things into her backpack. I exited the tent.

~ ☾ ~

As they loaded Kate's car, Evan led me out of earshot. He leaned down and whispered into my ear. "I'd really like to come with you to the hospital. Just to make sure you're okay." His breath tickled my neck and the smell of him surrounded me, a musky combination of antibiotic, sweat and man. I swallowed.

"I'll be okay," I said, fighting back a strange hollowness in my chest. "Amber and Kate will make sure of that."

"I'd really like to see you again, Sarah."

"I'd like that, too."

He smiled and his entire face lit up. "Great. I'll get you my phone number." Evan dug into his pants pocket and handed me a business card. I took it, glancing down to see his name just under the company title, 'Valente Developments, Inc.' "Will you phone me?"

"Sure." I grabbed my purse out of Kate's car and pulled out my own business card, with the name, address and phone number of the sporting equipment company I managed, SportInc, on the front.

For a brief moment, our fingers touched as he took the card. It sent a thrill through me, right out to the tips of my toes and fingers.

"Nice to meet you, Sarah." He helped me into the car.

As we drove away I looked back at Evan once more, standing at the side of the road, waving. I waved back.

"What's the story with him?" Kate asked.

I glanced over at her, as she looked back and forth between me and the road. I didn't even know where to start. All of a sudden, Kate's eyes widened and she slammed on the brakes. We lurched forward in our seats. I looked up.

Directly in the middle of the road stood a man, dark hair plastered in lank strips around his face, his heavy brow line low on his forehead.

He seemed to stare right at me with eyes black as

coal. I knew I'd never seen him before in my life, and yet he looked familiar to me.

"What is he doing, standing in the middle of the road like that?" Kate said with a scowl. She honked the horn three times.

He stood motionless, his hands deep in the pockets of a black trench coat. Then his chin rose and nostrils flared as he stepped aside to let us pass. We drove by, and as we did, his eyes glittered like shards of black glass, glaring. My stomach flipped in my stomach, because his gaze didn't move. He stared at one thing, and one thing, only.

Me.

~ ☾ ~

CHAPTER THREE

Once the doctor put two stitches into my calf and sent me on my way, Kate and Amber took me home to rest on the condition that I would give them a full disclosure of the day's events tomorrow, when I was feeling better.

The next day, Kate picked me up and we drove to Amber's childhood home, where I promised I would tell them everything. It wasn't that I was trying to hold them in suspense. I merely wanted to think over what had happened and come to some kind of conclusion in my own mind before I shared it with anyone else.

Plus, the added benefit of coming out with the incident at Amber's house was that I could talk about it with Amber's mom, Paulette, who was more of a mother to me than my own was. Not that I blamed my mom. She had always been so busy with SportInc while I was growing up, and now that I was in charge of the store in Slave Lake, and she and my father were in Colorado setting up another company, she simply wasn't available for advice or support.

Luckily, Amber's mother had taken me under her wing. Amber's parents were hobby farmers with a small berry orchard, a few horses, and a large vegetable garden. They lived close to the Wakina Reservation, where Paulette had grown up. Amber enjoyed the advantage of being so close to all of her relatives and saw them often, another reason why the pain of Jessica going missing worried her so much.

I stepped out of the car and was immediately met

with the cheerful sounds of birdsong. Each bird had its own tune, the sounds layering together in a sweet chorus of music. But the sound only served to make yesterday's experience seem even more surreal.

Gravel crunched underfoot as we approached the white, two-story farmhouse. Its old-fashioned wraparound veranda overlooked the massive, two-acre front lawn circled by several rows of raspberry bushes.

Amber's mother was off in the distance, pitching hay to her horses. She turned in our direction and began to amble toward us in green rubber boots. Paulette's pin-straight hair flowed around her shoulders, the sunlight reflecting off of it like black obsidian. She stood about six feet tall, but her commanding presence was offset by her gentle disposition. Ever since meeting her for the first time almost eight years ago, I'd always loved to talk to her. She was the embodiment of "Earth Mother" and the only emotion that seemed to radiate off of her was quiet and calm, like being immersed in a warm bath.

Today, Paulette's feelings were nothing like a warm bath.

Paulette's eyes were wide. "What happened?" Her rich Native American accent seemed exaggerated today, accompanied by an odd pitch.

Amber turned to me. "Sarah?"

Paulette placed a hand on my shoulder. She smelled earthy and sweet—hay, dirt and berries all rolled into one. Paulette looked at me as if she could peer directly into my mind. "What did you see?"

I glanced to Kate and Amber. Amber nodded, urging me on.

"Yesterday, I heard a child's voice outside the tent. I thought it might be Jessica."

Paulette's mouth dropped open. "Oh?"

"I followed the sound of the voice into the forest. The voice lured me to a house, and..." It was now or never. "I saw a spirit, or a ghost or something." Amber and Kate's heads jerked in my direction. I knew both of their gazes were pinned to my face, but I kept looking at Paulette.

"With bright yellow eyes," Paulette said, as if plucking the image right from my memory. My heart stuttered as emotions began to emanate off of her like gusts of burning sand. *She knows*. I felt like a weight had been lifted from my shoulders.

"Yes. Yellow eyes," I said.

"A horrible yellow color. Like bile." Paulette's voice had dropped to a near-whisper.

"Yes."

Paulette stared. "It's really true," she said, almost as if to herself. Then her pupils dilated and she appeared to be focusing on me once again. "You saw a Skinwalker."

I shivered as the vivid sensory experience of being invaded by that horrible pressure came back to me. I was at a loss for words.

She muttered something beneath her breath, and then looked at me. "Skinwalkers are evil people. People who practice bad medicine." Her alarm registered inside of me like a pit of quicksand.

Amber interjected to explain. "Bad medicine is the Indian version of black magic, Sarah."

"That was a person?" I asked.

Paulette nodded. "A warlock who has mastered the dark art of spirit travel. Some people call it astral-projection. They can leave their bodies and roam around in spirit form."

"That was a person who left his body?" I asked.

"Yes. And we call this 'skin walking'," Paulette said.

Something gnawed at my stomach. I stared at Paulette and then glanced at Kate and Amber who stood across from me, looking at me with concern. Was it true? Could that thing have been a warlock, practicing black magic? It seemed preposterous, and yet, there was no other plausible explanation. I felt as if I'd just been told I'd seen the Easter Bunny.

I turned back to Paulette, debating whether to tell her about what I'd done to the Skinwalker. I felt sweat break out under my arms, and my hands turned clammy.

"How did you get away, Sarah?" Paulette broke the uncomfortable silence.

I had to start with the background information if I wanted her to understand. "Paulette, did you know I can sense other people's feelings? Like they belong to me?"

"I wasn't aware of that, no," Paulette said. "But now that you mention it, I've always thought you were very perceptive."

"Sometimes those feelings are so strong, they really hurt," I said. "But this was something completely different. This time, I sort of...imagined throwing its dark feelings back at it, you know, with my mind? And then it just disappeared after that." I bit my fingernail, gauging her reaction.

Paulette's eyebrow quirked in the middle. "I don't think I follow you. You threw its feelings back at it?"

"Yes."

"And it disappeared, but you didn't see its flesh body?" Paulette asked.

"Yeah, it just disappeared. Does that mean he's still alive somewhere? Back in his flesh body?"

"Most likely," Paulette said.

"Why? Why was it there?"

"I think this has something to do with the newcomers." Paulette's eyes took on a vacant appearance. "Four strangers, who claim they are here to bring faith to our people."

"You don't believe that's the reason?" I asked.

Paulette shook her head, and a shadow passed over her eyes. "No. I know better. The whole community knows better. These strangers have come from the four corners, a place of great supernatural power, according to Navajo legend. Four U.S. States, Colorado, Arizona, New Mexico and Utah, that all meet at one corner. It's a location that has been a place of dark magic long before the man-made borders. It is said this part of our country is a portal to other dimensions, to the spirit world. Others believe the land is cursed by the Ancient Ones, the long-extinct Anasazi peoples. I don't know how it came to be, but either way, it's a Skinwalker hotbed." She snorted. "And everyone in Wakina thinks the story the newcomers have given is just a front for why they're really there."

I swallowed. "Why are they really here?"

"To enlist," she answered. "Recruit others who wish to learn the dark supernatural ways, the bad medicine of Skinwalkers." She paused as the words steeped.

"Do you think these Skinwalkers have anything to do with Jessica?" I asked.

Paulette let out a long breath and nodded, her mouth turned down at the corners. "Skinwalkers lure people by offering the power of bad medicine. But to become a full-fledged Skinwalker, one has to perform extraordinary acts of evil, usually a rite that involves breaking a cultural taboo." Paulette's voice warbled with the last two words.

"Like what?" I asked. I wasn't sure I wanted to hear the answer.

She paused, inhaling as if to galvanize the strength to answer. "Murder, sacrifice of... One has to sacrifice their own child."

Jessica's face flashed through my mind, her snapping brown eyes and flyaway hair that always fell out of its ponytail, her partially toothless smile. My stomach lurched. "Do you think Jessica's mother...?" I couldn't finish the sentence.

"Yes. We have feared the worst. That Sandra has been

lured into ways of evil by the promise of power. But until now, it was all just speculation."

"And now?"

"And now... Well, we know we have Skinwalkers, don't we?"

~ ☾ ~

CHAPTER FOUR

I placed another price tag on the pink Nike Sportband and set it next to the Ironman GPS watches in the glass shelf below the cash counter. I was back at work and despite the forty-eight hours that had passed since my unsettling confrontation with the Skinwalker, the memories of it continued to flash through my mind every few minutes.

I placed my head in my hands, trying to compose myself before I had to open the store and put on my work persona, manager of SportInc, capable, confident and able to make decisions. Unfortunately, today I felt more like curling up into the fetal position in my bed and hiding from the world.

My hands had taken on the rubbery smell of the watches, like warm condoms. I glanced up to the front door of the store, still locked with the Open sign facing inward. I had ten more minutes before I had to face customers, to act like I wasn't falling apart at the seams. Ten more minutes to get a grip.

Today was definitely a day I wished I had not been appointed store manager. If I was just an employee, I could turn my mind off and focus on surviving the day.

Unfortunately, when my parents had bestowed the great honor of making me manager of this store a year ago, my days of coasting ended.

I sucked back a gulp of coffee, its familiar bitter flavor tricking my body into believing it was the start of another normal workday, and yet, I didn't think I would ever quite feel the same about the word normal. I stared down at the neoprene pink band, the price tag stuck on sideways, thanks to my shaky hands.

Ugh. I threw all of the remaining Sportbands back into the box. I'd do it later.

Even though I'd been picking up other people's feelings, like a kick in the gut, for years, it didn't prepare me for the confirmation that there were supernatural beings like the Skinwalkers. Being a freak of nature always seemed like a piece of me that wasn't quite real, a part of me my mind only half-acknowledged.

However, my half-denial, half-acceptance didn't stop me from taking advantage of the gift. In fact, being able to immediately feel when someone was sexually attracted to me had proven invaluable, and over the years, I'd scored a few dates because of it. The ability also came in handy as the manager of SportInc, since I knew exactly which customers to focus my energies on.

But my ability came with a price, soaking up other people's emotions until I felt like a boiling tea kettle, screaming for release. Especially when faced with crushing hostility or suffocating contempt. Or perhaps the worst of all feelings: black melancholy.

I glanced around the store. Row upon row of hockey sticks lined one wall, the other wall, shelves of tennis shoes and cross-trainers. There was not a moving item anywhere, yet I just couldn't shake the sensation of being watched. Undoubtedly, it was my over-active imagination and I pushed the thought out of my mind altogether.

I reached into the purse I had locked away under the cash counter and dug out Evan's card. I considered what he had said, that he had bought the land and was bulldozing that god-forsaken, ramshackle old house right into the ground.

My watch alarm went off. Nine o'clock. I got up, and

with my sore calf, stepped gingerly over to the light switch and flipped on the huge overhead fluorescents, lighting the place up like a stadium. Taking a deep breath, I unlocked the front door, flipped the Open sign around, and returned to the cash counter, ignoring the spreading heat in my calf.

I turned to the phone and started to dial in my mother's cell, hoping she might answer it, just this once.

Before I even finished dialing, I was interrupted by a low, masculine voice behind me saying, "Hi."

I jumped. I hadn't even heard the overhead door chime. I turned around.

He'd come. Evan strode up to the side of the cash counter wearing a black suit, white button-down shirt and a vibrant blue tie that seemed to match the exact hue of his eyes. His mouth turned up into a thousand-watt smile. Instantly, my cheeks flooded with heat, and I ended my call.

"Evan! You came to see me."

"Of course," he said. His voice was smooth and his eyes twinkled. "How are you feeling?"

"I'm better. Sort of." I wasn't about to get into a lengthy explanation of my aches and pains here at work. "I got a few stitches, and with the help of Ibuprofen, I feel almost normal."

He chuckled. "Good. I was worried about you."

"Oh? Thanks." My heart stuttered. To get my mind off my racing pulse, I attempted to dig around and pick up his emotions once again. Unfortunately, it was like he had erected a huge glass wall around him and nothing was getting out. Why? How could he possibly evade me, when no one before him ever had?

Then another, stranger possibility entered my mind. Could he be willfully keeping his emotions from me? I brushed the thought out of my head as ridiculous.

"Are you in need of a Sportband?" I grinned and held

up the pink one I'd just finished tagging.

He rolled his eyes. "Yes, pink. Exactly what I was looking for." He winked. "Actually, I'm looking for a new GPS watch. Mine has been missing since we met. I'm guessing it must have fallen off and I lost it."

"Sure." I nodded, reaching under the counter for the new Ironman version and placed it on the counter in front of him. He picked it up, turning it over in his hand, bringing it close to his face to scrutinize it. Then he nodded and looked at me.

"Perfect. I'll take it." He handed me the watch with a smile.

I rang up his purchase, and as he punched in his pin number on the credit card machine, I gave him a once over. He looked more like a Guess model than the president of a development company.

"I'm going to be staying in Slave Lake for a while," he said.

My heart flip-flopped in my chest like a fish in a pail at just the thought of seeing this gorgeous man once again. "While you work on the land?" I asked.

"Yes. I'm setting up shop here, in town."

The thought of him being around here for a while had my blood flowing. "I forgot to ask you the other morning, what are you planning on doing with the land?"

"Development for recreational property. That place is an untapped gold mine. In the summer, there are water sports, fishing and hiking, and you know about the camping. Plus, great skiing and sledding trails in the winter. And so close to amenities, with it bcing just a few miles from the town of Slave Lake."

"But the land is already developed," I said. "There are already tons of cottages and a convenience store on that side of the lake."

"There's going to be a lot more than that, just wait.

Think of Las Vegas before it was developed. Just an empty desert in the middle of nowhere."

I grinned. "Casinos and strippers, too?"

He chuckled, a low, soft sound. "No. I'm just going to expand on what it already has."

"Good. Because I love that place just the way it is."

"You'll love it when I'm through with it, too. Don't worry." He grinned.

"Wow. It must be nerve-racking to be a developer, to buy land with just the hope that it will become valuable."

He patted his stomach, hard. "Guts of steel."

"Guts of steel, at your age?"

He chuckled. "Hey, I'm twenty-one. Plenty of time to develop intestinal fortitude."

I shook my head and smiled. "Where are you from, Evan Valente? I'm guessing not from anywhere around here."

"Eagle Creek, Utah," he answered.

Something niggled in the back of my mind at the mention of Eagle Creek, Utah. "You're a long way from home. Where are you staying while you're in Slave Lake?"

"I'm renting a hotel room by the month for now. Depending on how things go, I might consider buying something more permanent. What about you? Have you always lived here?"

"Yes. I'm helping manage this place. It's a family business. A few years ago it almost went under. I took over and turned things around just in time." I smiled, eliciting another broad grin from Evan. "So, I offered to stay and run the store for a year. Plus, I can save up for college."

"That's great, Sarah." Evan flashed top and bottom teeth.

"Sort of. Absolutely everyone I know has moved away

or is going to college. It makes it kind of lonely here during the winter months. But I'm moving to Grand Forks next year for college."

"What are you going to major in?"

"Psychology. I can kind of...read people, you might say."

Evan's eyebrows shot up his forehead. "Really? What do you mean?"

"It's sort of intuition, I guess." I shrugged, preparing for the kind of sarcasm a disclosure like this usually elicited from people.

"How does this intuition work?"

I looked at him again, carefully examining his features, the dimple on the left side of his face, the cleft in his chin, the crinkles at the corner of his eyes. "It's not working on you, actually."

"Really?" He canted his head to the side.

I shook my head. "Nothing."

The whirr of the fax machine started up, reminding me I was at work and should probably avoid getting too chatty with a customer. Even one as gorgeous as Evan Valente. "Is there anything else I can help you find, Evan?"

"Come to think of it, I do need a new pair of hiking shoes, seeing as how my favorite pair smells like vodka cooler throw up."

I tried not to blush as I thought of vomiting right beside him. "Sorry about that. Follow me." I led him to the wall that housed several rows of hiking shoes and boots. I turned around, and he nearly ran into me.

"What brand do you prefer? Saucony? New Balance?"

He stepped closer and looked directly into my eyes, holding my gaze for much too long for casual politeness.

"Indigo," he said.

"Pardon me?"

He blinked, as if composing himself. "Your eyes.

~ ☾ ~

They're indigo." His expression softened as he gazed into my eyes, his lips parted.

Air escaped my mouth. "Yes, they are."

"Very rare, that color."

I thought of my parents, both brown-eyed and brown-haired. I was definitely the genetic anomaly in our family, with my purple eyes and blond hair. I shrugged. "I guess so."

"They're gorgeous." He leaned toward me. I could almost feel the touch of his lips on mine. Then he took a step back and turned toward the wall of footwear.

"I guess I'll pass on the shoes for now. I have to get going. I have a meeting at the bank." He gestured to his clothing. "Which, of course, accounts for the stuffy suit I'm wearing."

"Good luck," I said.

He smiled and extended his hand to me. "Great to see you again, Sarah."

I glanced down at his outstretched hand, noticing a tiny, white scar in the space between his thumb and pointer finger. The scar looked like two inverted triangles. I placed my hand in his.

All of a sudden, everything changed. It was as if I was no longer in my own body, like I'd been taken back in time to a place I didn't even recognize. Images blasted through my mind, of Evan, screaming in pain as he writhed on the floor. Then the scene changed slightly and I could see that triangular mark on his hand, but now it was a raised, angry red.

My perspective changed again, and now I was no longer looking down at Evan, but rather, I was inside him. The world tilted, and then I seemed to be looking up at a face, blank and expressionless.

He let go of my hand, and all at once, I was back in my own body, my own mind. The images stopped. I was in the store, looking at him, his eyes squeezed shut tight.

~ ☾ ~

His eyes snapped open and he looked at me as if he'd just been punched in the stomach.

I almost collapsed. My heart fluttered, dizziness washing over me. I felt like I'd just hammered back six shots of tequila. What had I just seen? One of Evan's memories? Was it possible that in addition to being able to feel other people's feelings, I could also experience their life, as if seeing it through my own eyes?

If that were true, what I'd just seen from Evan could only be described as horrific. My heart pounded in my chest so hard, it was as if someone was trying to punch a hole right through my ribcage. My thoughts clawed around my mind for answers.

"What just happened?" Evan asked, breathless.

"I don't know."

The overhead door chime dinged as the door opened and two customers walked in. Evan immediately backed up, his legs unsteady. He placed a hand on the top of a clothing rack to steady himself as his Adam's apple bobbed in his throat.

"I, uh..." He cleared his throat, his eyes glassy. "Thanks for your help, Sarah."

He turned on his heel and strode out of the store. This time, I heard the door chime as he left.

~ ☾ ~

CHAPTER FIVE

"You saw that Evan guy again?" Amber asked. She sucked the last of her frothy pink drink through a straw. The mischievous look on her face was mirrored in the giddy emotions she gave off, emotions that were always especially loud when she was drinking. They resonated within me like a bouncy ball flying around in my stomach.

I downed another shot of "Sex on the Beach", hoping it would finally be enough to filter out the emotions of everyone here. Smooth at first, then tart, the booze finally burned its way down the back of my throat. The buzz-on was almost immediate, and the effect was wonderful, the way it almost obliterated all of the sex-obsessed feelings that seemed to roll off of nearly ever patron at the bar like a hot blanket being wound around me. *Sick.*

We sat at a booth right next to the bar. Amber held her glass up, signaling to the bartender who nodded and began to pour. He bobbed his head to the blaring country music from the loudspeaker.

Tables ringed the bar, booths along the wall and stools on the other side. Every few feet a brightly lit neon beer sign provided a dash of garish décor. Right in the middle was the dance floor, a little postage-stamp sized circle of parquet flooring that reminded me of an interlocking puzzle. Alongside it was a raised section with a few pool tables.

"Yeah, I saw him." I proceeded to explain his land

development business to Amber and Kate, who listened with rapt expressions.

"That's amazing. Nobody ever comes to Slave Lake. People only leave," Amber said. Our waitress, dressed in skin-tight jeans and a too-tight tank-top, brought us another round. Behind her, the giant flat screen on the wall lit up with random explosions of fuchsia, neon yellow and acid green, perfectly paced with the lyrics of the canned music.

Kate sat across from me on the bench seating, her copper hair shimmering pink from the neon "Budweiser" sign and the black light hanging on the wall behind her. Her teeth were glowing an unnatural white in the light, and every piece of lint on her black shirt stood out like a 3D movie.

"How interesting that you both were out in the bush that morning," Kate said.

I nodded. "I know. Quite a coincidence."

Amber sat beside Kate in the bench seat, facing the bar. She leaned forward in one fluid motion, her black hair sweeping the table. "Sarah. Look who just walked in." I turned in my seat. "And he's coming right over—"

"Mind if I join you?" asked a familiar voice, before I'd even had a chance to look.

I turned and smiled at Evan. "Sure."

He pulled a stool up to our table, his arms rippling with the movement. His very presence seemed to heat the air around me, his cologne eclipsing the bar smell of dirty jeans, stale beer and desperation.

I glanced at Kate and Amber, who both stared at him, bright-eyed. His dark fitted jeans hugged his legs, the denim slung low across narrow hips. A black t-shirt made of a material I couldn't identify hinted of the peaks and valleys of muscle beneath and a single silver chain with a dog-tag hung at his neck, a crest emblem engraved on it with the name Valente. This guy would look good in a burlap sack. Or nothing.

"You remember Kate and Amber from the campground?" I asked. They nodded in acknowledgement and exchanged niceties. Then Amber and Kate excused themselves and hit the dance floor. They'd been dancing together since we'd become bar age, both of them with the attitude that they weren't about to wait around for a guy to ask.

Evan and I watched as they twirled each other around, the only people dancing in the whole bar. Then they attempted to two-step, each of them fighting to lead. Goofballs.

I turned back to Evan. "How are you?"

He flashed that thousand-watt smile. "I'm great. You?" He inched closer and the atmosphere around my head seemed charged, like a swelling electrical storm. A shiver traveled through my body.

"Fine, thanks." I smiled.

"You look great." He gestured to my outfit.

I looked down at my jeans and a loose white shirt and glanced back up at him, cocking my eyebrow. "Thanks?"

"What? Not used to compliments?"

"Not when I'm dressed like a slob, no, not really."

He rolled his eyes. "You look awesome. Seriously. Want to dance?"

I stared at him, half-expecting he was kidding. But his face showed no trace of a joke. I glanced at the dance floor where Kate and Amber had begun to dance hip hop to the country beat.

I turned back to him. He held out his hand, across the table. Reluctantly, I took it and he led me to the dance floor where Amber and Kate made room for us, their expressions barely-muted surprise. People rarely danced in Slave Lake. Except for Amber and Kate, of course.

Evan placed his palm in my right hand and set his other hand on my waist. I glanced up at a set of smoldering eyes and immediately looked away, his gaze too intense. Unfortunately, by looking away, I realized that every single person in the bar was staring at us. Some people, who should have had their backs to us, had actually turned around on their stool to gawk. I felt like a fish in a fishbowl.

Evan leaned down, his breath caressing my cheek. I caught a silky coil of his scent, a rich, musky fragrance of expensive cologne, soap and his own unique smell. It was addictive. The hand on my waist snaked around to my back, pulling me closer. Heat radiated over my entire body as we began to move in slow, gentle circles. When the song came to an end, my arm fell from his shoulder. His hands didn't move.

"One more?" he asked as the music transitioned to a faster song, modern country with a dance beat. Kate and Amber were already dancing to it in a way that looked more fitting for a city club, Amber's arms reaching up and over her head, hips swinging. Kate had her own little groove going alongside her.

"Sure," I said.

He smiled and set his hand back on my waist, and suddenly we were in the fastest two-step I'd ever danced in my life. We moved around the dance floor at a dizzying pace, spinning circles around Kate and Amber who were laughing out loud watching us.

He twirled me several times, only to end up back in that break-neck, two-stepping pace once again. Now I was giggling to the point of breathlessness, my head spinning from the four shots I'd just downed and my racing pulse. He spun me three more times, and when the song ended, he lowered me into a long dip.

With his arm around my back, I was gently pulled up, our bodies touching from torso all the way down, so that even the tips of our shoes connected. I looked into his face, expecting to see a grin, but was met with a burning look that made my heart stutter and my breath catch. The whiskey on his breath was all I could think of, the heat of his mouth, so close to mine.

Then a sensation folded over me. A soft lethargy, like I was levitating, weightless. My eyes closed, and explosions of purple and blue light flashed behind my eyelids. I relaxed into the feeling.

"Are you okay?" Evan asked. I opened my eyes. He peered down at me, forehead wrinkled with concern. His skin was flushed bright pink.

My lungs began to re-inflate as my entire body tingled like I'd just had the best orgasm of my life.

Had he even kissed me? I licked my lips, but there was no taste of whiskey, no evidence of his mouth on mine. Obviously I'd had one too many shots. And yet, I felt perfectly lucid, his gorgeous face crystal clear before me.

"Uh...I'm fine," I said, my voice breathy. There had to be an explanation. Like maybe I was losing my mind. Or maybe my fainting spells were starting to happen again, ever since the stressful Skinwalker incident. Whatever it was, right now I had to make sure this perfect specimen of a man in front of me did not think I was a raving lunatic. I forced myself to speak, my mind scrambling for small-talk. "I...I had no idea you could dance like that."

The concerned look faded, and he flashed his perfect teeth. "Thanks. You're not too bad, yourself."

I dropped my hand from around his shoulder and backed up. He let go of me slowly, as if with reluctance.

"Come on. I need a drink," I said, motioning back to the bar where Amber and Kate had just sat down. We veered toward them.

Evan made eye contact with the bartender who nodded at both of us. "Scotch, on the rocks, please. What are you drinking?"

~ ☾ ~

"I'll have a Long Island Iced T—"

"Who's he?" A guy's voice said, close enough that I cringed from the volume. I whipped around.

Jeff Hansen. Town drunk that never seemed to do much of anything, other than sit in the bar, hit on locals and look pissed off. And boy, did he look pissed off. Emotions rolled off him like jagged pieces of glass, hurt and anger all twisted up into one gigantic ball of irritation.

"He's cool, Jeff. He's with me," I said. My heart started to pound as I remembered the last time Jeff had picked a fight. He'd bitten a guy's ear and torn part of it right off.

Jeff stared at Evan, his teeth exposed like he was snarling. "Is he treating you right, Sarah?"

"It's all good, Jeff," I said.

"You think you're pretty tough?" Jeff said through gritted teeth. He stepped forward and poked Evan in the chest. Evan was pushed slightly off-balance, and he took a step backward.

My stomach clenched. "Jeff, I said it's cool."

Evan straightened up. He had at least four inches on Jeff and well over thirty pounds. Jeff stepped back, and the sickly-sweet smell of weed came wafting off of his ratty jean jacket.

Evan looked down his nose at Jeff. "Back off, man." His jaw muscles popped in and out, and his hands balled up at his sides. The only thing Jeff had going for him was a bad attitude and liquid courage.

"Shut up, asshole!" Jeff slurred, a fine mist of spittle burst from his mouth and rained all over us. Jeff turned his head and flashed a snide grin, probably to impress his buddies who watched the spectacle along the sidelines of the bar.

"Jeff, stop it!" I said. Jeff ignored me completely, staring at Evan. I reached for Evan's hand, wound my fingers through his and tugged. “Come on. Let’s get out of here.”

Evan nodded, and we strode toward the exterior door. I glanced back to see Jeff running. He ran straight into Evan, knocking him forward.

Evan hit the crash bar of the metal door, his body weight forcing it wide open so that it squeaked when the hinges were pushed to their limit. My heart jumped into my throat as he stumbled and fell onto the cement outside. Immediately, he righted himself and jumped back to his feet.

Jeff smiled, eyes flashing. “I bet that hurt, didn’t it, tough guy?”

I ran toward Jeff. “Stop it! Just leave him alone!”

Jeff smiled at me. “Aww, you’re getting your little bi-otch to fight for you.” Then he turned back to Evan. “Tell you’re ho to shut her pie-hole, or I’ll shut it for her.”

“You’re going to wish you’d never said that,” Evan said, his voice a low, warning growl.

Jeff snorted. “You’re in my town. You’re gonna regret having a mouth.” His arms rose above his head in some kind of attempt to look intimidating, but to me he looked like a bird about to take flight.

“Stop it, Jeff.”

Stepping forward, Jeff hurtled his fist toward Evan’s face but Evan snatched his clenched fist mid-air. I lunged toward them, placing one hand on Evan and the other hand on Jeff’s jacket.

Instantly, the atmosphere around my head changed, filling with static.

The lights above the entryway flickered, humming like dying bees before building into a sizzling pulse. With a bang, the lights exploded in a rainfall of glass shards. I ducked to shield my face.

I opened my eyes and gasped. Jeff lay crumpled on the ground, his torso folded inward, his limbs pulled into a fetal position, moaning as he clutched his stomach. Then his face went slack, and his eyes rolled back into his head. Why was he on the ground? And why did he look like he'd been knocked out cold?

I glanced around, but all I could hear was the retreating sound of footsteps running outside, the parking lot no longer lit up by the overhead light.

"Evan?" I called out.

Silence.

~ ☾ ~

CHAPTER SIX

The following day, I was out at Amber's acreage once again.

"Sarah, I want you to meet my friend Noreen," Paulette said, leading me into her dining room. "She is a healer. After your experience with the Skinwalkers, I wanted you to meet her."

I followed Paulette in through the foyer. Today was overcast, the grayish shadows dancing on their beige walls. When we entered the dining room, the scent of starch hung in the air, fresh biscuits sat on a side table to cool.

Amber was already seated at the oak farmhouse table. Next to her sat a woman with frizzy gray hair past her shoulders, wearing clothing that looked like they were brand new, yet had been bought in 1987.

"Sarah, this is Noreen," Paulette said.

"Hi," I said.

"Hello." The gravelly voice seemed to match her grayish skin. I tried to pick up her emotions, immediately noticing her ability to contain them. They were compartmentalized, each one well defined: concern, curiosity and unease. What I did feel clearly was concern, judging by the way my insides were jumping.

"Have a seat." Paulette gestured to the open spot on the bench across the table from Noreen. I nodded and sat. Paulette lowered herself to the bench beside me.

Why was Paulette introducing me to this strange

woman? And what, exactly, did it mean to be a healer, anyway?

"Hello." Noreen extended her hand to me and I took it, her palm smooth and warm. "I am a fifth generation healer."

With the movement of our handshake, twisting blue veins popped up from under the paper-thin skin of her forearms. When she pulled her hand back, I took a long look at her. From here, it appeared her body was canted forward and her shoulders were turning in as if her skeleton had lost its ability to hold her upright.

"Paulette tells me you've had some frightening experiences."

"Yes." I swallowed back the sudden urge to cry, digging my fingers into my palm to distract me. Why in the world was I crying now? I barely even cried the day it happened.

"She says you were attacked by a Skinwalker outside Wakina?"

"In the old abandoned house at the far east corner of the forest."

"What you have been through has weakened your spirit." Noreen placed her hand on her chin and shook her head as she stared at a spot on the oak table. "You need a healing." Everyone around the table watched me, the ticking of the clock on the wall the only sound in the room.

Without waiting for my reaction, Noreen leaned toward me from across the table and looked at me with a milky quality to her brown eyes. "I'll need to touch your forehead. Is this okay?"

I nodded as I glanced down at her gnarled fingers clasped together. She rose and stepped around to my side of the table. Her scent wound around me, a rancid combination of stale cigarettes and lavender.

First, there was a long intake of breath before her

thumb pressed against my forehead, fingers on my scalp. "You will be—"

She stopped, her body quivering as if a tremor had passed from her head all the way down to her toes. I glanced up. Her mouth gaped as she stared into space.

"Something's wrong. They're telling me..." She gasped, pulling her hand from my head as if singed. She began backing away. Her eyes glazed over into a hundred-yard stare.

Paulette stood. "Noreen. What is it?" The tension in the air was like a corrosive fog. Feelings rocketed through me at such a dizzying pace I had no idea who generated them.

Noreen continued to back up, staring straight ahead, like she was seeing something invisible to the rest of us. She stopped when she bumped into the wall, her head jerking forward.

Paulette rushed to her side. "What, Noreen? What do you see?"

"The ancestors. They're afraid. Afraid for you," she said, leveling her gaze at me, gnarled finger pointing. My stomach lurched.

A tiny, high-pitched squeak emerged from Noreen's mouth and her voice dropped to a barely audible whisper. "Paulette, she needs the healing lodge."

*****

When I realized they intended to take me to Wakina, their home community, for the healing lodge, I insisted Amber come along for moral support. Paulette and Noreen began preparing me for the sweat lodge, a purifying and healing ritual scheduled for eight pm, by providing me with tobacco, so that when the time came, I could follow tradition by making an offering as a show of gratitude to the Creator.

Noreen and Paulette took us to a backyard at the home of Ernie, the medicine man. The four of us stood in his backyard at exactly eight, waiting while they instructed me on the formalities of the process of offering the tobacco to the medicine man before I entered the lodge.

His yard was at least two acres big, most of it natural grassland. There was a partially built doghouse on one corner of the property, and an old, yellow ten-speed bike set up against it. The yard was surrounded by trees that luckily cut down on the wind.

We stood in our skimpy clothes as part of the custom; Paulette had given us the choice of wearing shorts and a t-shirt or the more traditional option of nightgowns. Amber and I chose shorts and t-shirt, while Noreen and Paulette wore flowing nightgowns.

Ernie emerged from his house, the storm door slapping against the frame. He hobbled down the steps in bare feet, twisting his torso to the left as he clung to the hand railing as if he was stiff or injured. He was slightly built and weather-worn, the dark skin hanging from his frame, his body almost completely exposed in his tiny blue shorts.

When he reached the ground, he glanced at me. I saw wisdom in his wizened eyes, like he just knew things. I opened myself for his feelings, and what I received was like nothing I'd ever felt before. Soft waves of contentment lapped at the corners of my senses, almost as if he'd purposely sent them to me. I desperately soaked it in.

Two more people came out of the house, both robust men in their forties, each with two long, black braids cascading down their backs. Ernie nodded and led the six of us in silence through the backyard to the healing lodge at the edge of the tree-line.

It was dug into the earth, a round, low-domed shelter of white canvas and brown burlap stretched over willow branches that had been bent into arches. A warm fire

~ ☾ ~

greeted us, lighting up the dark trees that swayed below a swirling, gray sky.

Noreen and Paulette threw a bit of their tobacco into the flames, and Amber and I followed suit, an offering to the Creator and to the earth.

In a low, throaty voice, Ernie said something in his Native tongue, and then repeated in English, “We must give thanks to the grandfathers and grandmothers. Please pray with me.” He lowered his head, his hands clasped together. Low murmurings of prayers began, and I did the same.

“Now we smudge, to cleanse our bodies and souls.” Ernie led us in the ritual where we bathed our bodies with the smoke of the burning sage, breathing in the woodsy scent. He handed us each a braid of dried sage, and then gestured to enter the lodge.

Paulette and Noreen pulled back the brightly colored woven blanket that hung over the mouth of the dome. In I went, side-stepping the smoldering hot stones that circled the pitted ground. I sat down on a blanket, the thick wool providing little cushion from the hard earth beneath.

When Paulette closed the blanketed doorway, we were instantly plunged into a stifling, pitch-black interior. The glowing stones provided the only dim light in the insufferable heat.

Sage, willow and scorched earth created an unfamiliar blend of aromas I found both comforting and unsettling. Sweat formed on my brow immediately and moments later began to drip down my face in rivulets. Soon my t-shirt was soaked from top to bottom.

What if I had to go to the bathroom? What if I started throwing up from the heat? With Paulette, Amber and Noreen on one side of me, and Ernie and two other men on the other side of me, I would have to ask several people to leave in order to get out. *Damn it.* I forced my worries to the back of my mind and tried to focus on the process.

Ernie ladled water onto the smoldering rocks. Steam erupted, billowing out into the cramped space. Then he began chanting a song I couldn't understand. My head grew heavy and when I sucked in a breath, I found I could hardly breathe. My stomach twisted as I focused my mind on the braid of sage in my hand. I held it to my nose and breathed it in deeply, the scent easing my discomfort, but only slightly.

"It is time to request our anchors be pulled from the earth," Ernie said.

Paulette leaned over and whispered in my ear. "State the issue you want resolved in your life."

Each person took a turn, starting with Noreen. "I want freedom from the past," she said quietly.

Paulette went next. "Healing for Sarah."

Amber repeated her mother's words. "Healing for Sarah."

One of the men said, "Freedom from sadness." The other said, "Forgiveness."

It was my turn. "I wish to be free of fear."

The silence in the dark space was tangible, as if everyone simultaneously held their breath. A cramp coiled through my stomach.

"I need to get out," I said quietly, trying not to interrupt the others.

Paulette, Amber and Noreen responded immediately by crawling on their hands and knees to the opening and exiting the doorway. I followed behind and was struck by the cold air that immediately whipped against my face. I took a long, deep breath and opened my eyes.

The three women stood before me in sopping wet garments, their gazes evaluative. My heart began racing and my head spun. I bent over and faced the ground, just in case.

~ ☾ ~

"I'm sorry. I thought I was going to be sick."

"I understand," Paulette said. "It's your first time. You almost made it until the end."

"Will I be in trouble?"

Paulette and Noreen shook their heads just as Ernie and the three other men came out of the lodge and stood side by side, their bodies' slick with sweat.

Ernie turned to me, his short hair wet and pasted to his head. "I had a vision of the Skinwalker who attacked you. He wants your soul."

I suddenly felt like my skin was too tight for my form. "Why would it want my soul?"

He nodded, his jowls swaying from the movement. "Skinwalkers consume the souls of their victims, to remove their life force and take it for their own."

"But I thought it was random, that I was simply in the wrong place at the wrong time?" Fear had hitched itself to the back of my throat, making my voice sound strange and tight.

Ernie shook his head. "No. He was hunting you and you alone. He wants your life force."

I stood speechless, first wringing my hands, then running them through my hair.

Ernie placed a hand on my shoulder. "Skinwalkers are not bound by the physical rules of the material world. With each soul they steal, they grow stronger, serving only to make them desire more souls, more power."

I looked at Amber and then at Paulette and Noreen, who all looked at me with worry shining in their eyes. "This can't be true. Right, Paulette? This isn't true, right?"

"Ernie speaks the truth, Sarah," Paulette said.

Overhead, a lone raven cawed, a long, low screeching sound.

Ernie looked up and then back down, leveling his gaze at me. "You must be brave."

~ ☾ ~

CHAPTER SEVEN

I rolled up to my apartment in my ten-year old Honda Civic and stared at the empty street in front of my car. My eyelids seemed to have transformed into sandpaper and my legs to lead the closer and closer I got to home, worn out first from being overheated and then even more so when given Ernie's mysterious warning. I shoved the gear into park.

Movement from the corner of my eye caught my attention. Shrieks and laughter at top volume rang out, followed by the dry clink of beer bottles. My least favorite neighbors were partying on their balcony for the third night in a row. I hopped out, hoping they wouldn't see me.

"Sarah!" A low, slurred voice called out. I kept walking. A shrill whistle pierced the cool night air. "Yo! Sarah!"

Damn it.

"Hey, Darren, Jessica," I said, walking with purpose toward my front door. I didn't even want to pick up their emotions. With all of that beer swimming in their bloodstreams, their emotions would have been about as crisp as a wet sheet.

"Come on up and have a beer, sweetheart," Darren said.

"No thanks, Darren. I have to work tomorrow."

"Don't you ever take a day off?" He leaned forward, half-hung over the balcony railing, a lazy smile on his face, cigarette dangling at the corner of his mouth. The acrid stench of his Marlboros wafted up my nose and I cleared my throat. Jessica sat on a green plastic lawn chair, eyeing me as she took a drag of her own cigarette.

I wasn't exactly at work tonight, but they didn't need to know that. "Nope. No rest for the wicked," I said over my shoulder. I reached the door and stuck my key in the lock.

"Anytime you need a date, Sarah, you come on up. I'll show you a real good time," he said, then took a deep drag from his cigarette, creating a half-inch long heater that glowed red at the end. Exhaling, he blew the smoke out of his nostrils like a mad bull.

"Hey, Sarah," a voice said from beside me. I turned. Evan approached from the sidewalk by my car, his smile wide, eyes twinkling in the moonlight.

"Hi, Evan," I said.

Darren's leering smile dropped and his cigarette slipped out of his mouth. He caught it in a rain of glowing embers. I chuckled under my breath.

I turned back to grin at Evan. "What brings you here?" I asked.

"Out for a run. It's a great night for it, cool with a nice breeze."

"Would you like to come in?" I asked. "Or do you want to finish your run first?"

Evan's face lit up. "Or maybe you would like to come along? Maybe just a walk?"

I glanced down at my feet. At least I was wearing my tennis shoes. "Sure." I turned back to the balcony and the two watchful faces. "Goodnight, Darren. See you later, Jessica."

Jessica nodded and took another haul of her smoke as Darren said "Yep."

I nodded and we began walking down the street at a nice, ambling pace. I turned toward Evan. "I haven't seen you since you took off the other night," I said.

~ ☾ ~

"Where did you go, but more importantly, why was Jeff laying on the ground moaning?"

Evan made a grimace. "Uh, yeah. That." He shoved his hands into his pockets and looked at me through dark eyelashes. "After he pushed me into the door I gave him a pretty hard shove. When he hit the ground like that, I got scared I'd do something even worse to him that I'd regret and embarrass myself in front of you, so I took off. I'm sorry. Not very polite of me to just disappear like that, was it?"

I shrugged. "I was just concerned. It did seem a little weird."

Evan's eyes crinkled in the corners as he smiled. "I guess I'd better steer clear of the bar, then, shouldn't I?"

I chuckled. "That might be a good plan." My hair whirled around my face, wisps catching in my lip-gloss. The hairspray I used tasted like a combination of rubbing alcohol and mango. I stopped to pull my hood up and tuck the stray strands into it.

"You have really great hair," he said, watching me. "Have you been growing it for long?"

I smiled. "A few years."

He caught a wisp of it and tucked it into my hood for me. "It's so shiny, so healthy-looking." His fingertips remained on my cheekbone.

My heart fluttered. "Thanks." I turned and began walking once again, the rising body heat trapped inside my windbreaker warming me up. When we reached the edge of the park, the thick row of towering spruce trees butted up against the hard edge of the concrete sidewalk, marking where development immediately reverted back to a natural world of prickly green.

Dry spruce needles crunched underfoot, pine cones creating a slightly uneven terrain. The trees themselves were at least sixty feet tall, the branches on the thick trunks sprouting out above our heads. Each tree still had the spiky remains of old branches lower down around its trunk, creating the appearance of thorny sides.

Once through the trees, we entered a grassy area lit up by a single lamp pole. It was like we'd entered a different world, a world the wind couldn't reach and the sounds of the street were filtered out. We made our way toward a covered shelter and stepped inside. Shadows danced on the concrete floor as blowing branches passed back and forth in front of the overhead light. Beer bottles lined the two picnic tables.

"It looks like we missed the party." Evan peered out into the grassy area. "Is that a playground over there?"

I looked in the direction he was pointing. "Yeah. Why?"

His eyes flashed mischievously. "Do you want to swing? I'll give you an under-duck?"

I stared at him. "Are you serious?"

He held his hand out to me and I took it. Off we went, across the clearing toward the playground. At first he tugged gently, and then he let go and began to jog, running circles around me as I walked.

"Catch me if you can!" he said with a mischievous grin.

"You'd better run a lot faster than that!" I took off after him, and before long, we were in the middle of a game of tag. The burning pain in my calf was still sore enough to slow me down and my body strained to cope with the abrupt changes in momentum as I continually shifted direction to catch him.

Finally, I stopped and placed my hands on my hips. "Really mature, Valente," I said.

He winked. "Time for that under-duck?" He looked over at the swing set and then back at me, eyes flashing. "I'll race ya!" He took off before I had a chance to respond.

I watched him go, enjoying the view of his running

style. Perfect posture, wide shoulders, tight butt. I followed him to the swings where he held onto the chain and gestured to the seat as if he was offering me a chair in a fancy restaurant.

"Why thank you, sir," I said. "Now, what about my under-duck?"

I plopped onto the crescent shaped seat, my knees squeezed together, my feet sticking out at the sides, way too close to the sand-covered ground below.

"Scared?" he asked with a wink. His eyes glittered in the moonlight.

"Bring it on."

He went around behind me, grabbed the links of chain and pulled me as far back as the seat would go. Then he took off running, pushing me by the butt in front of him. He kept pushing until I was up so high that my back was nearly parallel to the ground below. A wild, weightless sensation followed, and my stomach seemed to fly up into my mouth, and then I was rushing backward toward the ground at a break-neck speed. I squealed.

Momentum took me right back to the start and when Even turned around to face me, he was grinning like a mad scientist.

"Holy hell, Valente!" I yelled.

"Scared now?" he said with a laugh.

I began to drag my heels in the sand to slow myself, and then I jumped off, landing in front of him. He reached out, and I took his arm, the momentum propelling me forward so that I spun him and then ended up in his arms.

"Scared, aren't you? Come on, just admit it." His eyes crinkled up in the corners.

I jutted my chin out in defiance. "No. Not even a little bit."

He chuckled and looked down at me, sweeping a stray hair from my face. I was suddenly very aware of how our bodies were connected from the waist all the way down.

I looked into his eyes, savoring his warm breath caressing my skin. His hand slipped around to the back of my neck and his lips touched mine, so lightly I could hardly feel it. Then I tasted him, the heady combination of mint mixed with spice flooded my mouth. I pressed my lips against his as my body turned into a live wire.

His lips crushed mine and I snaked my fingers through his thick hair. A light breeze swirled around us, ruffling his bangs against my forehead and tickling my skin.

Suddenly, my body turned buoyant, like I was floating, higher and higher. All around me was a warm, bubbly sensation, like every cell in my body was air soluble. Behind my eyelids, sparks of blue, purple and pink exploded against a stark black backdrop.

It was happening again. It wasn't just in my imagination or a response to stress. What was this? It didn't matter. The sensation felt good and I wanted more.

Then the silky, floating sensation began to break apart, as if it was splitting and thinning behind me, transforming into a hard, cold net. I shivered, as if my body had re-animated. A disconnected sense of panic rose within me, to try to hold on to that warm, dreamlike state for as long as possible. Immediately, I felt the whole of my body return, every joint, ligament and muscle.

I opened my eyes to see Evan's face, his fingers stroking my cheek while looking down at me with a gentle smile. His eyes blazed an indescribable electric blue.

"What happened?" I whispered.

"I don't know. It looked like you fell asleep. You looked so peaceful." He leaned down and kissed my lips again.

~ ☾ ~

"Are you serious? I just fell asleep in the middle of our kiss?"

I could see a slight flush in Evan's skin. "I guess it wasn't too exciting for you?"

I shook my head. He couldn't have been more wrong. In fact, I had never before been so excited in my whole entire life. "No, not at all. I was..." I looked around, but my head began to spin and the world tilted to the side. I stumbled backward, but he caught me.

"Take it easy. Are you okay?"

I shook my head and placed my hand on my forehead. "I don't know. I feel like I've been spinning circles for the last ten minutes. I'm dizzy, or disoriented, or...something."

"You look pale. Maybe we should get you home."

I half-walked, half-staggered back to my apartment with Evan beside me casting concerned, sidelong stares my way ever few steps. I had to admit, I was getting a little tired of this Evan helping Sarah pattern that had begun to happen with the two of us.

Once home, I turned to him. "Thanks. I think I'll head to bed."

"Is everything okay?" he asked, stepping toward me.

I nodded, looking up at him, at his gorgeous face. He looked into my eyes, and I felt like melting. The last thing I wanted to do was see him leave, but it was way too soon for the alternative. Plus, I was feeling a little...off. Maybe the heat of the healing lodge had dehydrated me.

Moving in to me, he placed a hand on my back. Eyes blazing, he leaned down and ever-so-gently brushed his lips against mine. Involuntarily, I pulled him to me, my hands reaching up and cupping his face so I could return the kiss, but this time, my lips pressed against his, hot and burning.

He pulled back and smiled. "You should get your rest. I wouldn't want you to have another dizzy spell."

~ ☾ ~

I fought off the pang of disappointment. “Goodbye, Evan.”

“Goodnight, Sarah.”

After Evan left, I went straight to sleep. It wasn’t until the shrill sound of my telephone ringing the next morning that I woke.

I grabbed the phone from my bedside table and knocked my reading lamp off in the process. “Hello?” My voice came out gravelly.

“Sarah.” Amber’s pressured voice buzzed through the receiver. “It’s my mom. She’s missing.”

I cleared my throat. “What?”

“She went to the Wakina Reserve yesterday to see my Auntie Lilly and check on what was happening with the Skinwalkers. But she didn’t come home last night, and she’s not answering the phone.”

“Where’s your dad?”

“He’s on the road and isn’t answering his cell,” Amber said, her voice tight.

“Maybe she’s staying with your auntie and forgot to tell you?”

“She wouldn’t just not phone me, Sarah. I’ve tried to call every relative I have out there, and nobody is answering their phone.”

I swallowed. “What do you want to do?”

“Can you come, Sarah? Can we go to Wakina to try to find her?”

My hands turned clammy at the thought of what I’d be walking into. Paulette’s words, “bad medicine”, rattled around in my head.

“I’ll be there as soon as I can.”

*****

Overhead, the sky was gray with mist, matching the dark cloud of fear that hung over the situation. Kate and I drove to Amber’s house and when we pulled into her yard, she was already outside of her house and running toward the car. We turned around in the driveway. Before we'd even come to a full stop, Amber had hopped into the back seat, and slammed the door behind her.

I turned around. Her skin was ashen except for her cheeks which were streaked pink right down to her jaw, presumably from crying. Hazel irises were surrounded by bloodshot whites, the lids rimmed with red. Waves of anxiety rolled off her, the undercurrent pulling down on me, like I could drown in it.

"To Wakina?" I asked.

"Yes." Tears spilled down Amber's cheeks. "Go!"

We drove toward the Reservation but within minutes were forced to slow down. A small horde of people were walking on the road ahead of us. As we got closer, we realized the horde was entirely composed of children and teenagers.

The closer we got to the Reserve, the more there were. Young faces stared at us, angry, afraid or expressionless. Not a single one of them was over the age of sixteen. Some of the older teenagers carried babies and toddlers. Why would so many children be walking along the road without adults? Despite the lack of evidence for my assumption, I knew instinctively this had something to do with Paulette's disappearance.

"What's going on?" Kate asked.

"It looks like they're leaving," I said.

Kate looked at me, her forehead creased. "Why would kids be leaving without their parents?"

I shrugged and shook my head.

"Stop!" Amber said. "That's my cousin, Jeremy."

Kate stopped the car beside the older teenager Amber pointed to. His buzzed-off black hair, dark skin and russet eyes were exactly the same as Paulette's. His whole face drooped.

Amber rolled down the window. "Jeremy. Where are you going?"

~ ☾ ~

"Auntie Paulette told us to go to your house. She said you would keep the little ones safe." He looked around at the group of small faces now surrounding the car.

"Is my mom okay?" Amber asked.

"No. It's the Skinwalkers." Those words caused both him and Amber to release a blast of fear, and I suddenly felt like I'd been hit by a rocketing bowling ball right in the gut.

Just hearing the term Skinwalker out loud was enough to send cold shivers up my back. Could the Skinwalkers have Paulette? Did they harm her? Was it too late?

"What's happening?" Amber asked.

"The adults are running the Skinwalkers out of Wakina," Jeremy said. His eyes darkened with fear and a shiver crawled up my spine. "They have them all locked in the community centre, and Ernie's praying for the protection of the community."

"Okay," Amber said. "Let the elders deal with it. Our interference won't help. Kate, why don't you take some of the younger kids back to the house in the car, and Sarah and I will walk with the other kids the rest of the way?"

Kate nodded, and Amber and I hopped out as a bunch of children jumped in. Kate turned the car around, carefully drove past us, and returned down the road to Amber's house.

Amber and I walked with fifteen or so children the rest of the way back. Once we were within ten yards of her driveway, I could see a lone figure, walking in the middle of the road. Normally, a person walking on a gravel road would be no cause for concern, but today, with what was happening, I felt...jumpy.

He wore a dark tailored suit and button-down shirt, hands in his pants pockets, his black suit jacket flapping in the wind behind him. Long, brownish-black hair swirled around his head in the misty breeze. I focused on reading his feelings. They felt black, cold and wet, like being plunged into the North Atlantic. As we passed him, he watched, head tilted to the side, staring. His face, chiseled and angular, had a distinctly European look that seemed familiar.

I stared ahead and marched right past him, bee-lining straight into Amber's house. I wasn't there for five minutes before Paulette came crashing through the front door followed by at least twenty people, including Noreen.

"Mom!" Amber said.

"Just a minute," Paulette said as she strode straight into the living room and closed the curtains. She proceeded to close every blind and curtain on the main floor. Amber followed her around, peppering her with questions that were largely ignored. People swarmed the house, crying as they retrieved their children.

"Mom. What's going on?"

Paulette whirled around. "They got away."

My heart sank.

"But how, Mom? How could that happen?"

"We had the stronghold. Or...we thought we did." Paulette's face crumpled and she sobbed. I'd never seen Paulette show so much emotion before.

"Mom? What happened?" Amber's voice was small. Strained.

"They counterattacked, cursing Ernie so he became disoriented and confused, long enough for them to get away." Paulette looked at Amber, her eyes watery. "Ernie stayed back to pray for some of the people who were hurt. But not everyone survived."

Air whistled past Amber's lips. "No." She shook her head.

Paulette stared at the floor and then stepped toward Amber and pulled her into her arms. Initially, Amber resisted, but then she gave in, melting into her mother.

A tear streaked down Paulette's face as she kissed Amber's head. "Auntie Lilly is gone."

~ ☾ ~

CHAPTER EIGHT

"Ready for a healing?" Noreen whispered to me.

She was the only one still there after everyone else had taken their children and returned to their homes. She sat down on the brown tweed sofa and turned toward me with her cloudy stare. I squirmed, still not used to the way she looked at me. Was I ready for another healing? I wasn't entirely sure I was ready to hear what might come out of her mouth.

I took a deep breath and exhaled loudly. "Sure."

She placed her thumb on my forehead and with her free hand, pulled a diamond-shaped pendulum from her pocket. She started to swing the blue stone back and forth and closed her eyes.

She swung the pendulum for what felt like five minutes, in complete silence. Blood rushing through my head sounded like thunder in my ears.

Finally, her mouth opened. "Indigo."

My mind whirred. Hadn't Evan said that same word just days ago? Her hand dropped from my face as her eyes popped open.

"The ancestors are telling me you're...an Indigo Child." Her emotional state was so weird, I couldn't even read it. It was like a glass of oil and water, fear, hope and excitement all together, but repelling each other somehow.

Noreen looked away, her expression unfocused. "Are you sure? Are you sure she's a true Indigo?" she muttered out loud as if speaking to someone unseen.

~ ☾ ~

My skin crawled.

She turned to me and leveled her milky stare on my face. "They're telling me you're in great danger."

"I don't get it," I said. "Are you talking about the color of my eyes?"

"No. Not your eyes," she said, her brow furrowed. "You do know what you are, don't you?"

Why did I feel like I was being accused of something, or like I was being tested on a question I was supposed to know but hadn't studied for? "What I am? No. I don't know what you're talking about."

"It does involve your eye color, yes. Eye color is the classic marking of the Indigo Child." Noreen's voice was even, but her face transformed into a deeply grooved frown. "It is said there is a very special kind of human who inhabits the earth, a completely new incarnation, one with an indigo aura."

"Okay?" My heart flittered.

"You are the next stage of human evolution." She eyed me as if deciding whether I could comprehend the weight of her words. "Did you know your aura isn't clear, like the rest of us, but instead, yours has an indigo tinge?"

"No." I shook my head.

"And when a person's life force is so potent, sometimes it can actually be manifested in the material world, like it has in your eyes." Noreen paused, the yellowed whites of her eyes visible above and below the milky brown irises. "I have never seen another Indigo Child. They are said to be very rare."

"Does that explain why Sarah knows what everybody is feeling all the time?" Amber asked.

Noreen turned to me. "Is this true? You feel what others feel?"

I shrugged, my face warming. "I do."

"Perhaps this is her gift as an Indigo Child," Noreen

~ ☾ ~

said. “It is believed that Indigo Children will show signs of a sixth sense.”

Was it possible that my freakish ability to feel the emotions of others was actually because I was this...Indigo Child? I bit my lip as I contemplated how to react. I was equal parts freaked out, annoyed, and angry.

I glanced at Amber. She was sitting partially hunched, her eyes narrowed as she watched Noreen. She sat up.

I took a breath. “I don’t know. This all sounds so—”

“So, is this Indigo Child thing a spiritual thing? Or is it an evolutionary thing?” Amber interrupted, biting her nails.

“Sort of both, if you will. She is more like a spiritual mutation,” Noreen said. “She’s definitely not like the rest of us.”

Amber’s eyebrow quirked. “Sarah’s a spiritual mutant—”

“You know what?” I said, interrupting her and getting up off the sofa. “I think I’ve heard enough of this today.”

“I know this is difficult, Sarah.” Noreen eyed me. “But take my words seriously. Please consider the fact that power of this magnitude commands great obligation. You must actively seek out your purpose in life and nurture your power.”

I glanced at Paulette who looked as shocked as I felt. I turned back to Noreen. “So tell me, Noreen, does this have anything to do with the Skinwalkers?”

Noreen’s posture slumped slightly. “I’m beginning to think it’s no coincidence the Skinwalkers have found a location to infest so close to you, Sarah.”

My heart thumped in my chest. Why would my being an Indigo Child have anything to do with the arrival of Skinwalkers?

Noreen’s head jerked up and her gaze was fixed on my face once again. “Be wary, Sarah. Skinwalkers are warlocks, and some are high priests and priestesses who have embraced dark magic." She reached out to grasp my hand, but I pulled away. "I know that Ernie told you how they like to consume the souls of their victims. If they have discovered you and your indigo aura, I have no doubt they want it."

~ ☾ ~

CHAPTER NINE

I had Evan over to my apartment, knowing I had to make a decision. It was time to either tell him what was going on with me or stop seeing him. Because when I saw him, I just couldn't pretend everything was normal any longer.

He sat down in my oversized chair, directly across from me in my living room. He was busy rubbing the ivory chenille fabric on the arm. "Soft chair. Very comfy." His smile lit up his entire face. "Maybe you should come and sit with me over here?"

"Sure." I smiled and joined him, the two of us fitting into the chair like it had been made just for us. I nestled into his chest, his heartbeat thudding against my ear. He began stroking my hair, his hand moving from the back of my head all the way down to the middle of my back.

How exactly was I going to bring up all of my issues without sounding like an absolute madwoman? The last thing I wanted was for him to be scared off and risk never seeing him again. But I couldn't go on pretending I wasn't scared as hell.

"I'm happy you invited me over, Sarah," he murmured. He switched to stroking my shoulder and arm, the sensation sending goose bumps all over my skin, my entire body warming.

I decided to limit the supernatural information just to the Skinwalkers. I didn't fully buy the Indigo Child theory yet, so there was no point in going there with him at this point.

~ ☾ ~

I took a deep breath. “I need to talk to you about something.”

His stroking ceased momentarily. “Oh?”

“I need to tell you what really happened that day we first met in the forest.”

Evan shifted in the chair, pulling his torso back from me slightly so he could look me in the eye. “Sure. Go ahead.”

I swallowed, knowing there was no easy way to say it. “I was attacked that day.”

Evan’s entire body stiffened and his eyes grew wide. He sat completely upright in the chair, furthering the distance between us. “Attacked? By who? Or what?”

“What I’m going to say is going to sound crazy, but keep an open mind, okay?”

Evan blinked and then nodded.

“Have you ever heard of a Skinwalker?”

His brow furrowed. “No.”

I placed my hand on his. “Skinwalkers are the name of a creature from Navajo legend; actually, not so much creatures, but people who’ve voluntarily turned to black magic with the goal of gaining power. Apparently, Skinwalkers are warlocks who practice evil, and one of those evil practices is spirit-travel. Astral-projection.”

Now Evan’s forehead was full of creases. “What does this have to do with you being attacked?”

“I’m getting to that part.” I squeezed his hand. “That morning, I hadn’t just fallen. I’d actually come face to...well...face with something. A creature with glowing, yellow eyes but with no body, no real form. It seemed to do something to me, like sink into me, into my body. I didn’t know what it was, but Amber’s mom, Paulette, says it was a Skinwalker, and that it was trying to steal my soul.”

“Are you serious?” Evan’s eyebrows had gone up high on his forehead and come together in the middle.

~ ☾ ~

"Yes. I'm serious." I glanced down at our interwoven hands that had grown clammy. I spied the strange mark on the webbing between his thumb and finger once again. He pulled his hand from mine.

"What do you mean when you say it had 'no body'?" he asked.

"It shimmered, kind of like the way heat shimmers off of pavement, without clear boundaries. But its glowing yellow eyes were clear as day."

"And it sank into you, like it was taking over your body, or...what?"

I took a deep breath and tried to steady my nerves. "Yes. It felt like it was sucking the soul right out of my body."

Evan pushed himself off of the chair and stood up, his back to me. "Have you ever had visions or seen or heard things before?"

Anger surged through me, but I tried to keep myself from showing it. I could hardly blame him for questioning the validity of what I'd seen. I would too, if it was me.

"No."

He turned around, his expression carefully composed indifference. "And you believe Amber's mom?"

I shrugged. "I don't know what to believe. All I know is that what I saw and what I felt was real."

Evan stepped back toward me and lowered himself to the ottoman directly across from the chair I sat in. He leaned forward and took both of my hands in his. "If you believe it, then I do, too."

Relief flooded my system, knowing he wasn't going to run away screaming, thinking I was a raging lunatic that needed psychotropic medication.

I looked down as my eyes began to sting, my throat choking up. "Thank you."

"Of course I believe you, Sarah."

~ ☾ ~

I blinked back the tears as one of Evan's hands touched my back, pulling me forward into a gentle embrace. His other hand remained in mine, on my lap.

That's when I spotted it again. That strange mark on his hand.

I cleared my throat. "Evan, what is that mark?"

His hand twitched, and the arm that was around my back fell to his side. "A scar."

I grasped his hand and held it up so I could inspect. "It looks so symmetrical. Almost like a burn?" I looked up to him, and his eyes were dark.

"It is a burn. My brother burned me."

~ ☾ ~

CHAPTER TEN

Before my conversation with Evan had come to a conclusion, Amber called to say an emergency search and rescue mission had been called on the Wakina Reservation. It was in direct response to the fact that the missing child's mother, Sandra, was now also missing in addition to her daughter, Jessica.

Evan and I headed straight out, wanting to do whatever we could to help the community. I'd been to Wakina enough times over the years to feel like I was an adopted community member, most of the people there accepting my presence despite my pale skin and blond hair. And I wasn't about to let Noreen's cryptic warnings keep me from living my life.

Don Whitehead, the Indian Chief of Wakina, stood before the men and women of his community to address them, waiting for the crowd of people who were raring to head out on the search and rescue mission to quiet down. The Chief waved his hands above his head and a hush fell over the group.

"We're going to break up into small teams of three or four to comb the surrounding area." His booming voice reached out, his tone strong and crystal clear, his ram-rod straight back and commanding presence absolutely oozing power and authority.

I was amazed so many people had turned out to volunteer for the re-initiated search and rescue mission to find Jessica and Sandra, especially since, if Paulette was correct in what she said, many of them thought the mother had actually sacrificed Jessica and joined the Skinwalkers.

I overheard two women whispering and I strained to listen without being obvious.

“Why should we look for her? We all know what she has done, what she’s become,” one woman said.

The other woman’s voice was quieter. “I know. Such a waste of time.”

Then a third, male voice interjected. “Don’t talk about my sister that way. She’s missing. That’s all we know for sure.”

I glanced over at them, and the two women looking at the man, their eyes wide. Both of them lowered their eyes and nodded to him before they turned and walked away.

“We need to spread out,” Don said, instantly sending a ripple of silence through the group. The hushed worry of the crowd slid in and out of me like a slippery tentacle. “But first, Ernie will lead us in a prayer to the Creator.”

Paulette, Noreen, Kate and Amber stood together as one small group in front of the community centre, while Evan and I lingered nearby. The slight breeze shimmering through the leaves was the only sound besides Ernie’s voice. Overhead, the navy sky was striped with gauzy clouds.

Ernie stepped forward and turned to face the group. He began a low chant that floridly grew in volume and pitch. There was something about that praying, chanting sound that tugged at my heart and gut, something that spoke to me on a most basic, visceral level. Without even realizing it, tears had sprung to my eyes, and my throat was all choked up.

When he was finished, he looked out solemnly to the people. “We are searching for our sister, Sandra. She is facing the darkness inside of herself. And if there is a chance our precious Jessica is still alive, we must find her. Bring them home," Ernie said.

Fear rippled through the community like a low hum of sheet lightning that spread momentarily, then receded, but didn't go away. The men and women nodded, exchanging quiet comments.

What would we find if we stumbled across Sandra? Was she a hostage, held against her will, as her relatives so earnestly believed? Or was she, in fact, turning evil and becoming a Skinwalker as Paulette expected? If I was being honest with myself, I had come to this search more for myself than anything else, because I wanted to know the truth.

Amber and Paulette paired up with Noreen and Kate, the four of them geared up in hiking boots.

"Be careful, okay?" I said to them as Evan and I prepared to search.

Noreen looked directly at me. "You shouldn't be here, Sarah."

Amber stepped forward and faced Noreen head-on. "Sarah's here for me. I asked her to come."

Noreen shook her head and glanced at Paulette. "Do you endorse this?"

Paulette looked at me apologetically. "I'm sorry, Sarah. But no, I don't."

"I didn't think so," Noreen said, turning back to me. "Don't you see you are putting us all at risk?"

I felt my throat tighten. "I'm just trying to help."

"Well, maybe you should help by leaving. You might not want to listen to me, but I know they're here for you. You're not helping us at all; you're only drawing them to us."

Amber placed her hands on her hips. "Noreen, that's not fair."

I placed a hand on her shoulder. "No, Amber. If she doesn't think I should be here, then maybe I should leave."

~ ☾ ~

Paulette nodded. “I’m sorry, Sarah. I think it’s for the best if you leave. But please, be careful.” Her gaze flickered to Evan.

“I’ll be with her,” Evan said as he twined his fingers through mine.

Noreen’s eyes narrowed before she spun on her heel and walked away, gray hair whirling, her pants showing off a wide strip of skin above worn-out tennis shoes.

“Let’s go, Sarah.” He grabbed the duffle bag he’d packed full of gear. We took off in the opposite direction of the crowd, back toward Evan’s vehicle.

Once out of earshot, I couldn’t hold my anger in any longer. “I can’t believe they don’t want my help. You’d think they would accept help from anybody who was willing to go on a rescue mission.”

“Maybe it’s safer for you this way,” he said.

I rolled my eyes. “Whatever,” I said, immediately regretting my rude tone. I looked up at his hurt expression. “Sorry. I’m taking my anger out on you, aren’t I?”

He shrugged and smiled with tight lips. “It’s okay, I know you’re mad.”

We kept walking to the parking lot behind the community centre, Evan’s vehicle nearly within sight.

An odd sensation flooded me, the back of my neck prickling, as if I was being watched.

I stopped and glanced behind me. Evan turned at the same time. Three men with backpacks stood behind us and began to walk in our direction.

Initially, I was certain they were part of the search and rescue team, but as they drew nearer, I realized there was something about their eyes, even perceptible from a distance, almost as if...they were glowing? My knees grew weak as my stomach twisted.

“Evan,” I whispered.

Immediately, the three made an about-face and

turned toward the trees that ran around the community centre, disappearing from view. A cold chill ran up my spine as my heart skipped a beat.

"Come on," Evan whispered, grasping my hand, pulling me in the opposite direction of the men. We continued toward Evan's vehicle, just around the corner.

When we reached the side of the building, the hair on the back of my neck stood on end. I turned around, blood pounding in my head.

Yellow eyes, vaporous body, a Skinwalker.

It rushed me.

I hit my head on the ground as its form began compressing into mine. The pressure built inside of me, expanding in my body like being violently filled with quick-drying cement, the force crushing the breath right out of me.

I clung to my physical body with every ounce of strength I had, but the Skinwalker's force mounted, pain shuddering through every muscle.

"*Subsisto tentatio indigentia*!" someone said. Was that Evan talking? "*Resisto*! *Resisto*!"

Immediately, the attack stopped. The pressure retreated with a loud creak of ligaments and tendons, the pain rifling, white-hot, every square inch of my body felt like it was lit on fire.

"Sarah!" Evan said.

I lay on the asphalt, my back pressed against pebbles and rocks, my head pulsing from the impact. I tried to push myself to sitting, but my aching body protested too much. I slumped back to the ground.

"Are you hurt? Can you walk?" Evan hovered over me with a wild look on his face.

I shook my head. "Not yet. Where is it?"

"It's gone." Evan leaned over me, peering into my eyes. "I'm going to get you out of here." He grasped me under the legs and back and picked me up, carrying me the rest of the way to his vehicle.

"What just happened?" I asked. "What did you say in that foreign language?"

"Foreign language?" His brow furrowed. "What?"

My mind whirred, trying to think of an explanation for what I'd heard, and why this time, the Skinwalker suddenly stopped. At the abandoned house, I'd imagined injuring the Skinwalker with its own feelings, but this time? I hadn't even had a chance to do anything before it just...stopped.

"Did you hear that voice saying *resisto* or something?" I grasped tightly to his neck as he began to jog.

"I didn't hear anything," he said, his voice pressured from running. "One minute that thing was sinking into you, and the next, it stopped. What did you hear?"

My chest tightened as I bounced up and down in his arms. "I heard someone speaking in a different language."

Evan frowned, but there was something strange about his expression. Something dark, as if he knew something he wasn't saying out loud. My stomach flip-flopped.

Then Evan glanced down at me, the dark expression completely gone from his face, replaced now with concern. Had I just imagined the strange expression?

"Maybe you heard the Skinwalker's voice in your head. He was inside you, wasn't he?"

My mouth opened, but I couldn't answer. Thoughts whirled around in my head, so elusive I couldn't latch on to any one of them. My head spun and my heart was pounding so hard in my chest I could hardly breathe.

"Sarah. Did you hear me? Maybe it was the Skinwalkers' voice you heard."

I forced myself to nod, but there was something about what he said that just didn't ring true. Evan slowed as we approached his vehicle but continued to look down

~ ☾ ~

at me, waiting for an answer, imploring me with his eyes.

I swallowed. "Maybe."

At his car, he lowered me to the ground. My muscles ached, the way they had when I was a kid after I'd jumped from my grandfather's hay loft. But my body was the least of my concern.

"Can you get in?" he asked.

I looked up at him, his eyes blazing beneath his worried brow. He looked genuine in his concern, like a caring boyfriend. He stroked the side of my cheek as he peered into my eyes, as if making sure I was okay.

I nodded and squeaked out, "Yes."

I slid in, and once Evan got into the drivers' side, we drove away. As we exited the Reservation, one lone man walked along the side of the road, the same man that walked along the gravel road by Amber's house. This time his dark hair was dry, long and curling around his shoulders.

He peered at us as we drove by. Nodding, his lips curled back, showing a flash of white teeth right before he walked off the road and slipped into the forest.

~ ☾ ~

CHAPTER ELEVEN

On some level, I knew it was a nightmare, but that didn't make it any less terrifying.

I walked down a long corridor, dimly lit by flickering bare bulbs. There were no windows, no rooms. I continued to walk. Where was I? Would I be trapped here forever?

The corridor came to an abrupt end with an empty waiting room to my right. I went in. The television was on, the volume so high it echoed off of the blanched walls and the pale furnishings. In the corner, something caught my eye.

I turned and jumped. Noreen sat in a chair, her empty gaze fixed on a wall of white. Her pupils were dilated to nearly the full size of her iris, creating a flinty tone to her thousand-yard stare.

She sat perfectly still, a white hospital gown over her clothing. Blood pooled beneath her feet, dripping off of the white fabric of the chair. The scarlet liquid soaked into her white socks. I tried to scream, but when I opened my mouth, nothing came out.

I turned and ran, barreling through the corridor, stumbling. The lights went out.

Suddenly, I was outside in the darkness. Spruce trees swayed overhead in the moonless night, the sharp scent of pine needles and balsam heavy in the air. To my left was the empty playground. I glanced to my right.

The man in black stood before me. My breath caught in my throat as he walked toward me, his mouth curled up into a sly smile, his white teeth glinting in the stark yard light.

Then, directly in front of me, three transparent Skinwalkers stood, bile-yellow eyes gleaming, blocking my access to the path out of the trees. I turned to my left. Evan stood, smiling at me, holding onto a chain-link swing, his head tilted to the side. I ran to him as the creatures around me closed in. I tried to scream his name, but again, nothing came out.

The closer I got, the more his smile fell. He held his arms out to me, his eyes black as onyx. I ran right into his arms. They were warm, and they folded me into him. I relaxed.

Then something changed.

Evan looked down at me, his eyes widening as his face began to move, as if something scuttled beneath his skin. His face became a strange mask, no longer Evan, but transforming into someone different, someone evil. The man in black.

He smiled at me, a predatory look to his grin, eyes glittering. I tried to push away, but his arms were a cage around me, squeezing me so my lungs were forced to empty.

His face began to distort, the skin bulging in places, stretched tight, shiny. Then the skin peeled off entirely and all that was left were the glowing yellow eyes and clear, shimming form of a Skinwalker.

I screamed.

~ ☾ ~

CHAPTER TWELVE

The next day, I shrugged off the bad dream and went to work. After my shift was over, I met Evan at the bar for a drink. Skinwalkers or not, I wasn't going to stop living my life. If anything, knowing I'd nearly had my soul sucked out of me made my resolve to live each day to its absolute fullest that much more solid.

"I suck at pool. Seriously," I said as Evan set all the balls into the little triangle. I'd only played pool a handful of times.

"I'll teach you. One lesson and you'll be set." He handed me a pool cue and grinned.

"All right, but no laughing at me."

Evan's smile softened. "I wouldn't laugh at you."

The way he looked at me made my heart flutter in my chest. Could he see how much he affected me by just looking at me? There was no doubt in my mind that he could read me like an open book. My cheeks continued to warm up, and now I was a little hot under the collar, too.

"Thank you."

He winked. "Why don't you break, and then I can see what's going wrong," Evan suggested. He leaned against the pool table with his cue. In his blue jeans, black tee, and dark leather jacket, there was a reason why every girl in the bar was watching.

I glanced around. Only fifteen or so people were here, being that it was middle of the week. I didn't really want my pool lesson to be observed by everyone in town.

~ ☾ ~

Public humiliation was not something I particularly enjoyed.

"All right." I leaned forward and placed my stick on the table, holding it in the weird little triangle I'd been told to make with my fingers, and aimed on the white ball. I took several little test movements, and then I hit it.

The cue nicked the ball on the right side, sending it forward with a sideways spin. It hit the triangle of colorful balls with a wimpy little click. The colored balls spread out, just slightly. I cursed and straightened up.

Evan was still watching the balls move, and then he looked at me, nodding. "I see what the problem is. I'll show you what's going wrong, if you'd like?"

"Sure. I'd like to not be the source of entertainment in the bar."

Evan chuckled, the sound lighting up the room around me. "Okay, let's start with your fingers."

He came up beside me and gestured toward the table. I leaned over and placed the pool stick on my fingers, the way I'd been shown by Tyler, my Ex.

"I think this is the main problem. See how your fingers are so unstable in this position?" He leaned forward and our bodies came into contact as he stretched out to touch my fingers. The weight of his muscled arm settled alongside me and when his hand touched mine, a palpable buzz glided through my body.

My breath caught. Evan's hand stopped moving momentarily, as if he felt it too.

He glanced at me, and then he went on. "If you set your hands up like this...." He moved in closer. "Do you mind...?" I shook my head as my throat went dry. The hard length of his body pressed into me, his breath warm on my cheek. His heady fragrance infused my senses, leather, mint, and man. I struggled to focus on the white ball at the end of my cue, too distracted by his warm fingers gently moving mine.

His hands were soft, but the skin calloused enough in places to show he didn't avoid hard work. Each finger was long and tapered, with perfectly shaped nails. He positioned my hand and the triangular shape between his thumb and forefinger caught my eye.

"Your brother, how did he burn you?" I pointed to the scar on his hand.

He took in a long, deep breath. "It was an accident while we were camping."

"That must have hurt."

He chuckled. "Yes. It hurt a lot." His gaze returned to my fingers holding the pool cue.

I debated questioning him further about the scar, why it was so symmetrical, and why it seemed to be a distinctive shape, but was so distracted by the sensation of his body alongside mine, the questions scattered in my mind and dissipated like smoke in the wind.

"There. If you can maintain that position while you concentrate on the white ball, it will make a huge improvement in your aim." He stood upright and backed away, and I instantly missed that warm heat against my left side. "Okay. Go for it."

I focused on the white ball, my thoughts tangled, and my breathing pace irregular. I hit it, and while this time it didn't spin, the shot was still weak. The colored balls barely even moved.

I looked at Evan, who smiled. Not a mocking smile...just a gentle, encouraging one. "Better. Now, let's work on your shot." Evan slid his jacket off and placed it on a chair, revealing ripped muscles beneath thin cotton.

He came up behind me and leaned into me once again. This time, his entire body pressed into mine. His warm, heavily muscled arm reached alongside mine once again, and I bent over, the sensation so intensely erotic, I felt dizzy. I struggled to even see the cue ball, much less try to hit it.

"Okay, so your fingers are in place," he said as he rearranged my hand slightly, my whole body tingling from fingertips to toes. "Now the key is to make sure you don't tip the end of your stick up or down. It seems like you're scared the cue will bite into the felt." He turned toward me, and his minty breath caressed my cheek. I turned, and our faces were within an inch of contact. It was almost as if a tangible buzz had ignited between us.

What was it about this man that had me so lust-drunk and crazily out of touch with my rational thoughts? His personality was as beautiful as his looks, and I knew that was a big part of it, but there just seemed to be something between us that defied understanding.

Evan nodded and smiled, his gaze dropping momentarily to my mouth. He licked his lips and then turned his head. "You'll need to let go of that fear."

He reached around me then, and with his right hand, placed it directly on top of mine at the back of the cue. Every movement he made I felt, every breath he took, every beat of his heart. With every subtle change in his body, his muscles tightened and released. My breathing staggered, my heart stuttering.

Oh, boy.

He turned his face into mine and then whispered, quietly into my ear, "Ready?" His breath tickled my cheek and heat rose within my body.

"Yes." I murmured. *God, yes. I'm ready to push you down to the floor and jump your bones.*

In a sudden move, he pushed our right arms forward and the loud crack of the balls connecting rang out. I blinked. The cue ball had stopped dead, while the target ball had gone directly into a corner pocket. Evan stood upright but remained pressed against me. I straightened and turned toward him. My left breast pressed against his chest as his right hand stroked my back.

"So that's how it's done," I whispered.

"It's that simple," Evan said, looking at me with eyes lit up like jewels. He leaned forward, his soft lips brushing mine. I gasped as my body became infused with heat, my skin tingling. I struggled to maintain my grip on the pool stick, my left hand snaking up his hard torso.

He pulled back and gazed down at me with a soft smile. I swallowed.

"Let's see what you can do." He stepped away from me entirely. I couldn't shake that odd sense of loss from his distance. I nodded, turning back toward the pool table, my thoughts jumbled, my body completely unhinged.

I walked around the table and back to the cue ball, now directly opposite Evan. I leaned over, carefully arranged my fingers, and glanced up at him. Evan nodded in encouragement. I took the shot, this time the ball connecting with its target just like it was supposed to.

Evan came toward me. "Perfect shot."

"Thanks." I smiled. "How about another lesson?"

Evan's face broke out into a sly smile as well, and he moved toward me, eyes blazing. Without a word, he folded me into him, this time the pressure against my back even more exquisitely tight. It seemed every inch of our bodies was touching. His rough stubble rubbed the sensitive skin of my cheek.

He turned his face toward me, his arms encasing me and whispered, "Focus, Sarah."

I took a deep breath, distracted by the warmth of our bodies, his raspy breath in my ear, the intoxicating scent of him. With every beat of his heart, mine echoed, until our heartbeats were unified, beating with exactly the same rhythm.

~ ☾ ~

“Focus,” he said, his voice smooth, melodic.

That soft languor filled me, and I was floating once again, carried away by a buoyant sense of ecstasy. I opened my eyes and gazed at the cue ball, my body buzzing.

I put all of my energy into focusing, into making that ball sail across the table and connect with the yellow one, which would go directly into the right corner pocket.

I pulled back, aiming.

Before I moved, the ball sprung into movement and rocketed down the table, crashing into the yellow ball and sending it toward the corner pocket. But instead of going in, the yellow ball skipped the table and hurtled through the air, knocking over my beer bottle and rolling to the ground behind the table. My beer bottle spun on the table for a moment, and then slid off, smashing on the floor into a thousand brown shards.

~ ☾ ~

CHAPTER THIRTEEN

"What the hell just happened?" I said, turning accusing eyes on Evan.

His own eyes had widened to the point where there was a circle of white around his blue iris, mirrored by his open mouth. He looked at the broken beer bottle, the ball on the floor and then at the pool cue in my hand. He blinked.

His lack of response sent a ripple of fear through me, setting my already erratic heartbeat into a further arrhythmia. "Evan. You saw it, too. Say something."

His mouth twitched, but before he answered, a waitress I knew as Cammie strode over with her bar tray and a big dishrag on top of it. Her light brown hair was piled high on her head, like a red carpet up-do that looked completely out of sync with her ripped jeans and tube top. She set the tray down on the table and looked at the two of us with a smile, as if sending a pool ball hurtling through the air without touching it happened every day. "Little mishap?"

Without waiting for a reply, Cammie got to work wiping the table when the bartender, Sam, showed up with a broom and dustpan.

Nodding to us with a bored expression, he bent down and began sweeping up the mess, his Bon Jovi 1992 World Tour shirt wet with sweat stains under the arms. Their silent cleaning only seemed to magnify the silence that was taking place between Evan and I, and I had to fight the urge to turn and run, putting this bar and Evan as far behind me as humanly possible.

Instead, I fought back the growing restlessness in my legs, determined to wait to hear Evan's explanation.

Once the glass was in the dustpan, Sam straightened up and nodded at us once again before dropping the contents in the garbage can.

"Want another beer, Sarah?" Cammie asked with a big smile. Her tray was now under her arm and her thumb was strung through a loop in her jeans.

"No, thanks," I said, plastering a smile on my face.

She nodded and looked to Evan, who shook his head. Then she shrugged and wandered away.

"Let's talk. In your vehicle," I said, grabbing my hooded sweater and pulling it over my head.

"Okay." Evan nodded and followed me out.

He opened the side door for me and once I was seated, went around and hopped into the driver's seat and stared straight ahead. "I saw it, too."

The strange sensation of my chest expanding built inside of me. "Why did that ball move?"

Evan's Adam's apple bobbed as he swallowed and slowly shook his head, his gaze fixed on the dashboard. "Would you believe me if I said I have no idea?"

I looked at him, wishing I could read him better. I focused on his feelings, and while they were tightly balled up, I could still sense a thread of confusion seeping out of him like a leaky faucet. "I believe you, but I wish at least one of us had some answers."

Evan's entire body relaxed, as if he was relieved I believed him. He turned to look at me, his eyes lit up like blue Christmas lights from the glow of the dashboard. "I wish we had answers, too. There has to be an explanation, right?"

I looked out through the windshield at the trees that ringed the parking lot and shivered. Would my life ever be normal again? Would I never be able to go on a date with a guy without something abnormal and unexplainable happening? I was beginning to think the answer to that question was no.

"I want to go home," I said.

"Sure." Evan put the vehicle in gear and we left, driving in silence.

As we passed the turn that led in the direction to Amber's house, I contemplated the possibility that this was related to Noreen's theory about me being an Indigo Child. According to Noreen, Indigo Children were expected to have a sixth sense, and that seemed to explain the way I could feel the emotions of others. But could it also mean I had telekinesis? Could I telepathically move material objects, like the ball? Somehow, it just didn't connect, because it had never happened before, and I hadn't even really tried to do it.

I debated telling Evan about the whole Indigo Child thing. He'd accepted the Skinwalker situation when I'd told him and had even been confronted by one already. So, perhaps telling him about Noreen's Indigo Child theory would no longer be such a stretch.

"I have to tell you something that is going to seem really weird."

Evan glanced at me as he drove down my street. "Okay?"

I took a deep breath to galvanize my courage. "Do you remember Noreen and Paulette from the search and rescue? Noreen was the one that told me to leave."

Evan came to a stop outside my apartment and parked. "Yes. What about her?"

"This has to do with the Skinwalkers." I looked at him and he nodded in encouragement. "She thinks they're here for me, because she believes I'm different from other people."

Evan's brow furrowed. "How are you different?"

"She thinks...I have a soul that is a different color

from everyone else, an indigo soul that's the same color as my eyes. She says...I'm an Indigo Child."

Evan's eyes glazed over a bit and he seemed to no longer be really seeing me. "What does that have to do with the Skinwalkers?"

"She says my soul is not only a different color, but that it is a powerful source of energy, too." I leveled my gaze at him. "Did you know I can tell what people are feeling?"

Evan's eye widened at first, and then his brow knitted together once again. "Pardon?"

I nodded. "I know. I told you it's weird. But it's true. I can tell what other people are feeling, almost all the time. It's like their feelings simply spill out of them and flood into my body."

"Hang on a second. Are you saying you can read minds?" Evan straightened up in his seat.

I chuckled. "No. But I can feel emotions, just like they're happening to me. If someone is sad, I feel like it's raining inside of my body. When someone is happy, it's like having a hot air balloon bouncing around inside of me. I can feel the emotions as if they are my own."

"No kidding?" Evan cracked the slightest smile. "Can you tell what I'm feeling right now?"

"Okay, so this is where it gets interesting. It seems that you are harder for me to read."

Evan's eyebrows shot upward. "Oh?"

"The first time I met you I was completely baffled. I had no idea why I couldn't pick up a thing from you."

Evan smiled.

"I have to admit," I said, "I was a little paranoid about it at first. But after that, I started to pick up on it more and more, as if your feelings had sprung a leak and you didn't notice." He chuckled at this. "Did you know you were keeping your feelings from me?"

He shook his head. "This is amazing. Unbelievable."

~ ☾ ~

He scratched the stubble on his chin. "No, I didn't know I was keeping my feelings from you. It's probably because I work so hard at controlling my feelings. I wasn't exactly brought up in an emotionally expressive family. I learned to shut most of my feelings down."

His expression changed for a millionth of a second to something that looked melancholic. Yet, there was no emotion that spilled out of him, only confirming his statement. "That must be why."

"So now you know about the Indigo Child theory," I said. "I can't say I've fully embraced the idea, but it does explain a few things. Anyway, the reason I've told you all of this is that I wonder if it has anything to do with that ball moving. And I know you've felt that strange energy exchange between us, haven't you?"

Evan blinked and then met my gaze head-on. "I've felt it. I haven't really wanted to admit it to myself, let alone out loud to another person, but yes, I've noticed something happen between us."

"I knew it," I said, narrowing my eyes at him. "And you played dumb this whole time. Letting me feel like a lunatic."

"Sorry." Evan nodded slowly. "Okay. Here's my theory." He twisted in his car seat so he was facing me. "There is an energy thing happening between us, right?"

"Yes. Before, it was like a sense of floating and pure pleasure. But today, it was more than that. The damn ball actually moved, Evan."

He nodded. "I know."

"So, you've felt that sense of intense pleasure, of floating?"

"I have. I didn't understand it, and sometimes, I thought I was maybe imagining it. But, yes, I've felt it every time you have. At the old house, in the park, today."

I searched his face for answers. "But today, the ball actually moved."

~ ☾ ~

"I think we can channel that energy between us like a current."

My heart thumped. "Say again?"

"It only happens when I'm around you. Never when I'm alone. I first noticed it that night at the bar. Do you remember during the incident with Jeff, how the lights flickered and then broke? I think that was the first time it happened."

I shot him a look. "Seriously?"

"I'm serious. It's like the two of us together create...electricity. I don't know how else to explain it."

"How, exactly, do we create this electrical current?"

He bit his lower lip and stared out the passenger window at the cookie-cutter houses. "I don't know if I can answer that question. But I've begun to notice that I can just...bring it to me. It's not something I do consciously. My mind and body seem to just know what to do to make it...happen."

"This is amazing. I tell you I'm an Indigo Child, and you tell me that together we create energy, and that there's a pretty good chance you can control it. Unbelievable."

Evan smiled and then let out a string of profanity, sliding his hand through his hair so that it stood up on end in peaks around his head.

"I know. Unbelievable." He grasped my hand. "Want to test it out?"

~ ☾ ~

CHAPTER FOURTEEN

I turned down Evan's invitation to test out our co-created energy, opting instead for going home alone and contemplating my ridiculous, outrageously strange life.

In my apartment, I decided to lie down, the weight of reality weighing on me. I stared at the ceiling in the darkness, considering what I'd confessed to him and his subsequent confession. It all seemed so surreal, the idea that there was a creation of energy between us and his belief he could control it. Was there any other explanation? If I truly was an Indigo Child with a powerful essence, was he something different, like an Indigo Child as well?

That niggling at the back of my mind continued as I weighed all of the information I'd received over the last few days.

Evan's arrival the day of the Skinwalker attack.

That voice that spoke the foreign language that Evan denied was his.

His strange burn mark that looked like a deliberate symbol on his hand.

His immediate acceptance of my explanation about being an Indigo Child and his own admittance of being aware of the energy connection between us.

Then it hit me. Evan was from Eagle Creek, Utah. Was it near the four corners?

I grabbed my cell and did a Google search. Sure enough, Eagle Creek was the closest community to the four corners.

~ ☾ ~

I dialed his cell number.

"Hello?" His fluid, low timbre immediately caused my heart to thump.

"Can I come over?" I said, trying to keep my voice even. "I've changed my mind. I want to take you up on your offer."

I could almost hear the smile in his voice. "Sure. Room two-twelve."

I arrived within twenty minutes.

His hotel room looked exactly like the one we'd rented on my eighth birthday when we'd had a swimming party here at the pool. A burgundy bedspread covered the queen bed, and brass lamps sat atop bedside tables next to the headboard. At least the oak desk had a new flatscreen television on it.

"Come on in." Evan walked over to two chairs on either side of a table by the large window, sat down and poured himself a glass of bottled water, dropping in a few ice cubes from the plastic container that sat on the tabletop.

"Want some water? Or maybe something stronger? I have a mini-bar over there." He gestured with his hand and then took a sip, looking at me over his glass, through a fringe of black lashes.

"I'm fine, thanks."

He nodded and set the glass down. "You just missed my brother, Stefano. I was having a meeting with him. He's only here for a few days to give me a hand while I make this land deal, and then he's going back to Utah."

"Can I meet him?" I asked.

Evan grimaced, showing his bottom row of perfectly even, white teeth. "I wouldn't recommend that. He's a little sketchy. I don't think you'd feel comfortable around him." He gestured for me to sit in the chair across from him. I did.

"Explain 'sketchy'," I said.

~ ☾ ~

"He's a little different. Intense. Not very talkative." Evan paused. "He doesn't like women, either."

"He's gay?"

"No, he's not gay. He just doesn't like women in general. He doesn't trust them. I guess it's because he didn't exactly have a great relationship with our mother."

"So, is it better now?"

Evan took a deep breath and ran his fingers through his hair, making it stand up in peaks all around his head. "My parents are dead."

"Oh, I'm so sorry, Evan," I said, reaching out to take his hand. He glanced down at our joined hands and a tiny muscle twitched in his jaw. "What happened?"

Evan cleared his throat, and out came a funny choking sound. "Excuse me. I'll be right back." He stood up and disappeared into the bathroom.

I spied his cell on the bedside table and gingerly stepped over to it and squinted to see what was on the screen. A little pang of guilt resounded through my chest. But I was here for answers, wasn't I?

The screen was still lit up, with several texts back and forth between Evan and one person who called themselves Valentedanti. What was that, a weird mish-mash of Evan's last name and...what? I began to read the texts sent earlier today.

Valentedanti: What is going on?

Reply: Nothing. At hotel alone.

Valentedanti: Where is subject?

Reply: I don't know.

Valentedanti: Find out. Now.

Then running water stopped. I turned and scuttled to the side of the bed, away from the phone. A piece of paper caught my eye, just barely visible where it was sticking out under the bed skirt. I bent down behind the bed to look at it. A phone bill.

~ ☾ ~

I read through the long list of charges, most of them to Utah, some to Arizona, some to New Mexico. But the most interesting was the one to Friuli, Italy. Was that where Stefano lived? Or other relatives?

Evan stepped out of the bathroom right at that instant. I let the paper drop from my hand and float to the floor, nudging it away with my toe.

He re-entered the room looking much more composed, the skin on his face slightly tight looking, as if he'd wet his face and then dried it off, rubbing as he did it.

"My parents died in a house fire when we were teenagers," he said, sitting down on the bed right beside me. "I was fifteen and Stefano was sixteen." His eyes were hard as flint.

"That's awful," I said. "How did the house catch fire?"

"It was the middle of the night, and we'd snuck out. When we came home, fire trucks surrounded the house. The whole thing had gone up so fast, there was no chance they could have gotten out. I hardly have a single thing to remember them by." Evan's eyes glossed over, and his gaze was distant.

I reached out and grabbed his hand once again. He started, looking down at our joined hands as if they were foreign to our bodies.

"I'm so sorry, Evan. To lose your parents like that at such an early age. It must have been so painful." My chest tightened as I watched him try to hold himself together.

He stared at me as his eyes shimmered with moisture. For the first time, I felt his emotions fully. His pain washed over me like a gale force wind, heavy, thick and endless. And there was something else in there, too. Cold and dark. Guilt? Had he been stifling his emotions this whole time?

He rose to his feet as if to hide his face, but I quickly

stood and grabbed his hand. He turned just as I pulled him in to me and our bodies collided. He looked down, his lips parted, his eyes blue fire. Our lips met in a slow, sweet kiss.

"Sarah, I want you," he whispered, his words echoing my thoughts.

His mouth met my neck, his hot breath creating delicious puffs of air that tingled up and down my spine. He backed me up to the wall.

My mind and body fought for control. Was it so bad that I wanted him and wanted to give in to my desire? My body stopped listening to this internal argument and took over.

I took in a rough breath. "I want you, too."

A low groan sounded in my ear as he kissed my earlobe and worked his way over to my jawline.

"You are so beautiful," he said in a low, husky voice. He reached up and pulled the clip out of my hair, the waves cascading down over my shoulders.

I shuddered as a sudden fear hitched itself to my mind. Lust-drunk and overwhelmed fought with morals and ethics. But I wanted him.

Evan placed a hand around the base of my head as his lips covered my mouth. I stifled a moan as he pressed himself to me, my back against the hard wall. The pressure of his mouth parted my lips, and his tongue gently probed my mouth, causing a warm, wet heat to ignite at my core.

The world evaporated around me, and all that was left were his lips, his hands on my body and my heart pounding in my chest.

"Am I moving too fast?" Evan murmured in my ear.

"No."

His fingers deftly pulled my shirt up, revealing my lacy black bra underneath. He slowly pulled my shirt the rest of the way over my head, running his hands down my arms and then unbuttoned my jeans. Before I knew it, I stood naked, my clothing a puddle at my feet. He drew in a long, deep breath as he looked me over from head to toe. I shivered under his gaze.

"You're gorgeous," he said. Then his mouth met mine again, this time hotter, more demanding.

I tugged his shirt up and off, leaving him bare-chested. I tried not to stare at where his low-rise shorts revealed a hard, flat abdomen. I undid his belt and zipper, and he stepped out of the remainder of his clothing.

He was beautiful, his skin supple and contoured with muscle. He was pressed to me in a heartbeat, grinding against me, the hard, cold wall on my back a stark contrast to the hot, demanding flesh on my front.

"God, I want you," he groaned, his warm, minty breath a soft caress over my face. He grabbed my leg under the knee and hitched it up around his thigh.

He backed me onto the bed where in the blink of an eye I was horizontal, the softness of the bedding on my back a welcome reprieve from the wall.

Evan was poised between my legs as I ran my hands up and down his thick chest muscles, up over the wide expanse of his shoulders, and then down his arms, corded and segmented. When I reached down, a low moan emerged from his mouth, his breathing coming more rapidly.

He slid down my body and kissed me, along my inner arm to my elbow, up to my shoulder, and then he pressed his lips to my clavicle.

Never before had I been filled with a desire so wild, so primal. I didn't just want him right now, I needed to have him.

"Sarah," he murmured. His face was a look of utter burning, only further igniting my need. I arched my body to his, gasping as that ache within me begged for him to be as close to me as possible. I lowered my hands to his hips and pulled him to me.

"Now," I whispered with a ragged breath.

"Wait."

Evan kissed me one more time, lightly, before pulling away. He lowered himself, kissing his way down the length of my body. I squirmed and panted as he kissed my most private, intimate parts.

When he reached over to the side table and tore open the condom package, a ripple of excitement tore through me. He put it on and before I knew it, he was positioned above me once again, his pupils dilated to an endless black. He leaned down to kiss me as simultaneously his body lowered. He pressed into me, hot and demanding, my flesh initially presenting resistance, but then giving way.

His body, his scent, filled my senses, the dizzying, spellbinding loss of control at the forefront of my awareness. I looked into his eyes, his expression primal, preoccupied, like part of him had lost all reasoning and sanity. His mouth opened as if to speak, and a soft groan emerged. He closed his eyes at first, and when he opened them, they were moist and shimmering.

We turned so I was on top of him. I leaned up, straddling his thighs and raked my fingers over his chest. Without warning, a strange impulse came over me, an urge, a yearning I felt deep in my core, at the root of my being. It defied rational thought.

"Let's do it," I said.

"Do what?"

"Do that energy connection thing," I said, panting. My heart staggered in my chest.

He looked at me, his brow furrowed. "I...I don't know how."

"You do, Evan."

"But what if I can't control it? What if it—"

~ ☾ ~

I cut him off. "Just try."

He leaned up, looked at me with eyes that smoldered a deep blue, and grabbed me by the shoulders. In one fluid movement, his lips crushed against mine, and he pulled my body back down to rest on top of him.

Then everything changed.

Like breathing in a wave of helium, my body seemed to float. Yet, I was distanced from myself, as if my brain had been severed and was held to my body by an ever-thinning thread. Floating streams of purple and blue light cascaded across my vision. Ecstasy rolled through me, the sensation better than any orgasm, any high. I reached for that pinnacle of pure pleasure my earthly body could never truly know.

When I touched it, the world fell away.

The next thing I knew, my cell phone was vibrating.

I opened my eyes. The hotel room was dimly lit, casting specters of shadow against the walls. The area was hot and smelled of aftershave, sweat and sex.

How long was I out? I glanced around. I was alone. Buzz buzz buzz. My phone. I glanced over to the empty bed beside me, the sheets rumpled. Water ran in the bathroom.

Buzz, buzz, buzz. I got up and stepped over our clothing to rifle through my jacket pocket, finally locating my cell. It was Amber. I turned the ringer off. I'd call her back later.

Evan exited the bathroom and walked over to me with a sexy smile, his nude body perfect, like a sculptural marvel. He was already hard and my own body echoed his arousal.

"Come here, gorgeous," he said, folding me into his arms. My breasts pressed against his chest, as his firmness hardened further against my hipbone. My hands snaked into his hair as his lips found mine. I wanted nothing more than to be back in that bed. His hands made their way to my breasts, his mouth to my earlobe.

I was back on the bed in mere moments and he was in me once again, and it felt so natural, so perfect. Like he was meant to be inside of me. Slow languid strokes warmed me, and I kissed him, our lips soft, wet.

Like being immersed in buoyant, warm water, it started again, but this time, I held on to reality. I remained lucid, half in my body, half out. He was thrusting harder now, and my hips met his with an intensity that needed satiation.

Crackling sounds erupted around my head as purple and pink stars shot across my vision. The bed vibrated beneath me and the clock on the bedside table began to jump, slowly moving forward until it fell off altogether, bouncing on the floor.

Bits of plaster began to fall from above us, raining down a light mist of dust. I pulled him into me. Harder. My nails raked down his back as his right hand gripped my hip. *Oh God!* His climax began, a low moan tearing from his throat as the current filled the small room, like it had been hit by sheet lightning. Vibrations buzzed through my entire body.

Everything began to shake and groan under the strain, the force escalating with every second. Dust fell from walls and fine, gray particulate rained down on me. Light bulbs shattered in the reading lamps. I turned to shield my face as the air crackled and snapped around my head.

Every hair stood on end, my skin a mass of goose bumps as the sizzling built into a crescendo, until the intensity reached its peak. His orgasm came with a wild shudder, his entire body spasming. I responded in my own trembling convulsion.

The electrical current evaporated all at once with an audible snap.

~ ☾ ~

CHAPTER FIFTEEN

Once in Evan's SUV, he hit the gas, and we started out on the back road toward my apartment.

I glanced around. Everything looked different to me, like the trees were clearer, colors more vivid. Even my hearing was different. Maybe our ability to connect and generate that power was having some kind of positive health effects. Not to mention the steamy sex.

I looked over at Evan. "Just so you know, I don't usually have sex with someone on the first date."

"Well, technically, it wasn't really our first date—"

Evan's words were cut off when *something* suddenly appeared on the hood of the vehicle.

"What the hell?" Evan yelled as he swerved to the right, braking hard.

My breath caught in my throat when I saw what it was.

The Skinwalker.

Like a cat on all fours, it stared at us with pin-prick sized pupils within those feral, yellow eyes, its vaporous form impervious to momentum or gravity.

The front tire went off the shoulder of the road, immediately lurching us to the right.

"Watch out!" Evan yelled over the rumbling of the tires. He turned the wheel sharply to get the car back onto the road, but momentum put us into a wild fishtail.

The Skinwalker's primitive feline position gave it an oddly animalistic appearance. It slipped right through the windshield, as if the glass wasn't even there.

~ ☾ ~

Evan ducked out of the way, and the fishtailing worsened, back and forth so fast I knew there was no pulling out of it.

We're dead.

Momentum spun us off the road, and we began to roll. When the ground approached my head, I jerked away. The door frame groaned as it hit solid ground, but as quickly as the ground was there, it was gone.

The car twisted and creaked as it rolled, shrieking metal against metal. My head hit the roof three times, my teeth biting the side of my tongue. Coppery blood filled my mouth, and I sputtered.

We stopped with a screeching thud. Belted in upside down, we dangled in our seatbelts. Blood pooled in my head, darkening my vision. Evan hung unmoving in his seat, his hair dripping with blood.

The Skinwalker squatted on the ground in front of the car, eyes fixed on Evan, glaring. It slid toward us, straight into the SUV, the hazy face within an inch of Evan's. A strange sound emerged from Evan, a wet pluck.

I screamed. Evan's face began to bulge as the Skinwalker's form tightened around him, pulling him out of his own skin as he hung, defenseless.

Instinctively, I reached deep within myself, and drew on my terror and rage, imagining my emotions as having the destructive properties of a bomb. My body, mind and soul worked in perfect unison as I mentally willed the feelings up and out of me and pushed them at the Skinwalker.

It froze.

The transparent arms flailed out backward as if it had been hit by a bowling ball, the translucent torso following, the clear, shimmering form whipped to the ground outside Evan's window.

The seat belt bit into my abdomen and the pressure of

blood pooling in my face pounded in my head. I ignored it.

Something inside of me exploded. I pulled at my horror, my fury, and threw them out at the Skinwalker once again, this time a low growl escaping my lips. The creature hovered over the ground while the vaporous body flickered in and out of sight, unmoving, as if it was caught in a vacuum between dimensions.

Evan came to, sputtering on blood. He blinked and coughed as he surveyed the wreckage around him.

"Sarah! What happened?" He coughed.

"It attacked the car, and we rolled. You got knocked out in the roll." I reached over to unbuckle his belt. "It was attacking you."

"Where is it?" His eyes darted about until they came to rest on the clear form just outside his door. "Why does it look like that?"

"I don't know. Let's get out."

Evan nodded, opening his door. He placed his arms on the car roof to hold himself from falling on his head. I undid my seat belt and hopped out as well.

We stepped toward the creature, Evan crouched down, and my mouth dried up.

"Evan! Don't—"

The creature's near-transparent form came into sharper view as it stretched its arms up. Evan jumped backward, out of reach.

Evan grasped my hand and static electricity began to snap around my head. The air around me grew charged, the atmosphere thick and difficult to breathe. The current was so powerful even small stones of gravel on the road began to vibrate.

Snap! The current came together with such a force that the air around me crackled and sizzled, as a million points of light zapped around the creature. The vaporous body slumped under the pressure, shriveling as if it were compacting against itself. The next instant, the Skinwalker's transparent form was gone, on its way back to its corporeal body.

I looked down at the empty space where the Skinwalker had been only moments before and then back to Evan. In that moment, his eyes closed, and he collapsed. I dropped to his side. His chest still vibrated from the energy that we had just channeled.

"Evan?" I cried. "Talk to me!"

~ ☾ ~

CHAPTER SIXTEEN

I leaned over him, my ear to his mouth, listening. Nothing. I placed my fingers on his neck. A pulse.

"Sarah," he whispered into my ear, his voice flat and devoid of inflection. I held his face in my hands, as a muffled sob emerged from my mouth.

"Thank God," I said, my voice breaking. I held him tight to me, afraid to let him go.

Fifteen hours, a tow-truck ride, and a visit to the hospital later, I was back at home in my apartment with Kate and Amber.

Evan had sustained a minor concussion, and we had both required stitches. Evan's SUV was in need of some serious body work, with the possibility of being irreparable. I didn't think I'd sustained much of an injury, but now that adrenaline had worn off, my neck was starting to stiffen. The doctor had warned me of this and prescribed a painkiller just in case. Unfortunately, I wanted to keep my wits about me and had yet to take one, sticking to plain old Ibuprofen instead, just in case. Just in case another Skinwalker came to visit.

"I'm sorry this happened to you and Evan," Amber said, looking at me like she was waiting for…something. I'd told her the whole story, about the way we could create some kind of energy field, and she and Kate accepted it as truth. I guess once a person has recognized the supernatural is real, nothing is surprising after that.

Kate piped in. "Me, too. We're just happy you're back

home in one piece. It could have been a lot worse, with the Skinwalker and the roll. You're pretty lucky to be alive."

I nodded. "Thanks. I'm relieved neither of us was seriously injured. It wasn't looking good, him hanging there in the vehicle like that."

Amber flashed a look at Kate, and then turned her attention back to me. Kate had the oddest expression on her face, like she'd been caught with her hand in the cookie jar.

"This electrical current thing we do has definitely come in handy, hasn't it?" I said, watching their expressions closely. "I'm sure if we didn't have it, we might not be here right now."

They glanced at each other once again.

Then Kate spoke. "That's the thing, Sarah. I know you see it as an advantage, and it obviously saved your life, but doesn't it seem a little strange? That you have this thing with Evan, but only when he's around?"

My whole body tightened. "What are you saying?"

"I'm saying maybe you think it's a joint power, but what if it's not?" Kate spoke slowly, as if choosing her words carefully. "What if it's just him?"

I glanced at Amber, who looked at me with her mouth in a tight, thin line. She shrugged.

"Do you think this, too?" I asked her.

"Look at this," Amber said as she shoved her cell into my hands.

Across the screen was an e-news article with the heading "Cigarette Sparked Fatal House Fire". I glanced up at Amber, who was looking at me intently. "Can you read it out loud so we can all hear it?"

I swallowed as I quickly scanned the article.

Then I began to read. "A man and woman are dead after a house fire in the small community of Eagle Creek, Utah, early Wednesday morning. Alesandro Valente, 39, and Gina Valente, 38, have been identified as the victims of the fire. Their sons, Stefano, 16 and Evandro, 15, were not present at the time of the fire, which broke out some time before 3:00 a.m. CST. The house was completely engulfed when fire crews got there, state police said."

I handed Amber her phone back. "I already knew about that. He told me everything."

"Oh really? Are you sure about that?" Amber flashed me a hard look and started flipping through the screens on her phone.

I rolled my eyes and glanced out my front window. My stomach turned as my mind was invaded by unwanted images of us completely eviscerating that Skinwalker in its spirit form. The thought of power of that magnitude in the hands of two human beings was suddenly enough to make my stomach twist with guilt.

Amber held the phone back up to my face. "Look at that."

I looked down and began to read aloud an article from a local newspaper, the San Juan Record. "Fatal house fire possible arson. A fire which killed a couple in the northern area of Eagle Creek early this week may have been deliberately lit. The couple was found dead in their home by fire crews. Police have identified a pair of suspects, known to be 'persons of interest'. Neighbors believe witchcraft was involved."

"Witchcraft? A pair of suspects? He has a brother," Amber said. "And did you know Evan and his brother inherited millions?"

I nodded. My head felt like it was floating through heavy oil. "He has a land development company..."

"Interesting that multi-millionaires live in a town as small as Eagle Creek that also just happens to be the stomping ground for Skinwalkers," Amber said.

My stomach roiling, I turned to face Kate.

~ ☾ ~

Kate shook her head. “It’s tragic, for sure. But I don’t think we can jump to the conclusion that Evan and his brother killed their parents for money. Or that they’re connected to the Skinwalkers. That’s a big stretch.”

I relaxed. “I agree.”

I turned back to Amber who had begun typing madly on her cell once again. “Are you in love with him?”

“I don’t know,” I said. Except that I did know. I could deny it to Kate and Amber, but I couldn’t deny it to myself. My heart told me my answer was a lie.

“Okay,” Amber said. “Let’s talk to my mom and Noreen about this. I want to know what they think about this energy thing and how you’re channeling it.”

“Just wait. I want to look something up.” I typed Friuli, Italy, into my phone, the name of the city on Evan’s phone bill.

Google brought up a number of hits, most of them describing the scenic, agricultural landscape. I clicked through a number of the pictures, fields of flowers flanked by mountain ranges that led to deep valleys with sparkling blue waters.

I then searched for “Alesandro Valente” and a link popped up, an article from a Friulian newspaper with the title, “*Alesandro Valente, sviluppatore terra*.”

I pulled it up and was met with a photograph of a gorgeous man, probably taken in the 1980’s, his hair a thick, wavy black, his bronze skin glowing, setting off his wide, white smile. Instead of Evan’s blue eyes, his were completely black. “Amber, pull up a translator. What does *sviluppatore terra* mean in English?”

Amber punched in the keys and then nodded. “Land developer.”

The article went on to interview Alesandro, and while it was in Italian, I got the gist of the article, that he owned and developed a vast amount of land in the Northern region of Italy.

~ ☾ ~

"Well, this explains all of the money Evan and Stefano inherited. Their dad owned tons of land in Friuli," I said.

"When did they move here?" Amber asked.

I shrugged. "No idea. Evan has no trace of an accent, so I assume it was a while ago."

Now that I really thought about it, Evan did have a manner of speaking that was different, but I'd always chalked it up to him being from a different region of the country than me, but never had I considered the different style of speech was because he was a recent immigrant.

"Do a search for Italian witchcraft," Amber said.

I glanced up at her, partly annoyed by her obvious assertion but also curious. I typed in some keywords. "Italian, Friuli, witchcraft." The search led to a book. The Night Battles: Witchcraft and Agrarian Cults in the Sixteenth and Seventeenth Centuries, by Carlo Ginzburg.

There was a description of the contents of the book. I read it out loud.

"The *Benandanti* (Good Walkers) were an agrarian fertility cult in the Friuli district of Northern Italy in the sixteenth and seventeenth centuries. Between fifteen-seventy-five and sixteen-seventy-five, the *Benandanti* were tried as heretics under the Roman Inquisition, and their witchcraft assumed as Satanist. The *Benandanti* claimed to travel in spirit form while asleep to struggle against the evil *Malandanti* (Bad Walkers) in order to ensure good crops for the seasons to come. Under pressure by the Inquisition, these nocturnal spirit travels (which often included sleep paralysis) were exposed as part of the witches' Sabbath, leading to the extinction of the *Benandanti* cult."

And then it hit me. Valentedanti . The name of the contact person on Evan's phone. Was it a coincidence that it sounded so similar to *Benandanti* and *Malandanti*?

"Wow." Amber's eyes were distant and unfocused. "Sounds like the Italian version of the Skinwalker."

It did sound like Skinwalkers, but what did that really tell us? Nothing. There was still absolutely no evidence that Evan was one of these *Benandanti* or *Malandanti*. We were grasping at straws because we were desperate for answers.

"What about the *Malandanti*?" Kate asked. "It doesn't say what happened to them."

I nodded. "You're right. It says the *Benandanti* are extinct, extinguished by the Roman Inquisition, but there's no mention of what happened to the *Malandanti*."

~ ☾ ~

CHAPTER SEVENTEEN

It was seven at night, and Kate and Amber had long ago gone home. On a whim, I decided to swing by Evan's hotel. I didn't expect to see him in the parking lot just as I was about to go in.

Evan was nearly at the driver's side of the vehicle when he spotted me standing beside my car. "Sarah! This is a surprise."

"I just thought I'd stop by to see what you were up to tonight," I said. It was weird. I wasn't technically lying, so why did I feel so guilty? "Rental car?"

He nodded. "I think the Mercedes might be in the shop for a while. Some pretty serious damage. Luckily, they can fix it, though." He looked at me intently. "How are you feeling? Any new pain from the roll?"

I took him in, from head to toe. He was once again model-gorgeous in his jeans and leather jacket. I was beginning to think this guy just couldn't look bad.

"I'm fine. How are you feeling?" I asked.

"Okay. But I've been better." He shrugged, rubbing an elbow.

It was time for a change in topic. "You said you were you born in Italy, right?" I asked.

His eyebrow arched. "Wow, this is an interesting conversation. If you wanted to talk, we could go in?" He gestured toward the hotel with his thumb.

I shook my head. Going in there with Evan would lead to one thing, and I had questions to ask him without getting sidetracked. "No, I can't tonight, sorry."

“Okay.” He nodded and stepped closer to me, a slight downward curve to his lips. “Yes, we moved here when I was ten.” His gaze matched the hue of the sky at that moment, a vivid, moody blue. When he reached out and placed his hand on the small of my back, I instantly moved toward him, almost without thought, like we were twin magnets, attracting each other.

I took a breath. “What city?”

He leaned in and whispered in my ear. “Paluzza.” The way he spoke the word, with a heavy Italian accent, drawing out the letter z so that it buzzed in my ear was enough to make my knees weaken beneath me.

I tilted my head toward him, his stubble brushing my cheek. When my lips came into contact with his, my entire body turned into a soft, rubbery mass of flesh. One of his hands slid up the back of my shirt to stroke the ticklish skin there while the other cupped my cheek. Involuntarily, my own hands snaked around his neck and I found myself pressed against him, his back against his rental car.

The sound of footsteps brought me back to the here and now. We pulled apart, his breath hot on my cheek, my body burning with need. I licked my lips and looked around. Whoever had walked by us was no longer in sight.

A stray hair caught in the breeze and blew across my face. He swept it away and leaned forward to tenderly kiss my nose.

“Sarah Ross. I think I’m falling for you.”

My heart felt like it had gone into an arrhythmia, and it seemed I’d suddenly forgotten how to breathe. Words I’d longed to hear my whole life, to be spoken by someone who I had such intense feelings for. And I wanted to trust him, with every cell of my being.

“Evan.” I smiled and kissed his soft, moist lips as quickly as I could manage. “I don’t know what to say.”

~ ☾ ~

He gathered all of my hair into a ponytail in his hands behind my head, to keep the wind from blowing my hair all about. “Was it too soon? I mean, was that totally creepy?”

I laughed. “No. Not creepy. I really care about you, too, Evan.” I pushed his bangs away from his face to keep the ends of his hair from blowing into his eyes.

“Good. I seem to find myself wearing my heart on my sleeve around you. I have to admit it’s a little disturbing.”

He looked so starkly vulnerable right then, so open and honest, I wanted to kiss him and tell him I loved him. But I couldn’t. Instead, I hugged him to me, my head nestled on his chest, taking in his scent of bergamot, fir and his own masculine musk. His chin rested on the top of my head, and his hands stroked the length of my hair against my back, right down to my waist.

I pulled away and looked up at him. “What region is Palazzo in?”

His head tilted to the side and his eyebrow quirked. “Wow, twenty questions?”

I shrugged.

“The province of Udine, if you must know,” he said. “It’s very pretty there. Lots of mountain ranges and hills. Many historic buildings as well.”

Was Friuli in the Province of Udine? If I asked one more question would he catch on?

“What region is Udine in?” I asked, throwing caution to the wind.

His one eyebrow went up, his gaze intense. “It’s actually part of two historic regions called Friuli-Venezia Giulia. Have you heard of it?”

I shook my head. “No.” I was growing much more accustomed to lying. “Do you miss it there?”

He chuckled. “Not really. Why?”

~ ☾ ~

"I was just thinking about all the things that have happened recently, with me and the Skinwalkers. And now your car is almost completely destroyed. I just have to wonder if Italy was safer, less...weird."

"It isn't less weird. Italy has its supernaturals, too."

Now I was getting somewhere. "Oh? Like what?"

He swallowed, and I could see his Adam's apple bob in his throat. "Actually, in Friuli, there are witches and warlocks. They're known as *Stregheria*."

~ ☾ ~

CHAPTER EIGHTEEN

"Where are we going?" I asked, holding a steaming cup of coffee in the passenger seat of Kate's car. It was four in the morning and still dark out. It had only been nine hours since I'd left Evan in the parking lot, and I'd barely slept. Kate and Amber had fetched me right out of my warm bed and now we were hitting the edge of town. The sun wasn't due to be up for another two or more hours.

"I'll show you when we get there," Kate said, her aqua eyes glowing turquoise in the dashboard lights. "We're going on a witch-hunt."

I swallowed and looked out the front window at the dimly lit street lamps that lit the main drag of Slave Lake. Every building had been there since the day I was born, but today, everything looked foreign, sinister.

"Witch hunt?" I asked.

Amber piped up from the backseat. "Evan might have a few secrets you didn't know about. I think it's time we see what this dude is all about."

I didn't know what to say. Kate nodded and drove to the hotel where Evan was staying and parked. Evan's rental car was in our direct line of sight.

"What are you doing?" I asked.

"Just wait," she said. As if she'd orchestrated the perfect timing, Evan and the man I'd seen from the road on two separate occasions was walking beside him. Was this Stefano? My heart stumbled in my chest. Not that he'd ever done anything other than stare at me, but there was something just wrong about him.

"Oh, God. How did you know?" I asked.

"I saw them together last night," Kate said. "Amber and I were doing some sleuthing without you. We didn't think you would allow us to spy on your boyfriend, so we sort of...did it behind your back. Sorry."

Evan and the other man got into the rental car and left the parking lot.

My skin began to crawl. It had to be Stefano, his brother, this man from the road. The first time I'd seen him was when Evan had found me out at the abandoned house, right after the Skinwalker attack.

That one made some sense. Perhaps they were out together, checking out the adjacent land. But the second time, along the road while the Skinwalkers infested Wakina? Stefano was always close to where the attacks took place, never seen directly at the location of the assault, but always nearby. Lurking.

Kate put the car back in gear and crept along behind their vehicle, making sure we weren't close enough that they'd see us. They turned left onto a road that led to the south side of town and kept driving for a few blocks until they turned onto a side street. Kate slowed to a snail's pace, and when they drove up into a driveway, she stopped.

"That's the old mechanic shop," she said. I strained to see. The landmark had once been a major town attraction. An old, 1960's Volkswagen Beetle stuck high atop a concrete pole, at least twenty feet in the air, lit only by a streetlight the next block over. Beneath it was the broken-down remains of the abandoned shop, white paint chipped and peeling, two large bay doors with rows of windows covered over with gray plywood. The concrete parking lot had crumbled with age and weather and had nearly turned to gravel.

Evan and Stefano got out of the vehicle and went

inside. Had they bought this shop, something for their development company? It was definitely possible.

As we sat idling, spying on my boyfriend, I had a little pang of guilt. I turned to Kate. “Now what?”

She shrugged. “I don’t know.”

“This is stupid. Can we go now?” I said.

Kate shook her head. “Just wait. Aren’t you curious what they’re doing in an abandoned building?”

I had to admit, I was curious. “We can’t see what they’re doing, Kate. And I’m not going to go peek into the windows and risk him seeing us.”

“There they are,” Kate whispered, hunkered down in her seat, her eyes just barely above the steering wheel.

I glanced up just as Evan and Stefano emerged from the building and returned to the rental car. The vehicle roared to life and backed out. When they began driving toward us, accelerating fast, I slunk down into the floor. Kate slid down in her seat as well.

We all held our breath, listening as the vehicle zoomed by. I waited another few seconds before sliding up. I definitely didn’t want Evan to see me snooping on him.

“They’re gone,” Amber said from the backseat. I sat up.

“Let’s go in,” Kate said, slipping her car keys into her pocket and unfastening her seat belt. Amber did the same.

My chest tightened at the thought of what we were about to do. “I don’t think this is a good idea. It’s breaking and entering.”

“So? It’s only a problem if you get caught,” Amber said, eyes glittering. “And besides, even if you did get caught, it’s not like your boyfriend would charge you, right?” Amber leaned forward, placed her hand on my shoulder, and looked me in the eye. “Stop thinking about it.”

~ ☾ ~

We hopped out of the car and quickly ran over to the shop. I grabbed the knob and pushed. It was unlocked.

Before we pushed the door open, I stopped and held it in place. “We shouldn’t do this.”

I shook my head and mumbled a string of profanity as Kate pushed the door open.

We stepped forward into the gloomy space, our eyes adjusting to the dark. Amber and Kate both pulled out their flashlights and turned them on. Directly in front of us stood the former checkout counter.

The walls in the entryway were painted white but over the years had started to darken, to the point where they were very nearly gray. To the side of the checkout was a concrete walkway where old, rusted car parts, metal rims, and steering wheels lined the shelves. The acrid scent of old grease mixed with dirt seemed to have permeated my airway.

We walked through to the back room. This space housed the garage, where two squared-off pits had been dug into the ground for working beneath the cars. Various mechanical tools were strewn about as well as empty oil cans, car parts, and other cast-offs that were never disposed of.

Why were they in here? What purpose did they have in an abandoned mechanic shop that didn’t even have power? Why had they come and gone so quickly?

We returned to the smaller room with the cash counter. There was another door off to the side. It was a large, three-stall bathroom with industrial-grade tiling on the floor that had begun to crumble into chunky green dust. In the far corner sat a duffle bag, a sleeping bag and a cooler. We stepped in and I turned around.

The entire wall beside the door was covered with my own face staring back at me. Pictures of me doing inventory at work, the photos obviously taken through the window, one of me helping a customer, another of

~ ☾ ~

me out during a morning jog, stretching. Cut-outs from newspaper articles over the years, starting as far back as when I was five and had made the town journal when I'd been at my great-grandmother's one-hundredth birthday, one of me throwing a basketball for the winning shot in my sophomore year.

There was a picture of me in my satiny blue prom dress taken with my ex-boyfriend, Tyler. Another was a half-ripped picture of me in my cap and gown, a page obviously torn from my senior yearbook. Beside it, other pages torn out where my friends had signed with various comments and phrases and inside jokes.

I sucked in a sharp breath. *Oh my God!*

My thoughts reeled. They were spying on me! They were profiling me and had pictures from years ago, before I'd ever seen either of them. What could they be doing with this information?

"What is all of this?" Amber whispered. "What kind of sick freak does this?"

I couldn't respond. My stomach seemed to coil up inside of me like a twisting snake. Sheets and sheets of foolscap were written on in perfectly-shaped cursive handwriting. The first one was dated two months ago.

"Sarah Ross. Indigo. Aura is one of the most potent known to the world. Only two others in existence, both are in hiding."

Another one, dated April 15th. He'd been watching me since April.

"Target appears to be unaware of her powers. Does not know she is the Indigo Child."

Then the handwriting changed to something more blocky, printed. It was dated three days ago. "The target is aware of her ability to read emotions. Does not have control of the ability."

Then right beside it, one dated from yesterday. "Target is easily suggestible. Slow siphoning does not destroy her. In fact, seems somewhat rejuvenated by it. This new finding is worth investigation before the devouring process is initiated."

My throat felt tight, as if words were screaming for escape, but my vocal chords had been cut. Regardless of whether this was Evan's writing or Stefano's, Evan was still privy to the entire thing. He was stalking me and for a reason.

Was it possible he merely wanted my aura, and he was working with his brother to get it? Could he have betrayed me, lying to me, telling me he loved me, while all along secretly plotting to take my life force from me? Was I merely a worthless shell that housed a commodity they wanted and would stop at nothing to get?

My mind told me to slow down, to think the situation through. Unfortunately, my gut instinct was insistently overriding my brain.

Just then, a roar of an engine and screech of tires breaking hard against pavement pulled me out of my harrowed reverie.

"Let's go," I whispered under my breath. We filed out of the washroom, into the entryway just in time to hear the creek of the doorknob. We took off to our right, through the door that led straight into the garage.

"Turn the flashlights off!" I snapped.

We continued to creep along the outside walls. Footsteps ensued, inside the entryway at first, and then fading away. Was he in the bathroom? We kept inching toward the end, where the holes in the ground came into view. The footsteps resumed. We were too far from the door at the back to get out, and there was nothing to hide behind. I looked at the holes in the ground.

"Jump in there!" I whispered, pointing to the oil-changing pits. Amber and Kate both nodded, and all three of us jumped in. We lowered ourselves down, half sliding on the crumbling concrete until we reached the dirt floor. The oily scent filtered into my mouth, tasting like rusty oil can.

Blackness engulfed us, the minimal streetlight that filtered in through a dirty glass pane in the back door providing no advantage in these holes. My heartbeat pounded inside my head. I glanced over at Kate and Amber who were crouching down in the filth, Amber holding her ankle and rocking back and forth, her eyes squeezed tight.

I placed a hand on her shoulder, mouthing are you okay? She opened her eyes and shook her head. I perked my ears to see what I could hear. Footsteps approached.

My heart battered against my ribcage, my legs shaking beneath me. Kate grabbed me with a Vulcan grip on my arm, staring at me, the whites of her eyes flashing. I stayed in a crouch position and placed my hand on hers and squeezed back.

Listening carefully, I was certain there were now two distinct sets of footsteps in the open space. One was from a hard-soled shoe, the other from perhaps a tennis shoe or hiking boot. My whole body vibrated. I focused my empathy on the two, trying to keep my fear from overriding my concentration. What I felt was distinct: one man was afraid, the other, oddly excited.

"They're not here, Stefano," a voice called out. Evan's voice.

The footsteps stopped.

There was no response. Silence was like a palpable substance that hung in the air around us, a caustic black cloud. The hard-soled footsteps resumed. Closer. They stopped once again. Breathing, slow and slightly raspy, could be heard even from within this pit. I held my breath.

"There's no one in here, Stefano. I told you!" Evan's voice. I was sure of it.

Why wasn't Stefano responding?

A squeak rang out, like nails down a chalkboard, and

~ ☾ ~

then the hard-soled footsteps resumed, receding. The soft soled shoes next. The sound faded away until, finally, we heard the squawk of the hinges as the door opened and clanged closed. I sucked in a deep, ragged breath.

"Let's go," Amber whispered, rubbing her ankle, looking relieved.

I shook my head, holding my finger to my lips and gesturing with my hands for them to stay put. I stood slowly, my whole body quivering like a trapped feral cat. I poked my head over the edge and waited.

"Let's go out the back door," I said in a barely audible whisper. I hoisted first Amber up onto the floor with my hands, then Kate. Then with as much spring as I could muster, I jumped up, getting my shoulder and elbow above ground. Kate reached down and grabbed a belt loop of my jeans and hauled me up the rest of the way.

We moved toward the back door, with Amber limping, taking great pains to do it as soundlessly as possible, just in case they were still in here. I opened the back door, and the eerie morning light hit our retinas. We started to run-walk into the junkyard behind the building, making our way along a chain-link fence around the side that led back toward the front of the building. The fence narrowed as it reached the gate, held closed with a rusted iron bolt-latch. As we neared it, I started to slow down, Amber and Kate behind me.

A shadow loomed across the ground directly in front of the gate. I stopped dead in my tracks, my heart lurching. I threw my arms out to the side to stop Amber and Kate from moving forward any further. Their pressured breathing fluttered through my hair.

The person came around the corner, starting with a pointed boot. Clad all in black, it was Stefano. He stood facing me, his head tilted forward like a cobra ready to strike.

~ ☾ ~

In a sing-song voice, he said, "Come here, little Indigo girl." His nostrils flared, and he smiled.

The only thing that kept him from me was the chain-link gate.

I involuntarily stepped backward and stumbled into Kate and Amber. We turned and ran, hurtling over tractor tires, and stumbling over bits of metal that littered the ground as we bee-lined toward the back of the fenced-off junkyard. I stumbled, stubbing my toe on a metal tube. Pain flared hot and fast, zipping all the way up to my knee.

Kate reached out to steady me as we continued to run, Amber in the lead. As we reached the back of the junkyard, I glanced up to the top of the six-foot fence where barbed-wire coiled.

Damn it!

I whipped off my jacket and glanced back to see Stefano finally break through the bolted gate. I turned back and threw my jacket up, trying to get it to land on top of the wire. It missed, and I tried again, my heart fluttering. Finally, on the third attempt, it hooked onto the little barbs and stuck.

"Go!" I said, pushing Kate forward.

She glanced back at me. "No, Sarah. It's you they want. You go first."

I examined her face, the expression of fierce determination, and then nodded.

Shaking, she held out her hands in a cupped position and I stepped onto her hands, my fingers clawed through the wire fence. With her hoisting, I threw my arm over the top and grasped the other side.

My jacket did little to cushion the barbs, and one dug directly into my bicep, another into my armpit. I barely felt it as Kate shoved on my foot and momentum threw my body up and over. Then my center of gravity shifted, and suddenly I was hurtling toward the ground.

~ ☾ ~

My hands grasped at the wires and I caught hold with my right hand, the weight of my body spinning, wrenching my arm right at the socket. My left foot hit the ground and my knees buckled. I fell forward, and landed palms-first into the dry weeds. Slivers embedded into the skin on my hands.

"Sarah! Are you okay?" Amber whispered.

I ground my teeth together. "Just a scrape. I'm fine."

Then the roaring sound of an engine began. I glanced up. To my right, Evan's rental car came to a skidding stop.

To my left, Amber looked at me from between the wires, her eyes wide. "Sarah, go! Hurry up, Kate!" The metallic clink of Kate's feet being repeatedly forced into the chinks in the fence told me she was scaling the fence at that instant. Amber's voice reached a new fevered pitch. "Get up, Sarah! Run!"

I pushed myself to my knees, my shoulder aching, my hands bloodied and torn. Evan's car door opened and slammed shut. He began to run toward me, and I forced myself to my feet.

"Back off, Stefano!" Evan yelled.

I glanced over to see Stefano picking up speed as he ran across the junkyard, his gait deliberate and stealthy as a jungle lion. Kate hit the ground next to me as Amber's feet rattled the chain-links.

"Sarah! Come with me!" Evan called out, his face red.

Amber hit the ground, and she and Kate each grasped one of my arms and began to pull me forward.

"Come on," Amber said into my ear.

We took off in a run. Footfalls began behind me.

"Wait! Sarah, wait," Evan said.

We kept running toward the car until we finally reached the side of it and slowed. Evan slid to a stop behind me.

I whipped around. "What? So you can devour my soul?"

~ ☾ ~

His expression changed, his eyes clouding over. “He’s coming. I can’t predict what he’ll do, Sarah. Just, please, please trust me!”

“Get in the car, Sarah,” Kate said, then she turned to Evan, her voice a low growl. “Shut up, Evan. It’s obvious you are only here to hurt her.”

“Sarah. You know I wouldn’t hurt you,” Evan begged. “I know I’ve lied, but I can explain.”

Clang! The sound of Stefano’s foot hitting chain-link clattered, ringing through my ears. I glanced back to see Stefano had begun to scale the fence in rapid-motion, reminding me of a spider. Evan was clearly trying to stall me so that Stefano could get me.

“Come with me, please!” Evan repeated, his voice ratcheting up an octave.

“Go back to your brother, Evan. Find another Indigo soul to steal.” I got into Kate’s car.

“Sarah,” Evan said, grasping the door and holding it open, “Let me channel your energy. Our power might be the only chance to stop him.”

I faltered, my insides twisting, the common sense part of me and gut instinct squaring off, at odds.

“Shut the door, Sarah!” Amber said from the front seat, but I couldn’t do it.

Something in my gut told me to listen to Evan. My gut overrode my brain, once and for all.

I glanced back to Stefano once again. My throat seemed to tighten and my vision narrowed. Stefano was nearing the top of the fence, his arms and legs moving steadily, unstoppable.

“We have our prize, Evandro,” Stefano called from the fence as his leg swung over the top.

Evan had stopped and turned back to watching Stefano as well, his eyes wide. He opened his emotions to me then, and I was hit by a wave of fear and worry so strong I felt my knees turn to water beneath me. He wasn't lying. He was afraid and worried, and he wanted me to know it.

Immediately, I got out of the car.

"Sarah? No!" screamed Amber.

I ran straight into his chest and when our bodies connected, I felt it once again. That soft pull at something inside me, something immaterial. Warmth surrounded me, a soft, warm pillow of light as my body grew vibrant and strong within his arms.

When I opened my eyes, Stefano was within ten feet of us.

Evan and I stood, facing off with Stefano, the two of them remarkably similar in height and build. The atmosphere around our heads began to crackle despite the mist. Chain-links rattled from the current that was generated from within us, the barbed wire at the top coming loose in sections and slipping to the side of the fence.

Stefano leveled his gaze at Evan and bared his teeth as he spoke. "You betray me, Evandro? You betray your *fratello*, your *famiglia*?"

"I'm sorry, Stefano. My loyalty is with Sarah now," Evan said in a low, grim voice.

Stefano's spine straightened, his fingers curling at his sides. "Evandro. We are all that is left of the *Malandanti*. Do not do this!"

"And maybe the *Malandanti* should be extinct." Evan said.

Stefano's eyes narrowed as his gaze raked across the two of us. "Mama told me you were born without a *caul*. She even hid that fact from Papa."

I felt Evan perceptively jump. "A *caul*? What the hell are you babbling about, Stefano?" Evan said, brows furrowed.

Stefano sneered. "She tried to protect you, the stupid woman. She tried to pretend you were one of us. But you weren't. I should have known you'd betray us sooner or later, Evandro."

"Don't be ridiculous. Don't blame this on some prehistoric superstition. I'm not turning on you. I'm telling you to stop, because this is wrong."

Stefano narrowed his eyes. "You were never one of us. Without the *caul*, you are not a true *Malandanti*."

"There is no us, Stefano. You killed them, remember? There's only you."

Stefano's lips pulled back, his nostrils flaring. "Evandro Valente, my brother, a traitor. Is that what you want? To betray me and to walk away from your rightful title as high priest?"

"I don't want it, Stefano. That was your ambition, not mine. I only followed you all these years because I thought there was nothing more for me." He tightened his grip around my shoulders.

"You are worthless, Evandro," Stefano sneered. "You are nothing without me."

"I don't think so. I think those are the words of someone who is desperately trying to hold onto his power." Evan's mouth turned up at the corners. "You saw what Sarah and I can do together, Stefano, didn't you? And you're scared as hell."

"It only confirms to me that you were never one of us, Evandro," Stefano said, his words nowhere near matching his emotions, the prickly wave of anxiety that rolled off of him confirming Evan's words.

I turned to Evan. "He's terrified. I can feel it."

Stefano's eyes flashed and his nostrils flared. "Shut up, Indigo."

Evan took a protective step forward, his own body shielding mine. "She doesn't have to tell me you're afraid, Stefano. I know you inside and out. You're scared because you have always thought you were the cleverest warlock, the most powerful. A mini god among mere mortals."

~ ☾ ~

Evan tilted his head to the side, and I wished I could have seen his expression at that moment. “But the reign of Stefano has ended, hasn’t it?”

“I have the Key of Solomon, Evandro.”

“Good. See, you won’t be all alone, will you? You’ll have your spellbook to cuddle up with. It’ll keep you warm at night.”

Stefano moved aside so he could see me. Evan’s body stiffened. I could see the side of Evan’s face once again, the hectic flush that had turned his cheek bright pink.

Stefano looked at me. “I hope she’s worth it, Evandro. She’s all you’ve got now.”

“You should leave. Now,” Evan said. “Before I kill you.”

Stefano’s eyes glittered. “You know I will never leave you alone, Evan. If you’re not with me, you’re against me. I can’t just let you live with your knowledge of the *Malandanti* ways, now can I? If you make this decision, for the rest of your days you will be my new target.”

Evan didn’t respond with words. Instead, the voltage around us increased until a snap of sheet lightning burst over us all, just above our heads.

Stefano staggered backward from the blow, righting himself as best he could. Then with a piercing stare at me and then Evan, ran off.

~ ☾ ~

CHAPTER NINETEEN

"What I'm about to tell you is going to change everything," Evan said, glancing over at me in the passenger seat of his car. He was still shaking after the confrontation with Stefano, but instead of settling down, it seemed to have grown worse. Amber and Kate had followed behind us in her car, undoubtedly there for me when I finally decided to get out.

"What?" I said sharply. "That you've been lying this whole time?"

"Please. Just promise you'll listen."

I turned to glare at him as he nodded. When the vehicle rolled to a stop at a red light, I realized I just couldn't take it anymore. I opened the door and got out.

"Wait, Sarah! No," he said, his voice muffling as I slammed the door shut behind me. I strode away as he cranked a hard right and roared around the corner, tires screeching as he came to a grinding halt at the side of the road. He got out and ran to me.

I whirled around to face him. "Why should I listen to anything you have to say? You've been lying to me this whole time. You and Stefano have been watching me, tracking me. You pretended to be my friend, like you had no idea what was going on. Like the time I heard you say something in Latin, you tried to tell me it was the Skinwalker's voice."

He held his hands up, palms out. "Wait, Sarah. I can explain, please."

My cheeks started to warm as a prickly sweat broke

out over my body.

"Start explaining," I said, my voice a low growl.

He bristled and looked down before facing me, his expression unreadable. Then he nodded in defeat and sat down on a sidewalk bench. I stood over him.

He looked at me. "Indigo," he said. There was an edge to the word, a pained edge. All of the air in my lungs disappeared. "Do you remember when I told you about my parents, how they were killed in a house fire?" Evan asked.

"Yeah. Your brother killed them. And probably with your help. So?"

He licked his lips and stared at his hiking shoes. "They weren't regular parents, Sarah."

"I'd already gathered that," I said with sarcasm. "After hearing what Stefano said to you, that much is pretty clear."

"I'll start at the beginning because I don't want to leave any detail out. This is my pledge to you. Complete honesty about everything." I rolled my eyes, but he continued, undeterred. "My parents came from Friuli, Italy. Several hundred years ago, our ancestors were an agrarian society. In the fifteen hundreds, warring began over the land, and crops began to fail. During this time, some of the people turned to the practice of magic, using it to summon the rain and the sun. They sought help to improve crops and help the residents of their communities." Evan paused.

"Well, my ancestors were into magic as well. But they used it for stealing. At first, they stole secrets from the more prosperous villages in an effort to improve their own crops. Then they began to steal livestock at night. Later, they perfected the art of spirit travel, and that's when the process of stealing the essence of other people began. They learned that their power increased tenfold when they stole the life force of other people. They very quickly grew far more powerful than the good *Stregharia*, or witches known as the *Benandanti*."

I shook my head, breathing through the sudden surge of anger that coursed through me. "I already know this."

His mouth tightened, as if finally coming to terms with what he was about to utter out loud. "I'm one of the *Stregharia* that practices black magic. I'm a *Malandanti*." He looked down, his shoulders turning in. Then he took a deep breath and began speaking once again. "The *Benandanti* and the *Malandanti* are both spirit-traveling shamans, but with vastly different goals. Over the years, the magic was perfected to the point where we could perform certain things unknown to any other witch or warlock in the world. The *Benandanti* have been gone for hundreds of years, but the *Malandanti* have remained, a secret from the Inquisitors and the world, and with time, we've perfected the dark magic and grown all the more powerful."

He looked at his feet and then back at me. I refused to speak, so he continued.

"We came to America when I was ten. My parents hadn't started training me, unlike Stefano, who they'd already been training for a year by the time we moved here. We came to Eagle Creek, right on the four corners. The meeting ground of Skinwalkers, the North American version of the *Malandanti*. Of course, their skills were rudimentary compared to our parents', and very shortly after we moved there, my parents became their leaders, teaching them everything they knew from hundreds of years of highly refined dark magic."

"Skinwalker School," I said wryly.

His gaze shifted away from me. "Yes, I suppose. Eventually, my parents became distracted by their new leadership responsibilities. I ended up being able to avoid the indoctrination that had already begun with

Stefano, who was dragged to all of the secret meetings. I remained innocent for an additional three years."

He ran a hand through his hair and then squeezed his temples with his thumb and forefinger.

I rolled my eyes. "Innocent?"

"I didn't know what they were doing then, Sarah. I knew something was wrong, but I didn't know what. But then it all stopped. When I was thirteen, everything changed." He turned his hands over in his lap. "That's when I got this." He held out his hand and I saw that mark again, that odd set of inverted triangles in the webbing between his thumb and pointer finger. "This is the Lucifer Sigil. The brand of Satan."

My stomach roiled at the thought of it. "Your parents branded you?"

A muscle in his neck twitched. "Yes. But the indoctrination was far worse than the brand. At least the burning only lasted for a few minutes. The pain of the indoctrination process lasted two years. Much longer for Stefano. But I avoided a lot of it, when...Stefano killed them." His voice cracked at the mention of Stefano's name. "At thirteen, I realized who my parents really were. I'd always felt distanced from my father and thought he was aloof, arrogant. He was only interested in talking to my brother, but my mother loved me. She used to sing lullabies at night and tell me stories."

He dug his fingers into the sockets of his eyes. "It seemed to me, overnight, she changed into someone I didn't even know. She wasn't who I thought she was at all. All she cared about was power. Revenge. Part of me died during those years. My innocence, my hope. And with it, it felt like all that was good in me died, too."

A strange lump stuck in my throat, and no amount of swallowing would dislodge it. "What is 'the *caul*' that Stefano referred to?"

"I have no idea what the word actually refers to, but

the *Malandanti* have many superstitious beliefs." He shook his head.

I evaluated his face to find a lie, some evidence of omission. There was none. "What happened after the indoctrination?"

"I changed. They changed me into a warlock, just like them. I learned the power of hate, revenge. I transformed into someone else. If I wanted to survive in that family, I had to."

I shoved my fingernails into my palm to keep myself from reaching out to him—either to slap him or hold him, I wasn't sure which. "What about the fire?"

He nodded sadly. "With the indoctrination, everything was very tense. There was a non-stop focus on acquiring power at the expense of anything remotely normal. We grew distant from our parents. Brought up on hate, we grew to hate them, too. One day, Stefano told me he had a way out. He didn't tell me what he was going to do to them, Sarah, but deep down, I think I knew what he was planning. I think I always knew he was going to kill them."

My voice came out steady, strong. "Tell me everything."

He cleared his throat. "In the middle of the night, he woke me up and told me to go to a friend's house, one whose family never kept their doors locked. I fell asleep on their floor. Little did I know that earlier that night he had drugged my parents with an overdose of sleeping pills. While I was gone, Stefano used a lit cigarette to set the curtains in their bedroom on fire. Then he took off." Evan's mouth tugged downward in the corners. "He knew what would happen."

"They burned," I whispered.

Evan's chin trembled. "They did. I was fifteen years old, and I was an orphan."

"God, Evan." I didn't even try to hide the disgust in my voice.

~ ☾ ~

"I know. But do you know what the strangest part is? I miss her. I miss my mother. Not the person of those last three years who allowed me to be tortured and brainwashed. But the woman who sang to me with the sweetest voice." Moisture filled his eyes but didn't come out.

My chest squeezed. *He's evil, Sarah.* I looked away from his gorgeous face. "And the land company?"

"We'd inherited my father's land, and all of his assets, and when Stefano was finally twenty-one, he took it over. We've got contacts everywhere," Evan continued. "And when Stefano first learned of your existence, through Sandra, we knew it was an opportunity. The indigo aura is unique and rare, and the power it offered was too enticing to overlook. So we came after you."

He looked at me with a hollow, empty look, his gaze going right through me, as if his mind was somewhere else entirely. Then he refocused on me, waiting for my reaction.

I bit my lip and took a breath to keep myself from shouting. "That very first day in the forest, with the Skinwalker in the house, what was the point of that?"

"He was there to subdue you. He was told only to take enough of your *élan vital*, your life force, to make you weak and compliant so Stefano and I could...finish you off."

My heart twisted in my chest. "So why didn't you do it? Why did you befriend me? Just to prolong the process?"

He shook his head, his eyes drooping. "No. It wasn't like that. When I found you after the attack, I was amazed you'd gotten away. Nobody I've ever known has gotten away before. And I had to know why."

I glared. "So you're a sick, sadistic, curious freak," I said with as much venom in my voice as I could muster. Then I turned on my heel and began to walk away.

~ ☾ ~

"Wait, Sarah," he said, jogging behind me. I quickened my pace but he kept following me and talking.

"Just walking with you that morning, I realized just how strong your *élan* truly was. Your indigo aura was so concentrated I could actually feel it. You were much more potent than Stefano or I expected."

With each word he uttered, my stomach tightened further.

"I wondered if you even knew about your powers, your true identity." He paused, and I stopped, turning around to look at him. His gaze fixed on my face. My cheeks began to burn.

"When I saw your eyes, your haunting indigo eyes, it was like a switch flipped inside my head. After that, I was hypnotized and couldn't break out of the spell. I can't explain it other than to say I fell in love with you at first sight. I know it sounds corny, but it's true."

"Do you really expect me to believe that? That you were going to basically suck out my soul, but when you saw me, you just—" I snapped my fingers, "—fell in love with me. Do you actually think by saying that, it's going to make everything all better?"

Evan shook his head. "No. I don't expect you to believe anything I say at this point."

I rolled my eyes. "God, I wish you'd just shut up and stop following me."

He ignored my comment. "Everything I've ever known, my understanding of who I am as a person, my whole identity, has permanently changed."

"Now what the hell are you talking about?"

"There's something about you... I can't explain it. It's like there's this connection between us."

"I think you're mistaking your ability to suck my soul out of my body with a romantic connection," I said with a snarl.

~ ☾ ~

"No. I've never experienced this before, not with anyone. You're different. Special." He looked at me with glassy eyes. "It's like we were meant to be together."

My breath caught in my throat, the pain of it all so hot, so raw, I wished I could hold him and hurt him all at the same time. I forced the next words out of my mouth, despite every bone in my body aching at the effort.

"Would you stop it with these ridiculous proclamations of love, already? You've just admitted to stalking me, and now you're going to expect me to just swoon? You're completely delusional."

His face crumpled. "I knew I couldn't hurt you the moment I met you. And now Stefano knows it, too."

My stomach lurched. "You're a liar, a manipulator, and a monster. Don't even attempt to garner my sympathy. I don't care whether your brother is going to hunt you down and turn you into ground beef. Do you hear me? I don't care!"

I mustered up every ounce of courage I had, reached into my inner anger, and solidified it, forcing it out of me and toward him, imagining hurtling it like a solid bowling ball aimed right at his gut.

He grimaced and bent forward at the waist as if he'd been kicked in the stomach, his body rocking backward. Then he straightened up, nodding. "I don't expect you to forgive me. I don't even expect you to understand. But you need to know Stefano is still after you, and only together can we defeat him. And now that I'm also on his hit list, I might not be able to stop him." He looked at me with wild, flashing eyes.

"Why should I care? You did this to yourself."

"I know." He looked away. "But it's not me I'm worried about. At least once I'm dead, I'll be free of Stefano." He looked back up to me, that crazed, frantic look still lingering in the depths of his eyes. "I'm afraid for you."

~ ☾ ~

I swallowed, anger coursing through my body, only matched by the fear that outpaced it. "I'll take my chances."

He placed his palms to his temples and squeezed his head. "For the shortest moment in time, I felt normal. With you, I almost believed I could have an ordinary life."

My mouth opened, but nothing came out.

He knelt in front of me and grasped my hands. "Say something. Please." He leaned in, and I felt myself pulled to him, to that familiar heat, that place where I lost all reasoning and sanity.

He was a liar. And just because he'd been forced to fess up didn't mean there were no more lies. Ever since meeting him, I'd been the victim of several attacks on my life. That was the only thing I was absolutely sure of.

I pushed him back by the shoulders. "I don't care, Evan Valente," I said, my eyes prickly and hot. "All I want is for you to get the hell away from me." I inched away and watched as Evan's composure crumbled. He looked like all the remaining hope inside of him had been punctured, like a flimsy balloon.

"I love you, Sarah. I've loved you since the moment we met." He slumped down to the park bench, placing his head in his hands.

I felt a pang, deep within my chest, the pain radiating up and out, until it pounded in the walls of my cranium. My heart was at odds with my mind, and it was making itself known. Could he be telling the truth?

The basic instinct for survival took over and overrode my heart entirely. "Leave," I said with as much confidence as I could muster.

"I'm sorry, Sarah. I'm so sorry." His eyes glittered as pain creased his forehead, his mouth turned down in the corners.

I felt a physical ache as I looked at his beautiful,

tortured face. What did it mean that I love him, despite the knowledge that he was truly a monster? What did that say about me? Was I a sadistic, self-sacrificing girl with a death wish?

I wanted so badly to run my fingers through his dark hair, to touch that dark stubble on his cheek, but instead, I stared at the self-recrimination that saturated ever cell of his being and forced myself to say words that my entire body fought against.

Choking on the horror that rifled through me, I swallowed a sob, then said, “Get the hell away from me.” I leveled my gaze at him, hoping he wouldn’t notice my trembling. “I want you to leave me alone. That means leave Slave Lake. And don’t ever come back.”

Head hanging, he nodded and walked slowly to his car, shoulders turned inward. Then he got in and drove away.

~ ☾ ~

CHAPTER TWENTY

"This is the last of my cookbooks to be unpacked," Amber said, jolting me out of a flashback of the last time I'd seen Evan over two months ago. I'd left Slave Lake, moved to Grand Forks to live with Amber and Kate, and begin college life.

Finally, an escape from small town and the sports store. My family had hired a new manager, and I was free to live my own life. Grand Forks, North Dakota boasted a population of over sixty-five thousand, a far cry from Slave Lake.

His face haunted my dreams every night, the color of his sun-gilded skin, the way his eyes sparkled like the ocean, his strong, powerful body.

Was Evan still alive, on the run, constantly looking over his shoulder like I was, afraid to make one wrong move? Had Stefano finally caught up to him and had his revenge on his brother? Was Stefano still looking for me? Or was it all a lie?

An ache in my chest told me my heart yearned for him, a yearning so powerful that at times I could barely breathe. Why did I care about him so much, anyway? He was a monster, wasn't he?

I clenched my teeth together to stop the ever-present scream of grief that threatened to tear itself from my lips. Would the pain ever stop?

"Uh, great," I said, scanning the remaining boxes.

"Here," Amber said, opening a zip-lock bag. "My mom baked us some cookies." Immediately, the sugarychocolate scent eclipsed the garlic smell that seemed to linger in the air of our new place.

She handed me a cookie, and I took a bite. Only Paulette could make a cookie that tasted this good. I relaxed, letting the sweet chocolate melt in my mouth, enjoying my last moments of irresponsibility. Tomorrow classes would begin.

"How has your mom been lately?" I asked. The first month after the death of Amber's Aunt Lilly, Paulette had been much more quiet, withdrawn. Now that it had been over two months, I hoped she would be feeling better. Kate came around the corner from the living room, her bare feet padding on the garish brown and yellow linoleum, to snag a cookie.

"Better than last month," Amber answered, biting into her own cookie. "But I'm sure it'll take some time."

A twisting knife seemed to jab into my guts—the horror of it all—Jessica, the Skinwalkers, and then Stefano and Evan. *Malandanti.*

Amber looked at my face as if trying to read my mind. Of course, there wasn't much I could keep secret from Amber.

"Any evidence of Stefano or Evan?" she asked.

My chest tightened. "No. Nothing."

"I don't know how you aren't paranoid," Kate said. "I'd be freaking out all the time."

I shrugged. "I am paranoid, but what can I do? I can't live my life waiting for the other shoe to drop, can I?"

"Are you still having Skinwalker nightmares?" Amber asked.

"Yes. I'm sure they haven't just suddenly decided I'm no longer valuable to them." I shrugged. "But at least we left right after Evan's big self-disclosure. We probably got them off our trail for a while, at least."

Amber chuckled. "Even if you'd tried to stay, I'm sure my mom would have dragged you from Slave Lake, kicking and screaming."

"I can't thank you guys enough for helping get me out of town, packing my apartment up for me, everything."

"The boys at Wakina were happy to help. You're a bit of a celebrity back there." Amber smiled mischievously.

When I thought of it, I was relieved the move had been so easy, because quitting my job and finding a replacement was far less so. It wasn't like I had any other option. I wasn't about to wait for Stefano to suck the life right out of me just because my parents didn't agree with my move. I hadn't told them what happened, because I knew exactly what their reaction would be. They would think I was insane and put me on psychotropic medications.

"Of course," Amber muttered. "We're here for you, Sarah. You know that, right?" Amber crossed the kitchen and wrapped her arms around me.

Kate followed suit and a second later her arms were around the two of us. I was in the middle of an Amber and Kate sandwich. "That's right. We're here for you."

"I know. Thanks, guys," I said. Kate gave one last little squeeze and then walked away, disappearing around the corner and into the living room. I heard the electronic sound of the television turning on.

"Plus, we have mom to turn to if things get freaky. And don't forget Noreen." Amber giggled and winked.

"Right," I said, smiling, "Freaky psychic lady who has forgotten what the inside of a bathtub looks like."

"We won't let anything happen to you. I promise." Amber whispered.

I shoved the final cookbook into the overhead cupboard and then sat down at the dining table, picking up one more cookie.

"Sarah! Come here," Kate said with a shriek. Her voice was so loud I nearly jumped out of my skin.

I ran around the corner of the kitchen and bolted into

the room, expecting her to be bleeding profusely, only to see her facing the television, her stare fixed. "Look!"

I looked to see the source of her outburst, and my throat snapped shut.

Evan.

It was a snippet on the local news, the headline reading, "New Development in Grand Forks", and Evan was in the camera frame standing beside a work truck, a piece of paper in his hands and pointing to something in the distance. My balance slipped.

"Turn it up!" I ordered.

Amber had followed me to the living room, and she grabbed the remote.

"A new community is currently under development in our wonderful city..."

The remainder of what the reporter said was lost on me as I stared at Evan on the TV. His shirt seemed to hang off of him, like he had lost weight, the tendons in his neck more pronounced, collarbones protruding under his thin cotton t-shirt. He looked disheveled, like he had just finished climbing a mountain, his hair wet and messy, skin ruddy.

Just then, he noticed the camera crew, and his eyes flashed for one tiny moment before he whirled away from the camera to step around to the other side of a truck so he was no longer visible.

A nasty-sounding guffaw escaped my lips, and I saw Amber's face jerk toward mine. I shut off the TV and sank to the ground, turning to Amber. She looked as shocked as I felt.

"I can't believe it," I said.

"I can't either." Amber had a new look of worry on her face, arched eyebrows raised high on her forehead. "What if he tries to find you?"

I was hit with an instant gut-spasm. "I don't know." I felt a tight little ball in the pit of my stomach.

~ ☾ ~

"Please, promise you'll stay away from him," Amber said, eyes flashing. Her worry rained over me like tiny pinpricks of hail.

"What if he finds me?" I said, my voice oddly flat. I took a deep breath as my stomach knotted up even tighter.

Amber's eye twitched as she leaned forward in my ivory armchair, staring at the empty TV screen. "Okay. Let's make a plan. Evan is in Grand Forks, probably with his *Malandanti* brother and their little gang of Skinwalker dung-rats who will be clamoring over one another to get to you first."

"Gee thanks, Amber. I feel a lot better now." I sat down directly across the room from her, on the sofa. Kate sat on the carpeted floor next to my feet.

"Just wait, I wasn't finished. I was just about to say, despite all of that, you have powers, too. You just don't know how to control them yet, right?" Amber didn't wait for me to answer. "But if you practice them, maybe you'll have a fighting chance, right? Show us. Show me and Kate."

"Show you what?" I looked over at Kate.

"Show us your Indigo Child powers." Kate spun on her butt, cross-legged on the floor to face me. "I think it's your best shot at dealing with this. Obviously, it's no coincidence that Evan's here in Grand Forks, and I think you need a strategy."

"But I've only actually used my powers, what, once, twice at the most? I have no control over them whatsoever. I don't even know how I did it. They just...came to me."

Amber stood up and stepped toward me, bending over to place both hands on my shoulders. "You can do it. Just focus on your ability to feel everyone's emotions."

"I already do that. The only time anything else has

happened is when I've been scared for my life."

Amber straightened. "Okay. So what happened that day in the car? When you had to fight off the Skinwalker?"

I thought back to that day, and the image of Evan hanging in the seatbelt upside down ran through my mind.

Instinctively, I'd reached deep within myself and drew on my terror and rage, imagining my emotions as having the destructive properties of a bomb. My body, mind, and soul worked in perfect unison as I mentally willed the feelings up and out of me and pushed them at the Skinwalker. It froze.

"It's hard to explain, but I think I used my own feelings to attack it."

Amber nodded rapidly. "Just do that with me and Kate, right now. All right?"

She backed into an empty area in the apartment, jaw set, hands palm-out in a defensive stance. Ready for what she expected was coming. From me.

This was not going to work. "But this is different," I said. "I'm not in danger."

"You're going to have to use your imagination a little here. Just imagine you're scared." She slapped her abdomen hard enough to make me wince. "Use me. Focus on me."

I stared at her, incredulous. "It's not going to work, you know." I rose to my feet.

She narrowed her eyes and placed her hands on her hips. "It definitely won't work if you're going to think negatively like that. Just try it."

"Sarah, Amber's right. Just try," Kate added.

"All right. But I have no control over the outcome. Don't say I didn't warn you."

Amber nodded in encouragement while Kate inched her way across the room, as if protecting herself from...

~ ☾ ~

God knows what. I wished I could have told her not to worry, but truthfully, I really couldn't.

"Here it goes."

I thought of my current state, frustrated. Annoyed. I allowed it to solidify in my mind, as if it was congealing into something more substantial, something I could almost grasp. Then I imagined pushing it up and out, until I could see it, in my minds' eye, flowing toward Amber.

"Well?" I asked, already knowing the answer.

"Nothing yet," she said, with a tight smile.

"Damn it!"

"Just try again. You'll get it eventually."

I started to get a headache as my mind tried to grasp something as elusive and fleeting as a feeling and make it tangible, concrete enough to psychically throw it. I covered my face and groaned.

"Concentrate. This is important. We may not have much time," Amber said with a stern look. "The sooner you understand your abilities and learn to use them, the more protected you are."

"I know, but it's like trying to catch a cloud. There's nothing to hold onto." My voice was becoming increasingly petulant. I hated sounding like that.

"Okay," Amber said softly. "Just try again, please?"

The heat of the room and the sweat dripping from my palms was distracting me. I couldn't focus. I clenched my teeth.

I closed my eyes and reached into my mind. The deep, festering wound of learning the truth about Evan, the grating sense of my own ineptitude all built up inside of me like a ball of volatile gasses. I pulled on it, pushing it forward, up and outside of myself. I continued to force that feeling out, willing it. Seeing it. I felt nothing.

I opened my eyes. The look of shock on Amber's face

transformed into pain, and she held her stomach as if she'd been kicked in the gut. She stumbled sideways, sputtering and sucking air in with a gasp as she reached out for the wall. A framed print of Old Faithful fell from its hanger and smashed when it hit the floor.

Oh, no! Kate and I ran across the room, and I grabbed her by one arm, Kate the other. Amber straightened up.

"You did it!" she wheezed between heaving breaths.

"I'm so sorry! Are you okay?"

"I'm fine," she said, smiling as she shook her head. "I'm just amazed you could figure out how to do it so fast. Wow. Noreen was right. Indigo Children really are evolved." She took a few deep breaths.

"Okay. I should not do that again, unless it's to a Skinwalker or a *Malandanti*."

"Don't worry, I'm fine." She cocked her head sideways as if to say don't be silly, and yet there was something in her eyes that refuted the look. She stiffened her posture and leaned forward defensively. "I have an idea. Let's try one more thing before we quit."

"What?"

"Why don't you try to get in touch with your terror, like that day in that abandoned house or in the car with the Skinwalker. If you can collect that terror, think of how powerful it would be."

"That seems like a bit of a stretch to me," I said.

"I don't think it's a stretch at all," Amber said. "Terror is a powerful emotion. Just think of the emotional flooding, the total freeze, and the adrenaline spike sending all of your systems into overdrive."

I contemplated her words. "But shouldn't terror eventually cause a person to 'fight or flight'?"

"Yeah, but it would give you a few minutes to fire up your next strategy," Kate said. I glanced at her, and she shrugged.

"What's my next strategy?" I asked.

~ ☾ ~

"Rage," she said with a smile. "I bet you could kill with rage."

I chuckled. "You can be so creepy sometimes."

Kate smiled and winked.

"Give it to me!" Amber said as she took on a jiu jitsu-style defensive pose.

This time I imagined channeling my rage, at nearly losing my life, at how Jessica Crow did lose hers, at Amber losing her Aunt Lilly, and finally, at Evan's betrayal. I forced the rage out and directly at her.

Amber's head flung sideways as if someone had slapped her, her body flying from the impact. She hit the carpet with a thud, her eyes rolling backward as her head struck the floor.

"Amber!" I dropped to the floor. She groaned and turned toward me, her arms hugging her body.

"Ow," she coughed out. Kate kneeled beside her, too, and shot me a look that screamed dumbass.

"I'm sorry. I shouldn't have done that," I said. Kate and I helped her up to sitting.

"Where did all that rage come from?" Amber's voice began gaining strength.

"All of the loss. The pain. The deaths."

Amber nodded, her eyes squeezed shut. "Good." She cringed when she pushed herself up to standing.

I shook my head. "I think we should stop, for both our sakes. I really don't want to kill my best friend." Kate and I brushed the dust off Amber's back.

"Okay." Amber rubbed the back of her head and winced. "We'll quit for now, but remember one thing, Sarah."

"What?" I said.

"Skinwalkers don't wait."

~ ☾ ~

CHAPTER TWENTY-ONE

Evan stood at the side of a giant, land-moving machine, arms crossed over his chest, checking his watch. Why I was here, at his land development site, I couldn't explain, even to myself. I just...came.

The land was mismatched, the rutty, partially graded brownish-gray clay and gravel in the middle in stark contrast with the cluster of trees surrounding it. Some areas were perfectly flat and smooth with a huge rolling machine atop them, probably awaiting the creation of a road. Other areas were still hilly and heavily rutted with tire tracks, where bobcats were busily flattening them out, the little machines like a myriad of worker bees, buzzing away.

The whole place was a cacophony of machinery, some whiny, some clicking, some roaring. Dust wafted up my nose and I sneezed, my mouth flooded with the earthy flavor of crushed rock.

I shouldn't be here.

He hadn't seen me yet, sitting in my car.

The mid-September sun hung low in the sky, the brilliant rays of light reflecting off of Evan's hair, highlighting the coppery streaks that peppered the near-black. Leaves quivered on the branches along the sides of the land, their colors ranging from lemony-green to burnt squash. Every so often one would fall, catching in the light breeze and rolling about in the air. While the heat of the sun warmed my face, the chill of the September air required that I keep my denim jacket on.

~ ☾ ~

In the light of day, I could really see him for the first time. He did look different. Thinner and more tired. He spoke to a group of workmen wearing bright orange hardhats, shaking their hands like a legitimate businessman. If they only knew.

I hovered out of sight, hiding in my car, parked behind the heavy machinery, my heart pounding in my chest as I watched him pack up his gear. He was still gorgeous, despite the change. In fact, he was almost more hauntingly beautiful because of his newly vulnerable appearance.

God. Why do I think like this?

He walked in my direction, and I sank back into my seat knowing that at any moment, he might discover me. He picked a binder off of the hood of a truck and turned away. He just looked so regular. Like a guy at work, not some warlock. A *Malandanti*.

Out of the blue, my skin began to prickle as a dark emotion flooded my senses, like a black eel that slithered up my spine. It was originating from my left, and when I turned, my gaze met a woman's.

She stood within ten feet of me, standing in the forest, motionless. Watching me. I had never seen her before, and yet she was familiar. She looked like a woman filled with highly distilled rage, her eyes glittering, her teeth bared.

Her eyes were all wrong. They sparked with something inhuman, and I knew I had seen those eyes before, but I couldn't place where. My stomach tightened at the sight of her.

Her black hair was pulled back into a severe ponytail at the back of her head, revealing noble, high cheekbones. Her skin was the color of dark-stained cherry wood, and her eyes were dark and fathomless as she stared, as if they could emblazon a mark right into me.

~ ☾ ~

Realization hit me like a punch.

The murderous mother of Jessica. Sandra Crow.

I trembled as I put the car in gear. I glanced back right before I hit the gas pedal and my gaze locked on her predatory eyes, like a cobra ready to strike. She stepped toward me with a wry smile as her eyes flashed with something unnatural.

“We are coming for you both,” she yelled through my side door window, her mouth pulled up like the snarl of a rabid dog. An icy chill slid up my back.

I hit the gas, turning my wheel hard to the left pulling a full U-turn. I glanced back one last time.

Evan appeared behind her, his expression wild. Eyes opened wide, he looked both surprised and fierce as his gaze flicked back and forth from my car to her.

She whipped toward him. They stared each other down, unmoving. Then she spun on her heel and ran into the bush.

He tore off after her, disappearing into the tangled mass of trees.

After a moment of indecision, I punched the gas and hit the road to exit the development.

I drove and drove, putting as much space between me and that woman as I could.

We are coming for you both. Her words rolled around in my head, over and over.

I drove downtown and parked the car, far from Sandra and Evan. I took a walk to clear my head and wait for some kind of solution to this situation to come to mind. Would I have to move again to get away from him?

I walked toward the bridge that hovered over the Red River.

The closer I got to the bridge, the more I felt pulled toward it. It was as if my self-control, my ability to turn away was fading from grasp.

~ ☾ ~

What was happening? The undulating river flowed slow and steady. My legs grew heavier and heavier. My feet felt weighted down, as if mired in concrete. Then, my mind felt detached from my body, like I was watching myself from somewhere else. The atmosphere around me changed.

I was being suffocated, all oxygen sucked away, leaving an airless vacuum in its place. My heart pounded like a wild bird caged in my chest. I turned, just in time to see Sandra, first her face and then her glowing yellow eyes as she transformed into a Skinwalker. How had she found me? How could she have gotten here so fast? I tried to run, but instead, I was frozen in place. I knew I should be scared, but I felt disconnected, my body unable to respond.

She entered my body with a snap. My feet began to move forward, toward the bridge. I attempted to gain some kind of control of my body, but in utter helplessness, I remained invaded, controlled. I approached the massive concrete structure that stood over the swirling, frothing river.

Once I reached the bridge, I was being pushed from the inside, my seemingly robotic legs wasting no time in climbing up and onto the ledge of the walkway. I heard the rending screech of tires braking hard on pavement. A car door slammed. Then someone hollered.

"*Resisto*!"

Evan? My foot stepped off the slab of gray concrete, my heart hovering somewhere near my mouth, my body now beyond the point of no return. I fell, my bodily sensations still with me despite my lack of muscular control. The air rushed into my face, whipping and lashing my skin as I fell, my arms and legs spread-eagle.

Something warm captured me, and I felt a familiar heat behind me. I suddenly knew there was nothing in this whole world that could harm me. A gentle languor stole over me as I bowed into the warmth. I could sense him, his energy signature, my awareness of him outside of normal human senses. Evan.

We rocketed toward the water and Sandra's presence left me with a suctioning sensation. I screamed as muscular control returned to me, my heart pounding in my chest. My eyes snapped shut as I felt myself being flipped mid-air. I opened my eyes, now looking up into strips of cloud against gray blue sky.

My body jolted with a sharp smack from behind as I sunk into the water. Freezing cold rifled through me like a shockwave. The wind was forced out of my lungs from the impact. I gasped for breath. Then everything faded to black.

The next thing I knew there was yelling all around me.

"Get something to stabilize his neck while I check for a pulse!" an urgent voice commanded, right next to my ear. My body ached. Something hard jabbed into my shoulder blade. I turned, forcing my eyes open. Two men in uniforms were next to me, moving about in a harried way.

"Miss, can you speak?" one of the men asked.

"Yes." I started to shake.

I twisted to look around. Evan was being pulled onto shore from where he lay sprawled on his back atop the rocks in a half-inch of soupy, brackish water. I tried to move toward him.

A hand was on my shoulder. "I think you should stay put, miss. What's your name?" It was the same paramedic.

I ignored him, instead focusing on Evan. He looked like a shrunken version of his former self, his muscular body looking compacted under the pressure of the landing. His skin was white, as if powder had been smoothed over it, his black eyelashes and stubble in stark contrast to his chalky complexion. His mouth was slack and parted, the purplish-blue backdrop of his lips dark against white teeth. Nothing in his appearance gave the impression that he was alive. He looked like death embodied. Cold, still, and flaccid.

A wild shaking began inside me, and a scream tore from my throat. I forced myself upright, ignoring every stab, every ache. Bruised and broken, I didn't care. I crawled to him, ignoring the men who tended to him.

"Miss, you need to stay away from him."

"Evan!" My voice was hoarse but had a pressured edge to it, a desperate edge that told me more about myself right at that moment than at any other moment in my entire life. I pressed on, pushing against the man's efforts to keep me from Evan. I shoved his hand off my arm. "Evan, no!"

I reached out to his face, praying for one last chance to look into his eyes, one more chance to see that smile on his lips, one more chance to see warmth in his cheeks.

He had to live. He was Evan, sweet, loving Evan, who, despite his horrible upbringing, still had to have something good inside of him.

I held my breath as I reached deep within myself, imagining my own soul entering his body, an energy transfer from within me to him, willingly given. The vibration began low in my belly and rolled up through my chest until it crackled from my fingertips, warming them against his cold, wet flesh.

Instantly, my hands felt something. His skin began to buzz in my palms as a pink flush swept across his skin. He took a breath, his lips parting as the air rushed in. Then his eyes fluttered open, his pupils dilating to pinpricks as they focused on my face above him. I burst into tears and leaned in to kiss him, his cold lips warming to mine.

"Sarah," he whispered. I kissed him all over his face.

~ ☾ ~

CHAPTER TWENTY-TWO

"How are you feeling?" I asked.

Evan had just woken up and was still in rough shape. After being bandaged up and my elbow set in a half-bent cast, I'd been discharged, free to go. But I couldn't leave. I had to see him. I sat on his hospital bed in my partially damp clothing that smelled like river water while everything else smelled like bleach, including Evan's green fabric hospital gown. It reminded me of a swimming pool.

"I feel like I was hit by a bus," he said, eyes closed. His body was completely still, his arm also set in a cast at his side. Despite his injuries and his vulnerable state, he still looked beautiful, the high cheekbones and chiseled jaw lending him the look of a sleeping Adonis. "How are you?"

"Broken elbow. That's it," I said, showing off my cast and sling. He opened his eyes for a peek, nodded, and then closed them again.

"Why did you do it?" I asked.

"Do what?"

"Jump after me."

He opened one eye to look at me. "Why do you think?"

Another pang hit me right in the chest at the thought of him jumping off the bridge to catch me. I didn't need to hear the words. His actions bellowed the truth. He loved me and would die for me.

"You could have died."

Now his other eye opened. "Very unlikely to happen, off the Sorlie Bridge."

I sat up, pulling away from him as the sensation of something thick and heavy stuck in my chest and spread to my stomach. My eyes started to prick.

"Were we committed under the mental health law for jumping off the bridge?" Evan asked.

"No. I told them it was an accident, although it took a lot of explaining for them to buy it." I placed my hand on his good arm. "Why are you here, Evan? Did you follow me to Grand Forks?"

"No. I've left you alone, like you asked. But I've been following them, and when they came to Grand Forks, I knew they'd located you."

"How did you know?"

"You told me that day in the store. You said you were moving to Grand Forks to go to university."

I mentally chastised myself for how much I'd revealed to Evan back then, in such a short period of time.

"Why was she there? Why was Sandra at the worksite?" I asked.

Evan closed his eyes once again, as if shutting out the world. "Stefano sent her to locate me while he was looking for you. She got away from me in the bush, got back to her car. So I followed her from a distance, as far away as I could without losing her. I knew where she would be headed to next. I knew she'd go straight for you."

"She went to the worksite for you, but once she saw me, she decided to come after me?"

He nodded. "And now she'll report back to Stefano where we both are."

"You couldn't have been too hard for him to find, with the company and the development and all. You were on TV, you know. Not very incognito."

Evan shook his head. "I've had an alias set up for a

while, with an alternate corporation and everything. I've got a number of developments going all over the country. He wouldn't have known where to start. And about that news cast, I didn't know they were doing a news story on the development. They just showed up that day. I didn't even see them before it was too late, and my face had been plastered all over the screen."

"So he found you."

"But he found you first, I'm sure of it."

A giant lump took up residence in my throat. "Okay. So now he's found us both." My heart stuttered. "Who does he want more, me or you?"

Evan took a long, deep breath and swallowed. "Right now, it's you. He knows the two of us have this power together. He saw it that day in the junkyard. And I know my brother. He'll do everything he can to extinguish it. Once you're eliminated, he knows the threat of our combined ability is dead, and he'll be that much more powerful in his efforts to defeat me."

I cringed. *Oh, God.* "This is the full truth?"

He stared up at me with an odd expression, his entire body still. "Full truth." He attempted to hold up two fingers on his cast hand. They uncurled pathetically. "I promise."

"Good. Because next time you lie, I'm going to have to seriously kick your ass. And I'm not kidding."

Evan chuckled, and then he winced. He moved his good arm to his ribcage.

"How are we not dead?" I asked.

He grimaced before answering. "I don't know for sure, but that electrical current we have... Maybe it created a protective ball around us or something."

I nodded as I considered his explanation. "Maybe."

He fixed his gaze on me, his eyes suddenly flashing. "What if that's true? What if it did create a protective ball?"

~ ☾ ~

He held out his good hand, and I took it. The moment our skin connected, I knew the current had begun, and that warm, bubbly sensation floated over me. Simultaneously, my skin began to buzz. But something was different this time. This time, I was channeling it, somehow. I didn't know how I was doing it, but it was as if the voltage was connected to my mind, like the more I wanted it to increase, it did. The more I wanted it to decrease, it did.

The vibration built into a throbbing sensation that, at first, hurt my elbow, but then seconds, maybe mere moments, later, the pain dissipated and then was completely gone.

We let go of each other.

I touched the skin of my elbow just inside the lip of the cast, which felt completely normal. I pressed on the tip of it that had only moments before been aching but now was completely fine. I glanced up to see Evan examining his own arm the same way.

"I think something just happened," I said.

He nodded, holding his cast up for inspection. He pinched the skin above and below the cast and didn't even wince. Then he pressed on his ribcage, and that too seemed to elicit no physical response.

"I think... Did we heal ourselves?" He looked up at me, beaming.

"Is it possible?"

He chuckled and shook his head in amazement. "I guess it is!"

I leaned down to kiss him, the first real kiss since that day, long ago in the hotel room when we'd first made love.

"Sarah, I don't think this thing we have, this ability, is a coincidence," Evan said.

"Then what is it?"

"Something is actually different about us, and I don't just mean the energy."

~ ☾ ~

*****

Evan's street overlooked a city park where enormous elms were spaced every few feet, creating a canopy of foliage in front of the homes. His place was the only modern house on the block, a white stucco structure with story-high windows on a massive curved front deck. It seemed like only hours ago we'd been in the hospital together, but in reality, that was almost a day ago. I rang the doorbell.

Evan answered, his hair wet as if he had just stepped out of the shower. Here he was, alive, skin flushed pink, his eyes radiant with life. My blood pressure spiked as his lips curled into a brilliant smile.

"Sarah." He reached out to me with his good hand, his soft palm enfolding mine into his. "Come in."

I did and the door shut behind me. "You look like nothing ever happened," I said.

"I know. I had to leave because the doctors were starting to prod me like I was some kind of freak of nature." He chuckled. "Which, I guess I am. What about you?"

"They said it was an error in diagnosis. That my elbow wasn't actually broken, it was just bruised." I rolled my eyes.

"Interesting," he said, examining my face. "How do you think we can do it? Heal?"

"I don't know," I said. "I'm not a scientist, and I don't have all of the terms, but I know energy is required in the healing process. Since we have the ability to manipulate that energy, maybe we can initiate it and speed up the process?"

"Together we manipulate energy," he said. "I don't even know what to say to that."

"There's really nothing to say, is there?" I asked, shaking my head.

"It just defies common sense, like all of the black

magic of the *Malandanti*. I've never known anyone to be able to completely control energy like that. Not even my parents, the High Priest and Priestess."

"Your parents were High Priest and Priestess?" I asked.

"Unfortunately, yes." He nodded. "Come in, I'll show you around. We can talk about it as we go."

The foyer was grand, two floors high, with a black iron light fixture dangling overhead. A huge floor-to-ceiling mirror hung directly across from a massive oil painting, making the entire space look gigantic. The flooring below my feet was glossy porcelain tile.

"This is beautiful, Evan," I said, knowing my mouth was hanging open.

"Kind of a step-up from a postage-stamp sized hotel room, isn't it?" A mischievous smile crossed his mouth. He led me to his living room to the left of the foyer. Slate gray walls made the space urban and modern, but despite the cool color, it felt warm and inviting. Dim lighting shone off the glossy hardwood floors, creating a mirrored effect. His dark brown leather furnishings looked straight out of a decorating magazine.

"This is where I hang out."

"Very nice," I said.

He smiled, and that inner radiance lit up his entire face. Just looking at that smile made my entire body roar to life, like turning a furnace to high heat. I feared my ability to keep myself from jumping his bones would crumble from just that look alone.

We entered his dining room, the dark wooden table and leather chairs mirroring the luxury of the rest of the house. Atop a side table sat a black and white photo of the two of us. It was a candid shot, one I'd never seen before. The picture had a tangible energy about it. My face was tipped up and smiling, and I was looking into his eyes as he looked down at me with a look of absolute devotion. My chest squeezed as I looked at that picture, as if within my chest was a giant hollow space that had been carved out when I'd learned the truth of why he was in my life. My eyes pricked with heat.

I'd loved him so much at that moment in that picture, when I was oblivious to the realities of who he was and what he'd done. I still loved him, but now, there was baggage.

"You saw the picture," he said, his voice quiet, curious.

I blinked, fighting the stinging in my eyes. "It's kind of hard to miss," I said, my voice bursting from my throat with a croak.

He looked at me with the saddest eyes, the edges drooping. I was almost overcome with the compulsion to kiss him. Stifling the desire felt like denying myself oxygen.

"It's my favorite picture of us." He walked over and straightened it.

"I can't... I can't believe you have that picture up."

I watched him smile and shrug, seeming to be at a loss for words. "I know. Kinda creepy, especially since Stefano took the picture. And then to keep it up after the girl told you to get lost, it really dials up the creepy factor, doesn't it?" He looked down. "I just couldn't stand to not see you every day."

I stared, words whirling about in my head as a tennis ball-sized sensation built in my throat.

"Come on," he said, placing his hand lightly on my back, urging me forward.

He led me to the adjoined kitchen where I slid my hands along the cold, black granite countertop. My back warmed as Evan approach me from behind. He put his hands on my shoulders and squeezed. The pressure was exquisite, a mixture of pain and pleasure all in one. He continued his massage down between my shoulder blades.

~ ☾ ~

"You're tense," he said.

"I know."

"You've been through so much." Regret tinged his words. "Sarah, I'm sorry. For everything." An odd choking sound warbled his words.

I turned around, the strange lump in my throat preventing me from responding.

"It's time to talk, isn't it?" he asked, looking down at me, his lips mere inches from mine.

I nodded. "It is."

He led me to his dining room table. "What do you need to know? I'll answer any question you ask."

I sat down directly across from him and swallowed, hard. "What can the *Malandanti* do, and how are they different from the Skinwalkers?"

Evan took a deep breath and leaned forward, his chest touching the edge of the walnut-colored wooden table. "The *Malandanti* spirit-travel, like the Skinwalkers, but the roots of our society are far more advanced. Our magic goes beyond spirit travel. Really, the possibilities are endless. It's merely a matter of skill and access to the proper incantations."

Anger surged within me, faster and hotter than ever. I dug my nails into my palm. "And how do you access the proper incantations?" I said, trying not to sound like I was speaking through clenched teeth.

"The Key of Solomon," he said. "It's a book of spells. I believe it is the only remaining evidence of the *Malandanti*'s existence, aside from Stefano and me."

I thought of the confrontation between Stefano and Evan that day Evan fully admitted his guilt. "And Stefano has the book, doesn't he?"

His head bobbed slowly, up and down. "Unfortunately, yes." A chill ran up my spine, and Evan, as if sensing it, reached across the table for my hand.

So Stefano had an advantage, and always would as

long as he had the book. Images of Evan dressed up in some strange red robes and uttering an incantation swirled through my head. I knew this was completely from my imagination, but it sickened me, nonetheless.

The question was, would I ever be able to look at him without these images? Would I ever feel about him the way I felt about him at that moment in his photograph? My heart wanted it to be yes, but my head was overruling my heart these days.

Evan squeezed my hand. "But don't worry. What we can do when we're together, it far outweighs any spell I've ever known. Together, we're untouchable, and Stefano knows this. And he's scared as hell."

"This is all so bizarre, Evan."

"I know. Imagine growing up with it. Believe me, the fact that it was bizarre wasn't lost on me, even as a child."

I peered at his face. "What about that first time we met, after the attack? You were siphoning my energy then. Why didn't you just steal my soul? Why did you stop?" I said. "And don't say it was because I intrigued you."

He nodded vigorously. "I'd never actually attempted the soul-stealing before you, so I didn't really know what to expect." I felt the urge to interrupt, but I suppressed it. "So when I siphoned it off slowly like that, I didn't realize that wasn't how it's supposed to work. I started the process, the way I'd been taught to, where you steal a portion, enough to subdue the victim, you, so you could be taken back to Stefano. But that's not the way it happened at all. What did happen was something almost...involuntary."

"How?"

"It was very strange." He swallowed. "At first, I was confused, disoriented. Instead of your soul merely filling me with your power, my body and mind felt totally euphoric. I knew immediately that it wasn't supposed to happen that way."

"If you'd never done it before, how could you know that?"

Evan shook his head. "I've seen Stefano do it numerous times, as well as my parents. I can tell it is pleasurable in a way, but it also hurts at first, with the increase of energy inside your body. Nobody's supposed to have more than one soul reside within them. It's an abomination against nature. The body initially revolts, and it takes a while for the body to adapt."

"And you had no pain?" I asked.

"No. And the weird thing is, I knew you didn't either." He shook his head once again, this time running his hands through it so that it stood up on end. "Usually the victim is in agony and holding onto their soul with every instinct they've got. But I could actually feel your euphoria. And I knew you weren't holding back, letting the energy flow out, but it was like the energy flowed in an out between us, like we...like we..."

"Like we were one," I said, finishing his sentence for him.

His gaze locked on mine. "Yes. Like we were one entity, sharing our souls with each other."

A thrill shot up my spine at the visceral memory of that shared euphoric moment. It was beyond description.

Were we sharing our life forces? If we were, for what purpose? For purely pleasure-seeking? Was it possible that the energy we generated was actually connected to our ability to share our life forces?

He let go of my hand and leaned back in his chair, sucking in a deep breath. "It seems like another lifetime, watching my brother, my parents, stealing souls for their own selfish purposes. Like someone else's life. Like a bad dream that I keep wishing never really happened."

~ ☾ ~

He squeezed his eyes shut. "I wish it had just been a bad dream."

An image of his parents, also dressed in red robes, ropes tied at their waists, standing in a dim room lit by candles, a young Evan lying on a pyre in front of them, flashed through my head. Again, I knew this was my imagination getting the best of me, and I also knew I'd better replace it with a more realistic image before the made-up one stuck.

"So once a soul is stolen, how does it get brought back to your own body?" I asked.

He looked like he was about to throw up. "The evil soul is like a magnet, it just keeps the victim's soul stuck to it, like gravity. When you soul-travel back to your own body, it comes with you, unable to resist."

"Sick," I said, imagining two souls, one dark, black, and suctioning, floating through the atmosphere. I re-focused on Evan, who still looked as white as a sheet. "How much do you know about the history of the *Malandanti*?"

Evan looked at my face, his expression unreadable. "It is said that long ago, in the fifteen and sixteen-hundreds, *Malandanti* were cannibals as well as necromancers." My still tender stomach roiled once again. "I knew Skinwalkers would do just about everything evil under the sun for their powers. Of course, I thought necromancer meant sex with dead people, so how much worse can it get?"

Evan laughed, long and hard. It was the first real belly laugh I'd heard from him since before...the confession. "That's necrophilia. But then again, these were people who ate other humans. I wouldn't put it past them."

"So they read minds, cast spells, and of course, those crying child sounds that lured me out of the tent that morning," I said.

~ ☾ ~

Evan shook his head. "Only the Skinwalkers use the crying child sounds to lure their prey."

"Okay, so the *Malandanti* just eat people? Great family legacy, there." I realized it sounded like I was trivializing a very bad situation, but what else could I do? If I really thought about it too seriously, I'd probably end up in the fetal position and wailing at the top of my lungs.

"That happened in the fifteen-hundreds, not now," he said. Despite his correction, his face still looked sheepish. "But the Skinwalkers are a whole different breed. There are as many differences as there are similarities."

I rolled my eyes. "Like what?"

"Did I tell you about the corpse powder?" he asked.

My guts twisted at the thought. "Corpse powder. Is that...?"

He nodded. "Powder from corpses. But it gets worse. It's actually white powder."

"No! Bones?"

Evan's face was contorted from disgust. "Ground bones from infants."

"Ugh! That's disgusting!" I crossed my arms over my chest, trying desperately to ignore the rising gorge in the back of my throat. "What was the indoctrination like?" I asked.

Something dark flashed across his eyes, but it was gone the very next instant. "It's very painful, a story that ends in me becoming a very sick, twisted individual."

"Right now, I have an image of your parents dressed in red robes and chanting incantations over your body. Can you please replace it with the truth?"

He nodded. "It's not that far from the truth. The only difference is the robes. There were no robes. Just pants and shirts."

"You were lying down?"

~ ☾ ~

His eyes glittered, as if a very specific memory had just crossed his mind. "Not just lying down, I was tied down. The process is painful, with the branding and all."

"God. Your parents were monsters."

His mouth pursed. "Yes, they were. Well...you know how it ends for my parents."

I shivered as I imagined Stefano as a sixteen year old, willing to murder his own parents, watch them burn. "How could he do it? Set his own parents on fire?"

"He was sick. I can't really describe it any other way. Brainwashing in childhood to evil, it makes you immoral. Insensitive to other people, uncaring. The only person he cared about was himself, and maybe me, a little bit." Evan bit his thumbnail as his gaze remained glued to the table before him. "But I can't help but feel like my parents just experienced the consequences of their bad karma."

I stared at him. He looked hard. Cold. "You say that like you think they deserved to burn to death."

"No. That's not what I meant," Evan said, eyes penetrating. "I just think that...when evil breeds evil, the outcome is unpredictable. I loved my mother. I think there was something good in her, however small it was. And that was the part that I loved."

"You mentioned karma. What about your bad karma?" I said. "You must have killed some people in the years since your indoctrination?"

Evan's face went off-centre, as if he was biting the inside of his cheek. His eyes took on a faraway look. "Never. Lots of soul-travel and black magic, spells and all that. Lots of setting things up for Stefano to do the devouring. So, in that sense, I've been an accomplice. But I've never stolen another soul, and I've never killed another human being."

"Hmm." I evaluated his face, his glassy eyes, the corners of his lips drooping. Was he lying?

~ ☾ ~

As if reading my mind, he nodded slowly. “I know, hard to believe.”

“But what about your heritage? Your *Malandanti* magic? You’re just going to walk away from all of that power?”

“I don’t want it,” he said, looking down. “And I can’t go back. I won’t go back. The moment I met you, everything changed. I started wanting something more, needing it. That life of evil, it wasn’t me, it was them. It just wasn’t until I met you that I realized it.”

“What were you like before you met me? How were you different?”

He shook his head and took a deep breath. “I can’t explain it. It’s like I had something inside me, something good, and it was clawing to get out. I felt like I was living inside a dark cloud, and I couldn’t see my way out of it. I like to think there was always good in me, just like my mother, but after the indoctrination, it became totally out of reach. I have to get this evil off of me. Sarah, I want you to stay here. With me.”

*****

Amber and I stood together in the kitchen putting our food together on the counter top. I poured milk into my bowl of Cheerios and took a deep breath, thinking about how just yesterday, while at his house, Evan had suggested I stay with him while both of us were targets of Stefano and his minions.

“Evan wants me to stay with him for awhile,” I said, half-wishing I had earplugs at this particular moment in my life.

“He wants you to stay with him? Is he freakin’ delusional?” Amber’s voice had grown in volume unnecessarily; I was right beside her. She glared as she made a sandwich, cutting it in half with so much violence it was as if she was imagining slicing right into Evan.

~ ☾ ~

"Yes, he is delusional. He thinks we can just go back to what things were like...before." I walked out of the kitchen, hoping the conversation would trail off, but with no such luck. She followed me into the bathroom.

"I hope you sorted that out." Amber stared at me. "You did tell him there was no way you would do something so stupid, right?"

"I just told him no." I stood with my hand on the bathroom doorknob, hoping she might take the hint.

"You need to say more than that," she said, unmoving.

What would Amber say if she knew the truth? That I'd accepted Evan back into my life, and that we were all but back together? The thought of that conversation made me internally shudder. She was definitely not ready for that. "We've been through this before, haven't we?"

"I know, I know. He saved your life and blah, blah, blah. And now it seems like you are unable to stay away from him," she said.

I rolled my eyes as I reached for my hairbrush. I had to get ready for class and it didn't appear she was taking the hint. Then I was struck with how my brush looked different.

"Hey, did you use my hairbrush lately?" I asked, changing the subject from Amber's rant.

"No. Why?"

"Because somebody cleaned it. Look, all the hair is pulled out of it. It's clean. It almost looks brand new," I said as I turned the black brush over and over in my hand.

"Maybe Kate cleaned it. She's always grossed out by your brush."

"Yeah, maybe it was Kate." I called her over, and she came out of her room in her purple pajamas, a Cosmopolitan magazine in hand. "Did you clean my hairbrush recently?" I asked.

"What are you talking about?"

"Somebody cleaned my hairbrush. I went to brush my hair and it was clean, there was no hair in it at all."

Kate glanced at Amber, who shrugged, and then back at me. "Good. That thing was disgusting. You should have done it a long time ago." Kate's eyes scrunched up, her nose crinkled.

"You didn't do it?" I asked as a shiver slid up my back.

"No, but Amber probably did it." Kate turned to Amber.

"I didn't," Amber said.

An icy sensation started to expand in my body. My hands began to shake.

"Could it be...?" Kate asked, her eyes growing wider and wider.

~ ☾ ~

CHAPTER TWENTY-THREE

"Okay. Check this out," Kate said as she turned the laptop on the floor toward us. She sat cross-legged, leaning forward to read the news online. We'd all decided to cut class and spend the rest of the afternoon scouring the headlines in Grand Forks for anything else weird or suspicious.

"Did you see the headline about that flight of sick passengers?"

"No, what happened?" Amber asked without looking up from her phone.

"On a flight coming to Grand Forks, several passengers came down with a mysterious illness," Kate said.

"What kind of illness?" Amber asked, her interest in science keeping her from actually studying it.

"They don't know," Kate said as she scrutinized the screen. She looked like a circus performer, folded in on her body like a human pretzel. "It says public health is involved. They're concerned it could be the start of an outbreak."

"What are the symptoms?" Now I was interested.

"I've never heard of this condition before." Kate squinted her eyes at the screen. "It's called catalepsy."

"Does it say what catalepsy is?" I asked, scuttling across the floor so I could sit next to her.

"It's a condition of muscle rigidity and sudden loss of consciousness."

"That's a weird set of symptoms for such a large

group to have all at the same time," Amber said. I noted she had also closed the gap between herself and the laptop as well. "Where did the flight depart from?"

Kate looked at us both, her expression grim. "Cortez, Colorado."

A sharp intake of air whistled past Amber's lips. "Cortez is near the four corners," she whispered. A shiver of ice slid up my back.

Kate continued to read, not even reacting to what Amber said. "All of the remaining people from the flight are being held in quarantine."

Amber and I looked at each other, her fear and worry washing over me like a caustic haze.

I took a deep breath. "Skinwalkers or *Malandanti*?"

*****

Evan and I agreed to meet along the path of the river, the giant elms still full of yellowing leaves. The branches reached out to the sky like slender threads snaking about aimlessly, creating a beautiful chaos of lemony leaves. I wanted to know what his take was on my cleaned hairbrush and the flight with cataleptic passengers.

Evan approached, looking gorgeous as usual, wearing dark jeans and his brown-black leather jacket. The silver dog-tag with the Valente crest flashed in the sunlight, momentarily blinding me when the sun hit my eye.

"Hi," he said, handing me a paper cup of hot coffee. "Black, just how you like it."

"Thanks." I took a sip of the frothy liquid.

"What did you want to see me about?" We began to stroll along the riverbank.

"I wondered if you've been following the news story about that flight from Cortez, Colorado?" I watched his expression carefully.

His posture stiffened as his brow furrowed. "No, I haven't heard anything about it."

"Do you know where Cortez is?"

"Cortez is the closest airport to the four corners. It's only thirty-eight miles from where I used to live in Eagle Creek."

I nodded. "Over half of the passengers went into some kind of catatonic state." I went on to explain what Amber, Kate and I had read in the news. His eyes darkened as the story unfolded. When I finished, he put his hand to his face, rubbing the dark stubble of his jaw, his eyes downcast, deep in thought.

"What do you think?"

"I don't know. I'm sure Stefano had a hand in this," he said.

I nodded. "There's more."

He nodded, his entire body motionless as he listened.

"My hairbrush, it used to have a lot of hair in it, but earlier today, it was completely clean."

His eyes widened and he let out a string of profanity. "Now I know its Stefano. He's getting parts of your essence to do a spell."

"What's he going to do? Make a voodoo doll that looks like me and poke it with pins?"

Evan shook his head, his eyes blazing. "Don't underestimate this, Sarah." His electric gaze remained fixed on me. "I wonder…" His words trailed off as he continued to evaluate my face, as if there would be some kind of answer there. Then he crossed his arms in front of his chest. "Have you been practicing your abilities since last summer?"

"I have, actually."

He bit the inside of his lip. "Good. The more practice, the better."

A slow, steady clack of footsteps approached us from behind. An icy sensation began to build inside of me, starting at my core, climbing up my back and spreading through my neck and scalp. Evan immediately grasped me by the waist and pulled me to him with violence. I didn't even have to turn around to know who was there. A chill blasted through each and every nerve ending. I turned toward the footsteps. Stefano.

I grabbed Evan's hand, and we turned to run.

"Evandro. Wait," Stefano called out.

We continued on, both of us running full-out, Evan yelling over his shoulder, "I don't think so."

From behind us, Stefano bellowed, "*Resisto*!"

Evan came to a grinding halt, stumbling forward as if his legs had suddenly become mired in the grass below us. He righted himself before he fell and turned to face Stefano.

"What do you want, Stefano?"

"Evandro. Miss Ross. So nice to see the two of you on this fine September afternoon," Stefano said. He approached us, boots clicking against the asphalt trail.

I tugged at Evan's hand, but he didn't move. My throat tightened with every step.

"What the hell are you doing here?" Evan said through gritted teeth.

"Well, brother," Stefano said. He stared Evan down. "Why don't you give me a proper introduction to your girlfriend?" His eyes glittered in the sunlight, like shards of cold, black glass.

I glanced over at Evan, who had stiffened. Despite the warm sun, I was freezing.

"Just leave us alone. You know very well that everything has changed between us. Sarah and I can defeat you now."

"Then why aren't you moving?" Stefano said with a twitch at the corner of his mouth.

Evan grimaced and then clutched my hand tight. Immediately, the earth beneath our feet began to vibrate, the quivering sensation moving right up through my toes and into my knees. Then Evan stepped toward his brother. "You underestimate our power."

Stefano's eyes widened and a ripple of shock passed over his expression, so quickly I barely saw it. Then he smiled once again and turned to address me. "I suspect you don't realize just how naughty your boyfriend really is?"

I glared at him and clamped my lips together, determined not to take his bait.

"She knows everything," Evan said. "You can't manipulate her, so don't bother trying." Evan let go of my hand and stepped forward, into Stefano's physical space. I reached out to stop him, but it was too late.

Stefano immediately grabbed Evan by the throat. "Don't bother? Why not?"

I lunged forward and attempted to pry Stefano's fingers from Evan's neck, but his grip was too tight.

With his free hand, Stefano reached into his pocket and withdrew a switchblade, and then with a quick twist of his arms, Evan was spun so he was facing me, his eyes bulging from the blood building in his head. My hands were flung away in the motion, the switchblade nicking my pinky. It stung, like a paper cut.

"Our mother lied to save you," Stefano said, the blade pressed firmly to Evan's throat. "If father had known you'd been born with no *caul*, he would have sacrificed you immediately, the way he did the family cat."

Stefano's expression was wild, his eyes glittering like hematite. He grinned. "For fifteen years she kept the truth from him, protecting you. And for what? Just so you can turn on me? I don't think so."

Evan choked, his throat emitting a strange gurgling sound. Stefano loosened his grip, but just slightly.

Evan sputtered out his words. "I learned from the best, brother. Betrayal is the Valente family legacy."

I was ready to pounce, my arms at my sides, knees bent as I waited for one small change in Stefano's posture that would allow me some advantage, some way to rip the knife from Evan's throat. But I wasn't going to risk the blade severing his carotid, and the way the skin was depressed beneath the knife, it was very close. I was motionless, every muscle in my body as wound up as an over-tightened guitar string.

Before I could see what Stefano was doing, he grabbed Evan's hand and stabbed it with the knife. Blood began to drip off of Evan's fingers and thumb.

With the blade finally off of Evan's neck, I rushed at Stefano, trying to wrench his arms off of Evan, but he spun me around and shoved me forward. When I hit the ground, my neck jerked backward, my wrists taking the impact.

"Don't even attempt it, Indigo," Stefano said, practically snarling.

I spun around to see his entire arm was now around Evan's neck in a sleeper hold. I jumped to my feet but kept my distance while Evan tried to pry his hands under Stefano's arm.

I looked directly at him, holding his gaze. "Please, let him go. I'll do anything."

Evan's mouth opened and closed, but nothing came out.

Stefano sneered but loosened his grip once again. Evan began to wheeze as he sucked in a ragged breath. The dark red was fading from his face, his skin now a bright pink.

Evan's voice came out in a ragged whisper. "Sarah, no."

Stefano stared me directly in the eye, his chin jutting out. "And to think our mother covered up the truth to save you. A traitor. Stupid woman. At least she deserved what she got."

He smirked the ugliest, most sinister grin I'd ever seen.

~ ☾ ~

"I just wish I'd told father when I found out, so he could have slit your throat and bled you out, just like I did to Fluffy, your cat." He gave Evan's neck one more squeeze. Evan grimaced, his entire face bulging. My heart stuttered.

"Stop this, please! You're killing him," I said, completely unable to hide the desperation in my voice. "I'll do anything."

His face transformed into a mask of cruelty, his lips pulled back from his teeth, eyes narrowed. His arms loosened, and with a move of violence, he shoved Evan to the ground.

Without warning, Stefano was on me. My back hit grass and rock, tiny pebbles biting into my shoulder blades.

"Just relax," he said with a grin. Immediately, his *Malandanti* spirit form sank into me. It was quick, but I didn't miss the unmistakable glowing yellow eyes, just before my entire body was engorged with his *élan vital.*

It all went much faster than with the Skinwalkers. This suction was immediate, forceful and decisive. A burning heat shuddered through me, as if my entire body was on fire. Pain rifled through me as my ligaments popped with the stretching and pressure, and my bones strained. I could hear screaming. It was my own voice, but it sounded distant and detached. Every inch of skin stretched to the brink of its elasticity, and I knew at any minute, it would tear.

"*Subsisto tentatio indigentia*!" Evan's voice rang out.

The suction stopped, and slowly, the burn in me began to recede. The pressure flip-flopped, like he was doing a somersault inside my body.

And then he was out.

Back in his own body, he sprang to his feet and whirled to face Evan. I sat up, dizzy.

"You think one incantation is enough?" Stefano said,

laughing. “I came out willingly, little brother. Do you really think you can match me? I’m the closest thing in this world there is to a *Malandanti* High Priest.”

Evan cleared his throat, but it didn’t help remove the gravelly sound. “No, but maybe this will.” Evan reached his hand out to me, and I extended mine.

The second our fingers touched, an explosion erupted, the ground rumbling beneath us, shaking the trees enough that they creaked and groaned. The ground heaved, a giant fissure cracking apart at Stefano’s feet, and he lost his footing. Lurching forward, he grabbed the nearest tree trunk, causing a rain of dried leaves to shower over him.

He turned to us and glared. “Smoke and mirrors. This is nothing more than a dog-and-pony circus act. But one fact remains. If I’m already inside of her, there is very little your power can do, can it?” Then he chuckled.

My stomach lurched.

“Get out of here, Stefano. Before Sarah and I turn you into a pile of ash.”

Surprisingly, Stefano didn’t respond, but his head tilted to the side. He was looking at, no, *staring* at something. Evan? His brow was furrowed. He lunged at Evan, one hand around the livid red skin of his neck and the other hand clamped over Evan’s dog-tag chain. The Valente family crest.

I grabbed Stefano’s elbow, but with lightning reflexes, he shoved me backward. Already unsteady on my feet, my tailbone hit the grass, a ripple of pain rifling through my spine.

Evan pried at Stefano’s fingers, which only caused Stefano to squeeze Evan’s chain tighter, leaving angry red gouge around his neck.

“Your family crest,” Stefano said, grasping the silver dog-tag once again. He rolled the silver pendant over in his hand. Then his head jerked up and he muttered a word, directly into Evan's face. It sounded something like, "*A mortis.*" Evan's knees buckled beneath him, his eyes rolling into his head.

"Evan!" I screamed, launching myself at Stefano, but before I got there, he grabbed the chain of Evan's dog-tag and yanked. Something exploded. Stefano was thrown backward and stumbled into a bush.

Stefano stared at Evan, his mouth agape. "No." Stefano's eyes flashed. "No, it can't be."

He righted himself, disengaging his body from the bush as his gaze remained fixed on Evan. He inched toward him, stepping as if walking on eggshells, like Evan's body contained a contagious disease.

"Get the hell out of here!" I screamed.

His head jerked toward me, eyes widened. Then with one more glance at Evan, he took off running, his shoes clack-clack-clacking against the sidewalk until he disappeared out of view.

~ ☾ ~

CHAPTER TWENTY-FOUR

I ran to Evan's side. "Your hand. You're bleeding," I said.

He nodded and slowly began to sit up, moving his hands defensively to his throat, one bloody hand painting his neck with a brilliant crimson stripe. He croaked before words finally came out.

"Why did he fly backward from me? I didn't do that on purpose. Did you do something?"

I shook my head. "No. Why did he cut your hand?"

"I don't know."

I grasped his bloodied palm and examined it. The slice was superficial, enough to open the skin but not a serious wound. It seemed to have created a tear right through the Lucifer sigil. "First, he cut this brand, then he ripped your dog-tag off, and then...something exploded, throwing him backward into that bush." I gestured toward the six-foot tall hedge with tiny yellow flowers.

Evan looked down at his bloodied hand as well. "Why would he cut through the brand?"

I shrugged as I watched him touch the red skin on his neck where the chain once lay. Then he glanced around to the ground beside him, running his fingers over the blades of grass. He came up empty-handed. "He took the chain."

I nodded. "Did you see his reaction?" I used a napkin to wipe off the blood before I bandaged him up.

Evan looked as confused as I felt. "I know." His brow

furrowed as his gaze went unfocused, his eyes tracking back and forth, looking at nothing in particular. “I can’t imagine anything causing a reaction like that from Stefano.”

“He saw something,” I said.

“I know, but what?” Evan’s hands returned to his neck and he held them there, grimacing. I rubbed his back as I leaned in to scrutinize his face. His eyes had never looked so blue, so electric. It was as if twin sapphire flames had been lit behind his retinas.

“I don’t know...” I leaned forward further, looking. “Evan. Your eyes... They look so different. I’ve never seen them look like this before. They’re the most brilliant color of blue. I could swear you’re wearing contacts.”

“I’m not.” His hands dropped to the ground, and he pushed himself to standing.

With his hands away from his throat, I finally saw the red streaks across his neck, the exact length and width of Stefano’s fingers.

Once upright, Evan’s gaze raked over me. “Something’s different about you, too.” His eyes squinted and widened, and then he repeated it again, as if he wasn’t able to clearly focus.

“What is it?”

His forehead creased as dark eyebrows shadowed his eyes. “I can’t see your Indigo aura anymore. It’s like it’s...gone.”

“It’s gone?”

“It looks that way.” He scratched his head. “I’ve always been able to see it.” His eyes darkened. “I don’t understand?”

“Do you think Stefano could have taken my *élan*?”

“No. You wouldn’t be walking and talking right now if he had.”

I shrugged. “I don’t feel any different. Are you sure it

isn't just the light? Maybe it's obscuring your vision somehow?"

He shook his head. "No. Normally I can see it anytime, day or night. It's so strange… It almost makes me wonder if my ability to see it had something to do with the Valente Crest."

Very curious.

Could the crest have been providing some kind of evil power? Was that what kept that dark shroud of evil with him, like he was wearing a cloak of black magic, with no awareness that merely taking it off would release him?

"Did you ever take it off before?" I asked.

He nodded. "Yes. Many times. But this has never happened before."

"Who gave you that crest, anyway?" I asked.

"My mother. She gave it to me right before the indoctrination. She told me never to take it off because it protected me from jealous warlocks who might want to hurt me, like the *Benandanti*."

"But I thought the *Benandanti* were extinguished?"

He shrugged. "They are, but I never really questioned it, until now."

"I wonder if this is related to what Stefano said about you being born without a *caul*." I glanced up at Evan who was deep in thought as well. "Maybe this was something else your mother did to protect you, to protect the secret?"

Something changed in Evan's eyes, a glimmer of recognition. "I wonder… So you think the object did something to veil my secret from my dad?"

"Maybe?" I said. "Do you know what the *caul* is yet?"

"Yes. I looked it up. It's the amniotic sac. In *Malandanti*, the belief is that after birth, the amniotic sac, or *caul*, is partially covering the face of the newborn. Only those with the *caul* are true *Malandanti*."

~ ☾ ~

"So you are the only one who didn't have it, and your mother knew this would put you at risk, so maybe she created a magical object to keep you safe?"

"An amulet," he said, his eyes oddly vacant. "I think you're right. She may have cast a protection spell on the crest and made it into a talisman to protect me from my father. And later, from Stefano."

"Do you think your father would have really killed you—just because you weren't one of them?" I asked.

"I don't know. But my mother may have thought so."

"But what about when you were a baby or a young child?" I asked. "You said you got it when you went through the indoctrination, right?"

He nodded. "Yes, but I had a baby bracelet on until I was three, and then a few anklets until I was a teenager. She always made sure I wore them, even in the bathtub. In fact, I remember when I was three and I managed to get the bracelet off. She screamed at me for so long, I was terrified to ever take it off again."

"That's it," I said. "Now your protection is gone, and so is your ability to see things as a *Malandanti*. Your mother's amulet both protected you and cursed you with its power."

~ ☾ ~

CHAPTER TWENTY-FIVE

We went directly to my apartment after the confrontation with Stefano.

"Maybe we should wait for me to stay with you until we can tell Amber and Kate," I said. We were inside my apartment, having just made the decision for me to stay with Evan on a semi-permanent, perhaps permanent basis, and the thought of just packing up and leaving without even telling them felt entirely wrong. Pressure mounted inside me, and my head started to throb at my temples.

How would they react? Would they be angry? I knew if it was me, I would probably be protective and mad as hell.

"Do you want me here when you tell them?" he asked, but before I could answer, a key turned in the lock of the door. *Too late.*

"Hi, Sarah...?" Amber's voice quickly trailed off as she saw Evan. Her face transformed from happy-go-lucky to a glare in the blink of an eye. "What is he doing here?" She spoke as if he wasn't even in the room.

"Amber," I warned.

She looked at Evan with slitted eyes, her mouth a tight, thin scowl. Kate appeared in the doorway behind Amber, her expression much the same.

Amber stepped forward, glaring at the two of us. "You're together?" Her eyes had widened and now the whites flashed in the light.

"Things have changed." I stared back, holding her glare.

~ ☾ ~

"Oh, things have changed, have they?" Kate's voice was cold, sarcastic. "A change that involves getting back together with a warlock?"

I glanced over at Evan, whose expression hadn't changed. I turned to them. "I guess so." My hold on calmness was thinning and the shaking of my hands told me that one more thing and my very last frayed nerve might snap.

"Why are you? Why, Sarah?" Kate asked, her forehead crinkled, her frown exaggerating her prominent cheekbones.

What could I tell them that wouldn't fall on deaf ears? How could I possibly make them understand the situation from my perspective?

"Look. I know this is going to be hard to hear, but Stefano is after me again, and I've decided to stay with Evan for a while. I'm going. Today."

Two very distinct gasps erupted simultaneously. Amber and Kate both gawked at me as the blood in my face began to burn.

"Sarah, no," Kate said.

"I'm sorry, Kate. I'm sure you don't understand my reasons, but please believe me when I say I've put a lot of thought into it. This isn't a rash decision."

"This is ridiculous," Amber said through gritted teeth, her face flushing bright pink. "A few weeks ago you two weren't even speaking, and now suddenly, you're not only together, but you're moving in with him? Have you lost your mind?"

"Like I said, I know you don't agree, and I get that." I breathed in deeply, ignoring my fluttering hands. "But believe me when I say this is for my own safety."

"No, it's not," Amber said. "Don't you think it's kind of coincidental that Stefano shows up and is after you, and luckily Evan is here at exactly the right time to save the day?"

~ ☾ ~

"Amber, I—"

Kate interrupted me. "How can we accept this decision when we know he's only going to hurt you in the end?" Behind her, Amber shot a glare at Evan. He shifted his weight, but said nothing.

"I appreciate how you're both trying to look out for me." I placed a hand on Kate's arm. "But I need to do this. Please, trust me."

Amber suddenly stepped toward Evan, and his entire body went rigid. She jabbed her pointed fingernail directly into his chest.

"And you," she seethed, "you might have her under your spell, but I can see right through you."

Evan grasped her hand and gently removed it from his chest. He glanced at me before responding. "I understand why you think that, Amber. But you don't have all of the facts."

"I have enough facts to know you're evil and you're using our friend for your own sick, sinister purposes." Amber was nearly snarling now, her teeth completely bared.

It was my turn to step in. "Enough, Amber."

"What about all of the bad things that have happened?" Amber flashed me a pointed look.

"Look, there are things you just don't know." My voice was getting louder, firmer. "You know some stuff but not everything. Now, you have to trust me."

"Then tell us," Amber said.

They stared at Evan like he had leprosy, but his expression remained impassive.

I nodded at him, a silent communication passing between us. "Soon. But not yet." Evan and I turned toward the door.

"Just one more thing before I leave," I said as I turned back to face them. "Did either of you borrow my mascara or nail file recently?"

~ ☾ ~

Amber looked at me like I had completely flipped my lid, and Kate cocked her head to the side.

"What the hell are you talking about?" Amber muttered.

"I'm missing my mascara and nail file."

Kate shook her head. "Are you sure?"

"Yes," I said. Kate and Amber exchanged glances.

"No," Kate said.

"Of course, I didn't," Amber said, her voice lowered. Both sets of eyes stared at me with a look so concerned I found myself feeling slightly unbalanced. "He's got it, doesn't he? Stefano?"

I swallowed. "I think so, yes." I turned to reach for the door handle.

Amber stared at me as one tear slipped out of her left eye and streaked down her cheek in a crooked black line. "He's really after you, isn't he?"

I nodded.

~ ☾ ~

CHAPTER TWENTY-SIX

We drove to his house, my car right behind his black Mercedes. I wasn't sure if it was the old vehicle, fixed up, or a new one. And right now, I didn't really care. Butterflies that felt more like wasps spreading within my stomach began backing up into my throat. My bones seemed to have been removed and were replaced with mush.

Overhead, the sky cast an eerie blue glow over the trees.

Evan hopped out of his SUV and opened his trunk to retrieve my belongings. I stepped out of my car, and Evan folded me into his arms before he picked up my bags and led me in.

I looked around at my new home with a sudden strange feeling. Two weeks ago, I never would have predicted I'd be here. Or at least not willingly.

"Let's go upstairs. I'll show you the bedroom," he said. I swallowed. He must have seen the look on my face because his voice immediately softened. "No, I didn't mean...for that. I just mean, so we can put your bags down and you can get settled in."

"Right. Of course."

He led me up the stairs to a landing where three doorways led to separate bedrooms. He led me past two empty ones to the final doorway at the end of the hall that led into the master bedroom.

It housed a king-size bed with a luxurious sleigh-style headboard in the middle of the room. The bedding was a steel gray with threads that gleamed silver in the light. An oversize dresser made of a shiny cherry colored wood and accented in silver ran along the wall. The hardwood floor was covered in a room-sized area rug in masculine colors of rust, burgundy, black and brown.

"This is my room, and you can sleep in here. I'll take the guest bedroom. What do you think?" he asked, pulling me out of my reverie. I turned to face him.

"Nice," I said. "It's so...you."

"I hope that's a good thing?" He smiled.

I chuckled. "Of course." I set my bag down beside the door and stood there, not knowing where to go.

He set the rest of my luggage on the leather upholstered ottoman at the bottom of the bed. Then he turned to me.

"Is everything okay?" His eyes widened with concern, and suddenly I felt like I had a lump lodged in my throat the size of a grapefruit. My eyes pricked.

What could I say? I wasn't fine. I had doubts I would ever be fine again. Part of me didn't want him to know my fears, but part of me knew he could probably see my distress in everything I said or did.

I swallowed and cleared my throat. "I'm scared, Evan. I don't know what's going to happen."

His mouth tightened, and he nodded. "I know. But I'm not going to let anything happen to you."

"Stefano is going to come for us."

Evan's eyes shadowed. "I'll protect you, no matter what. He'll have to go through me first."

"We can't be inseparable forever. Eventually, he's going to get one of us alone."

One single tear sprang from my eye and ran down my face in a hot line.

Seeing my tears, he reflexively reached out to me. "We can't think about that right now. We can only focus on what we know right at this moment. And at this

~ ☾ ~

moment, when we're together, we're undefeatable." He kissed me on the top of my head and wrapped me in his arms.

I melted into him, my body conforming to his contours. Our connection, the vibration, was immediate. I was overcome with such an intense love for him, I felt as if I were parasailing.

"There's no need for either one of us to sleep in the guest room," I said as I snaked my hands through his hair, pulling his face toward mine, kissing him like it was my last day on earth. Because for all I knew, it could be. I crushed my lips against his, until he was breathless and wide-eyed. I continued on, my mouth hot and eager to taste him.

I backed him up to the bed and looked into his eyes. His mouth was parted, his breathing heavy with arousal, giving him a raw, primitive look that nearly took my breath away. I looked into eyes that blazed with deep intensity, like blue fire, echoing the fire that had ignited within me.

I pulled his shirt up and over his head and threw it to the floor. Then I followed with his pants, tearing his clothes off with such force I wondered momentarily if I'd hurt him. But he did nothing to stop me. In fact he did the opposite, handing over complete control, his mouth curled up in a sexy smile.

I looked at him then, naked and vulnerable, his eyes shining. His body had changed since I'd last seen it, more defined with weight loss, his stomach flat and hard, hipbones protruding. But every square inch of him was segmented muscle. I pushed him back on the bed and crawled on top of him.

I raked my hands over his torso, luxuriating in the hills and valleys. His eyes closed as I started to kiss him, his breathing growing ragged and pressured. A heady sense of power bloomed within me as a sparkling heat spread throughout my body. Within moments, he'd removed all of my clothing as well.

He reached up to caress my breast, but I grabbed his wrist and held it down. "No," I whispered, leaning forward to kiss him. "Don't move."

He smiled a slow, sensual smile. "Okay."

A savage hunger filled me, and I felt consumed with the urgency to have him. Within seconds, I had a condom out and on him. Then I pressed my heat against him, and his mouth opened, a low moan escaping his lips.

He audibly swallowed. "Oh my God."

Evan arched his hips and ground into me, the pressure lighting me on fire. My need for him ached, and I ran my hands down his hard chest, savoring the warm, supple skin.

Then I leaned down, dusting his throat and chest with kisses, moving along the hard planes of his stomach and down.

"Sarah," he groaned, his head tilting backward in ecstasy. A gasp emerged from his mouth.

He pulled me up, and I kissed him, his hot mouth mirroring his body heat.

I lowered my hips to his, and as flesh met flesh, an ever-expanding sense of urgency filled me.

"I've missed you so much," he murmured into my jaw with a slight hitch in his voice.

"Shh."

Lightning exploded behind my eyes, in rays of purple and blue sparks.

*****

Afterward, I held onto him, needing to be as close to him as humanly possible. I never wanted to leave those arms. A pang of guilt shuddered through me as I traced a line down to his stomach, which was flatter and harder than before, and out to his hipbones, angular and protruding.

~ ☾ ~

He smiled his thousand-watt smile and pulled me to him, our bodies pressing against each other once again. He lay on his side, caressing my lips, nose and cheekbones with his fingertip. I stroked his chest, working my way up to his throat, where my finger touched the aggravated gouge in his neck from Stefano yanking off the chain.

A low growl escaped his lips as the thrumming sound began to emanate from our bodies, our joint anger and frustration coming together in a powerful, unexplainable way.

"I can't believe that happened," he said as he swore under his breath. My finger traced a circle around the reddish-brown mark, careful not to touch any part of the actual injury.

I looked into his eyes. "Let's try to heal it."

His pupils dilated as his mouth turned up into a smile. "Great idea. Why didn't I think of it?" Our combined humming began to intensify into a palpable buzzing. "Let's do this."

I closed my eyes as the vibration built into high-wattage crescendo, the current singly focused on the crusty cut on the side of Evan's throat. The pulsation intensified so that it was a refined line that waxed and waned, the intensity varying with dizzying speed. And then suddenly, it was over.

The sore was nearly gone now, the scab fell off and the red parts faded to a whitish-pink. I placed my fingertips on it, and found that the skin underneath was no longer warm to the touch. It was silky and smooth, completely normal once again.

My chest swelled with the accomplishment. "I think we're really getting the hang of this healing thing."

Evan smiled, but the sentiment didn't reach his eyes. "If it weren't for Stefano, we wouldn't have needed to heal it." His jaw tightened. "We have to stop him. There

~ ☾ ~

has to be a way to make him stop, no matter what."

I yawned, Evan's face fuzzing in and out of focus. "We can take him. All of them," I said with much more confidence than what I actually felt. Truth be told, I would have chosen hiding in a hole within the earth than facing the Skinwalkers or Stefano even one more time.

"We'll take them," I heard Evan say, right before sleep charged up and took over.

*****

The sound of water running woke me. I glanced around the dim room, disoriented.

I'm in Evan's room.

I turned toward his side of the bed. He was showering. I pulled his pillow to my chest and hugged it, the smell of him embedded in the fabric. Fresh soap and musky aftershave immediately set off memories of last night's lovemaking, the feel of it still lingering in my thoughts and tissues. I found myself almost giddy with the overwhelming sense of euphoric happiness.

I loved this man, and the emotional sensations attached to that love were so different than anything I'd ever felt before. With Evan, my love was at a cellular level, a most basic, fundamental emotion. To be without him, would be like trying to survive without oxygen. I was never going to let him go again, no matter what.

I got up and threw on a thick terry-cloth robe that hung on the door of the walk-in closet. The fabric felt smooth like butter on my skin, and it smelled of him. Of man. I wrapped myself in it, draped in Evan. There was a flat screen TV that sat atop his dresser and I turned it on, flipping the channel to the news.

"Public health officials have released the surviving passengers who were originally in quarantine after the unknown illness of United flight eight seven one. The victims of this mysterious illness are either comatose or have died. It is expected that the few remaining survivors have mere days, or hours, to live."

A new restlessness filled me, as if I was standing in ocean tides. There was no evidence whatsoever that this had anything to do with me, and yet, somehow, I just knew it did.

The water shut off and Evan emerged from the bathroom in a towel, his torso covered in a wet sheen of dampness. Despite his recent weight loss, he still looked like a meticulously sculptured Greek god, his body the epitome of the male perfection.

"You're up." He flashed a smile as he sat beside me on the bed.

"I was watching the news just now. They've released the remaining passengers from quarantine. Most of the people who had the so-called mysterious illness have either died or are in comas, expected to die any minute," I said.

His eyes took on a faraway look and clouded over. "When did they release them?"

"Today."

Evan stood and began to pace, cursing under his breath.

I grabbed his hand as he walked by. "Please stop pacing."

"I'm thinking. Pacing helps me think."

Sitting down on the bed, he stretched his socks apart to put them on, and I caught a glimpse of the partially destroyed scar on his hand, his brand. My hand, as if of its own volition, reached out to touch it.

My finger jolted as if singed from the contact, while my mind simultaneously flashed with an image of Evan, his face contorted in a silent scream. I let go. A low groan emitted from deep in his throat, a moan of resistance, but he held out his hand anyway, giving me perfect access to his scar.

~ ☾ ~

The skin looked as I remembered it, thick and ropy where it had knitted back together. Ignoring the still reddened slice right down the middle of the mark, I tried to focus on the original design. Immediately the memory of it came into sharp focus.

The newer skin of the scar was white, the old skin outlined darker pink around it. A large, upside down triangle was on top, with lines through it, creating another set of triangles inside it. I shuddered as I tried to imagine the pain of being burned to the point where it would leave a life-long mark like this.

I placed my thumb directly on top of it. Emotional pain flooded in, like getting stabbed with a blunt-edged blade. These were Evan's feelings shuddering through me, not my own. Shame and horror temporarily blinded me, but I held my thumb firmly on top of the mark on his hand.

The image of Evan's hand, the skin more youthful and smooth, came into sharp focus, a hissing sound and wisps of smoke rising from a branding iron pressed to his skin. Red-hot pain blasted through my own hand, as if I was feeling this situation myself. Was I experiencing Evan's own memory? Was I seeing and feeling what it was like for Evan that terrible day where he'd been branded by his own father?

Then Evan's body went from rigid to slack with the removal of the instrument from his skin. The blistering mark was clear on his hand, his skin red and angry.

Next, I was seeing Stefano's face. But there was neither pain nor fear in his eyes, only a steely indifference as the red-hot branding iron sizzled on his flesh. Once it was removed, a slow smile crept across his face, a smile mirrored by the brander himself, an attractive man who appeared to be in his forties, with the same thick dark hair and angular jawline as Evan. But his eyes were black and glittering, like Stefano.

~ ☾ ~

Never before had I felt such an intense stab of betrayal, the kind of deep betrayal that comes only from a place of love; the betrayal of a father harming his own son.

I removed my hand and the image evaporated. Reality came into focus before me so fast I felt immediately nauseous and dizzy from the transition.

"I saw it. And I felt it. All of it," I said in a husky whisper.

"What did you see?"

"I saw you getting branded. I felt your agony." I reached up to his face with an instinctual need to soothe him. "I saw Stefano. And your father."

"What did the room look like?"

"There was...a blue carpet," I said.

His eyebrows shot up. "You saw? Sarah!" His mouth moved and bunched together at the side of his face as if he was biting the inside of his cheek. "That was our house in Eagle Creek." His eyes flashed with something dark and fierce...like sadness.

He leaned forward and placed his head in his hands. He looked so vulnerable just then, half-naked and full of shame. "I wish I could erase that day from my existence."

"I wish you could, too." I stepped forward and held his hand, then brushed my lips against his.

He broke the kiss off and looked at me with a perplexed tilt to his brow. "I feel different. I feel... After you did that, held my brand, went through my experience...I feel different, better somehow."

"Really? Better, how?"

"It just doesn't seem to hurt anymore when I think of that situation. I feel like it has been almost erased, but not... Because I can still remember it. But there's no pain attached to the memory. Weird, isn't it?"

"Weird."

He squeezed his eyes shut before he went to the closet

and put on a pair of jeans and a t-shirt.

I had an awful thought, completely out of the blue. "Do you think Sandra Crow...you know the corpse powder? Do you think she did that with the bones of Jessica?"

Evan gazed down at my upturned face and stroked my cheek. "I wouldn't put it past her. The Skinwalkers, the *Malandanti*, these people are despicable. They'll murder their own children for the power. Grinding bones is nothing to them."

My stomach roiled. No wonder Sandra had looked more snake than human that day she was beside my car, out at the development. No normal human being would murder their own child and grind their bones into powder.

"Just the thought of it makes me feel like puking," I said. "Do you think there's any humanity left in them?"

"No. There are different levels of evil, and with each level, the individual is further and further from human," Evan answered, his eyes suddenly fixated on something.

"What about Stefano?"

"Yes, Stefano has lost his humanity." He nodded. "With each despicable act, they are closer to becoming full-fledged demons."

"Demon? As in the devil?"

"Not the devil, as in Satan," Evan said. "But yes, an actual demon."

"What about you? Are you part demon? What despicable acts have you committed?"

He swallowed loudly. "So far, I've done nothing active to remove my human emotions, my empathy."

"You're okay, then?"

"I'll never turn demon, no. Unless I murder someone or do something equally heinous. But I can never go back to your average Joe, either."

"What does that mean?" I asked, the anxiety in my

chest creating an oddly tight, pulsing sensation. I stared at him. “Evan, I don’t know what you’re saying.”

He reached out and swept a lock of hair out of my face and behind my ear. His eyes were moist. “I think you know, and you just don’t want to accept it.”

“Are you condemned...to hell?” I asked.

He nodded.

I shook my head and swallowed back the tears. “It doesn’t seem fair. You were born into a family of warlocks. It’s not like you had a choice.”

“I know,” he said, pulling my face to his so we stood forehead to forehead. “I’m sorry.”

“No, Evan. Don’t say that. We will find a way. There’s always a way, right? God forgives.”

“I know, but—”

I interrupted, my blood pounding through my veins. “We’ll see a priest, we’ll get you baptized. We’ll do something, Evan. Anything.”

“Don’t, Sarah,” He looked at me, eyes blazing like luminous gems. “You’re only torturing yourself.” He wound his fingers through my hair, pulling me to his lips with vigor.

When our kiss broke, I had to remind myself to breathe. I couldn’t accept that Evan was condemned. My mind searched for answers until I thought of something that just didn’t make sense.

“Evan, I’ve been thinking. Why would your mother need to give you an amulet to protect you? I mean, if your dad didn’t know about the *caul*, why would she have to protect you after you were born? It’s not like the *caul* is something that stays on your face, right? How would anyone know one way or another?”

Evan’s eyebrows pulled together in the middle, and his gaze went far away. “Good point. I don’t know, for sure. But we know she had to keep the truth about me not being a true *Malandanti* hidden from my father.”

~ ☾ ~

I stroked the stubble on his jaw. "I think there's something different about you, Evan. Something Stefano saw that day, that neither of us can see. You said you can't see my aura anymore, right? Well, maybe that was part of the spell placed on the crest, the ability to see with the eyes of a true *Malandanti*. Now that the amulet's gone, your ability to see my aura is gone too, right?"

He appeared contemplative. "You're right." He got up and shook his head, running his hands through his hair. "I'm going to go outside for a minute. I need some air," Evan said. "Just call if you need anything, okay?"

"Sure."

After he'd left the room, I headed downstairs and looked around at the books on his bookshelf. I picked one up entitled The Broken Joy.

Somebody tapped my back. Not on my shoulder, but down lower, on my spine. I whipped around to see who had touched me. Behind me was an empty leather seat.

Nobody was in the room.

~ ☾ ~

CHAPTER TWENTY-SEVEN

It happened again. Now the nudge felt like more of a jab, as if the tip of a knife blade was pressing firmly into my lower back. I reached around to touch the spot. It was hot.

The sensation of the blade tip changed to more of a hot poker, and my back ignited into a concentrated point of fire. I tried to stand up, but pain blasted through me, fast and furious. I sat in place, unable to move, barely able to even think.

What was happening to me? I tried to scream but found that the pain kept me from being able to suck in enough air in my lungs. What came out sounded more like a yowling maimed animal.

I pulled out my phone and texted Evan who was in the back yard.

Something's wrong.

He came crashing through the back door after I'd barely even lifted my finger off of Send.

"Sarah!" Evan raced toward me, his palm slapping the wall behind my chair as he jolted to a full stop. Immediately, he dropped to his hands and knees beside me, and his fear blasted through me, like being smacked in the face with a brick.

"My back! It's burning." I moaned, almost unable to move from the pain. He reached down to me and picked me up under my arms.

"Your back?" Evan's voice was wavering, frantic. "What happened?"

~ ☾ ~

"I don't know. It just started to burn. It feels like someone is pressing a hot knife to my back." Every movement exacerbated the pain. "I want to lie down. Help me upstairs. To the bedroom. Ouch!"

"Maybe we should go to the hospital?" Evan said.

"No," I said feebly, my voice growing weaker as the pain in my back increased in intensity to the point where it now felt like someone had inserted a burning ember into the skin at the base of my spine. "This is Stefano. The hospital can't help undo a spell."

His brow creased, his mouth open. "Should I carry you?"

"No. I'll walk. Just hold me up."

He nodded as he placed his arm under my own and around my upper back, taking most of my weight. I stood hunched at first and then forced my feet forward. Each footfall sparked a new blast of pain to shoot down my legs, the heat now spreading around to my hips and waist. I barely made it up the stairs upright, and as soon as I reached the top, my legs nearly buckled. But Evan had me by the waist and kept me from falling.

Then without asking, he picked me up, carried me the rest of the way to the bedroom, and laid me on the bed. I turned to my side and pulled my shirt up so he could look.

"What the hell is that?" he said, his voice tremulous.

"What does it look like?"

"It's a huge red welt that is visibly growing, like it's...bubbling." He moved around so he could see my face.

"Oh, no!" I said, rapidly losing my ability to manage the pain. "Can we channel the energy, to heal me or something? Hurry. Make the pain stop." I moaned once again. Everything around me was turning dark. I used sheer will to stay in the moment. "Please, Evan."

He immediately took both hands and placed them on

the small of my back. At that moment, I was willing to do anything to stop this fiery, bone-crushing pain. A low rumbling began in my back, a vibration that was slow and wide. The current ignited between us, channeled through Evan, from his hands and into my back, thrumming between us.

Dread gripped me. Could we control it while he was this stressed out?

The burning fire became just a fevered pressure that spread and thinned before completely dissipating throughout my body, so that now it was just a general sense of heat instead of a focused spear of pain.

Every inch of my body relaxed, and my head slumped forward. I was dripping with sweat.

"Thank you," I said in a whisper.

Evan fell onto his back on the bed. I turned to face him. He had his hands over his face and began rattling off a blue streak of profanities under his breath. Relief rained over me, his relief, and for a moment, I felt almost buoyant.

My relief disappeared the second I saw the sheer terror in his face. "It was Stefano, wasn't it?"

He nodded, his eyes dark and unfathomable. "It reeks of dark magic." He stood up and began to pace back and forth across the room. "Pain doesn't just come on out of the blue like that." He walked over to me, as if looking at my face would provide some vital clue. "Stefano. It was a spell. He grew something inside of you."

My throat felt as if it closing down. "No."

His jaw was like a stone carving.

Now it was my turn to curse. "I can't believe this. We have to kill him. There's no other way. He's going to continue to torture us. He doesn't even need to be around to torture us, and this proves it. He could probably be in the Antarctic and still launch some kind of voodoo attack."

~ ☾ ~

"I know. We have to stop him," Evan said. "But you know what that means, right?"

I stared at him. "What?"

"If I kill my own brother, I will have done it. Committed a heinous crime, an unforgivable sin."

He would become part-demon. I swore again. "Then I'll kill him."

Evan's mouth opened and closed repeatedly, as if he couldn't decide how to respond. "How is that any different? You kill him, or I kill him. There's still a penalty to be paid for taking a life."

"I'm willing to take that chance."

Evan shook his head. "No. It's too risky. I told you how the soul darkens with each evil act."

"It's different with me. I'm not a *Malandanti*. It won't affect me the way it would ruin you. I'm the good guy, killing a warlock in self-defense."

"No," Evan said, his jaw firmly set.

"This isn't about you letting me, Evan. I'm telling you."

Evan's mouth dropped open. "No. Please don't, Sarah. There are consequences to actions like that."

I waited, contemplating his words. "I know you're worried, and I appreciate your concern, Evan. I do. But I'm not afraid."

"You should be afraid." Evan shook his head, biting down on his bottom lip. "I just... All I know is that when I started the indoctrination, my parents drilled into our heads over and over that to be full-fledged *Malandanti* and have access to every power imaginable, one must aspire to the ultimate goal. Murder. Committing murder raises one to the highest rank below priest and priestess, and it immediately opens up our new abilities. So the thought of you killing someone... I just can't accept it."

A sudden idea flashed into my mind. "Maybe there's another way."

~ ☾ ~

CHAPTER TWENTY-EIGHT

Twenty minutes later, I called Paulette and told her what I was thinking, insisting Evan cooperate with my plan. When we drew closer to Amber and Paulette's house, she was at the end of the driveway already waiting for us. We slowed so she could pull out in front of us.

"I don't know about this, Sarah," Evan said, his voice low. In his vehicle, we followed Paulette's blue Caravan to the Wakina Reservation. "In my experience, healers like this Ernie usually don't know the half of it. They think they have insight into dark power, but they really don't."

"What other option do we have?" I asked pointedly. "You don't want me to kill him, and I don't want you to be a demon, so that only leaves us with the option of involving others."

"But they don't...," he started and then stopped. His gaze remained fixed on the road, his eyes hard like flint. "I'm just worried. Nobody has a vested interest in you the way I do."

I cocked my head to the side, looking at him. He shook his head, glaring at the road ahead.

"Besides, do they have any idea what they're dealing with?" he asked, but before I could respond, he rambled on. "I doubt it. If they did, those Skinwalkers wouldn't have gotten away."

"To me, magic is magic. It's no different. The only difference is that Ernie and Noreen use it for good, and the *Malandanti* and Skinwalkers use it for evil."

"Not quite. Remember the part about transitioning into a demon with each evil act?" he said.

I felt cold despite the vehicle's heater running. Outside, gnarled trees lined the highway, everything dead and brown, the leaves having fallen off in the last few days. Shaggy evergreens stooped under the heavy fresh snow.

We drove the rest of the way in silence, following Paulette to Ernie's house. Finally, we reached a sign on the side of the road that read, "Wakina Reservation Welcomes You", where she turned onto the reservation road.

"Let's just give him a chance, okay?" I said. Evan nodded, albeit with reluctance.

Paulette pulled her van up to Ernie's little old house that looked exactly the same as the one beside it, as if they were built at the same time, all like little square boxes. Since the last time I'd been here, he'd painted part of the exterior buttercup yellow. The other half, from about head height to the roof, was still a weather-beaten gray.

Two black dogs wagged their tails and slobbered as they waited for us outside the house. The yard was filled with various projects, a half-built doghouse, a partially stripped table and chairs, and a swing-set on its side with one leg removed.

Paulette stepped out of her van and motioned us over. We got out of the Mercedes and followed her up the spongy front steps. I stepped gingerly and tried not to think about the pain of my calf being sliced open during my first experience with a Skinwalker.

Paulette knocked on the brand-new steel door, and Ernie answered. As I saw him again, I realized I couldn't really guess his age. His skin was leathery and wrinkled as it hung off his bones, every square inch of his face a criss-crossing of creases. His eyes, dark and watery, seemed wizened with time and experience. But there was something about his gentle smile and his calm energy that was eternally young. He gestured us in.

His home smelled of bacon and onions, as if the odor had been permanently baked into the olive green carpet underfoot. The house was so small that the entire living space was visible from the front entrance. The kitchen cupboards looked hand-made out of deep orange pine and the brown laminate table reminded me of the tables that were sometimes rented out for social events in Slave Lake.

"Sarah, you remember Ernie," Paulette said as she motioned back and forth between us. "Ernie, this is Evan."

Ernie nodded, his dark eyes averted. "Please, have a seat." He led us to his living area and sat on one of the folding chairs. We followed him, and Evan and I sat on the tweed sofa.

I focused on his feelings and felt nothing but composed calm.

He turned to me. "Paulette tells me you've been cursed with bad medicine? She said you had a pain in your back but with an unknown cause?"

I nodded. "I think so." Evan grabbed my hand and squeezed with the gentlest pressure.

Evan cleared his throat. "My brother is behind all of this."

Ernie nodded. "Paulette told me about the *Malandanti*. Very, very old magic. I once heard about the good walkers and the bad walkers of Italy. They are powerful priests and priestesses." He leveled his gaze on Evan.

"Yes." Evan went on to tell Ernie about his family, the indoctrination and his parents' role as high priest and priestess." His mouth formed the words with unconcealed contempt.

"And you?" Ernie asked pointedly.

Evan looked down. "I've never been directly responsible for a murder. But I have done soul-travel."

Ernie nodded. "Old Medicine. Ancient power." He stared at Evan for a second too long, and then under his breath, said, "But that doesn't explain the likes of you, young man."

I glanced at Evan, who stared, confusion crossing his face.

"Pardon?"

"We'll deal with you later," Ernie said with a wave of his hand. His eyes seemed to refocus as he shifted his gaze from Evan to me. "First, we need to do a counter-curse of good medicine to protect you, young lady." Ernie looked at me with watery eyes. "But first, we must cleanse your spirit with a smudge."

My breathing quickened, and I glanced at Paulette, who nodded. "Okay."

"I'll get the smudge." Ernie stood up, hobbling as he left the room.

"Offer the tobacco now," Paulette instructed. I pulled the bag of chewing tobacco she had given me out of my pocket.

When Ernie returned, he placed a length of dried, tightly braided greenery on a plate atop the coffee table in front of us. I offered the tobacco, and he nodded in acceptance as he dug into his pocket to retrieve a lighter. He lit the braid of green on fire. An earthy, sweet odor wafted up my nose, and I had to stifle an involuntary cough, in case it was rude.

"Sage. It's a cleansing plant. It will clear out any dark energy." Ernie put his hands into the smoke, and with cupped hands, pulled it toward his head and body as if washing with the swirling gray smoke.

"Now you," he said, beckoning me with his hand, each

finger knotted at the knuckle. I knelt in front of the coffee table and repeated what I had just seen. He nodded in approval. Then Paulette did the same.

Ernie turned to Evan. “You too,” he said. Evan leaned toward the table and completed the ritual as well.

The old man began to sing in a throaty voice, the sound foreign and strange to my ears. His voice changed octaves rapidly, but there was a solid pacing to the song. I was moved by the sound, my eyes watering as something transcendent overcame me, like I was bathed in illuminating power.

Then Ernie stopped and opened his eyes. “Come,” he said, gesturing to me with a gnarled finger. He put his hands to my forehead.

“I will do the holy chant.” He began to recite something in an unfamiliar language. “I need to extract the evil from you now.”

I turned and pulled my shirt up so he could see the mark on my back. Ernie set his hands on my back and began kneading the skin. The sensation it produced felt like nails digging into my flesh. I flinched, my back spasming from the pain. A gasp escaped my mouth.

He abruptly stopped. “There is something in there.”

My heart thumped against my ribcage. “What is it?”

“I don’t know,” Ernie said. “Will you allow me to extract it?”

I took a breath. “What will you do?”

“I need to make a small opening where the object is so I can pull it out,” Ernie said. “It will hurt, but I think it’s necessary.”

I glanced at Paulette and she nodded. “I think you should, Sarah.”

“I don’t know,” I said. My voice sounded strange to me, as if I was talking within a bubble of water.

What was inside of me? How would he get it out? By slicing me open and digging it out?

~ ☾ ~

"I'll go get the supplies while you think about it." Ernie got up and disappeared from the room. When he returned, he was holding a razor blade and some rubbing alcohol.

Evan stood up. "Wait."

Ernie stopped, mid-stride.

"What are you going to do with that?" Evan asked.

Ernie met Evan's gaze with confidence. "She needs the cursed object removed. The bad medicine will poison her from the inside out. I need to open her skin to get it out."

"No!" Evan's eyes flashed. "You can't just cut her open."

Ernie's voice remained even. "If we leave it in, it will fester. The negative energy coming from this magic is very powerful. I can't be sure, but she may have only hours, or even minutes, before it kills her. But I think you know that, don't you, young man?"

Evan interjected. "I'll take you to the hospital. Come on, Sarah."

I ignored Evan's comment. "I might only have hours or minutes?"

Ernie nodded, his eyes downcast. "I don't know. There is no guarantee you would make it to the hospital."

I glanced over at Evan, whose eyes were spitting fire. Yet there was something within the depths of those eyes, something that looked like helplessness and fear. Those feelings registered inside of me loud and clear, like an itchy wool blanket.

My mind raced. Do I take the chance to get to a sterile environment but risk dying on the way? Or do I believe this medicine man's warning and allow him to cut me open? While the thought of it turned my stomach, I hardly felt I had any other option.

"Do it," I said.

~ ☾ ~

"Sarah!" Evan said, eyes wild.

"You can take me to the hospital immediately after," I said. "At least then it will be out. They can clean the wound and put me on antibiotics if necessary."

Evan looked back and forth between me, Ernie and Paulette, and then sat down, nodding his head, eyes drooping.

I lay down on my stomach on his sofa, and Ernie placed the tip of the blade on my back, at first a gentle poke that turned into something not so gentle on an already tender spot. The blade went in, white-hot.

I squirmed, the instinct to get away from the pain so overwhelming I had to dig my fingernails into my palm to distract myself. Heat was replaced with pressure as his fingers dug, pinching and pushing. A moan involuntarily escaped my mouth.

Evan rushed to my side and knelt on the floor, his hands gripping my shoulders.

"Sarah, are you okay?"

I screamed as the pain hit a crescendo, and with one final gushing sound, something was plucked out.

"A bone," Ernie said, matter-of-fact. I turned as he set a bloodied white bone on the coffee table in front of me and immediately began to tend to my back. Something wet rubbed the area and a fiery burn a moment later. A dry bandage was then pressed against my back, and my shirt was lowered.

"How?" I gasped.

"This bone was made to grow within you by a very powerful spell, ancient magic I've never seen before, and I don't understand. It's a way for them to connect with you, to torture you from afar," Ernie explained.

Revulsion shuddered through me. I turned to Evan, to see his expression. His skin had turned pale, the whites of his eyes glowing, his mouth a hard, thin line.

Ernie set the bone in an empty ashtray and poured

lighter fluid on it. Then he set it on fire.

"Why burn it?" I asked.

"You have to destroy the cursed object," Ernie said as the bone went up in flames and then turned to ash.

I closed my eyes and mentally checked my body. I felt as though something had been lifted from me, like a shroud or veil, and I felt lighter somehow. It was like I was suspended in mid-air. The ever-present knot of tension in my stomach disappeared.

"Thank you," I said, my voice no longer sounding like it was inside a bubble of liquid. I hadn't felt this good in weeks.

"You're welcome," he said with a nod. "Don't allow them to take any more of your belongings. Especially your hair, nails, blood or saliva. Those ingredients contain your vital essence. They can create some very powerful curses using mere fragments of your person."

I nodded in understanding. Finally, the mystery of my missing hairbrush made sense. I stood up, but Ernie's wooden walls spun around my head like I was on a merry-go-round. The entire room tilted.

Everything went black.

~ ☾ ~

CHAPTER TWENTY-NINE

I opened my eyes.

A sea of white surrounded me. White walls, white floor, white blanket. The turquoise bed sheets were the only color in the tiny room. The hospital? My thoughts reeled. The last thing I remembered was being at Ernie's, and then...nothing.

Fear built inside my chest as I lay on the hospital bed, the hard mattress beneath me no source of comfort.

I sat up. The hospital room was dark and silent. There was a single chair in the corner, a small closet and a tiny sink with a mirror near the door. I stood, my feet cringing from the cold industrial tile.

The acrid smell of bleach filled my nostrils, but that wasn't the only smell. Something else seemed to linger just beyond my ability to identify it. Out of the corner of my eye, I thought I caught a movement. When I turned to look, there was nothing.

I moved toward the door and looked through the small glass opening to see the dim fluorescent lights in the hall outside my door flickering.

A stretched shadow loomed from the hallway, appearing against the wall like an ominous bent skeleton. It was still, looking like it was someone standing motionless, just out of sight. I strained to look. The lights went out in the hall, further obscuring my ability to see in the near-blackness.

A cold, black sensation crawled into my chest like an unwanted parasite. I was instantly flooded with foreign feelings; raw rage commingled with regret so torturous that the combination felt like the organism had grown into a gigantic wraith within me. I'd never felt such emotions before in my life, and I knew they didn't belong to me. I fought back the sensation of wanting to claw right out of my own skin.

The shape closed in on my door, and I backed away. Emotions rifled through me, intensifying with every inch closer the person came. Then the face came into sharp focus as the small amount of light coming from the window in my room shone on her face.

Sandra Crow. The Skinwalker. The monster that sacrificed her own child stood within three feet of my door. Her face twisted with a rage so wild her expression became something that barely even resembled a human being. Every nerve in my body buzzed on high alert.

I jumped out of her line of sight, but it was too late, we'd already locked eyes. So with feigned bravery, I moved back, facing her again, knowing the glass would provide no barrier.

I'd held off Skinwalkers before. Surely I could do it again? I swallowed hard.

Sandra bared her yellowed teeth at me, that sinister smile more feline than human. Her eyes glittered as she winked at me, a gesture that caused my heart to jump. With her fingernail, she tapped the glass directly in front of my eyes. I blinked.

The doorknob began to turn. I backed up and took a deep breath, my legs shaking. *I can do this*. The door banged open as she pushed it aside. She inched toward me, a predatory lilt to her gait.

"For once, I have you alone," she said through gritted teeth.

My heart squeezed inside my chest. *Show no fear*.

"You, and soon, that traitor boyfriend," she said, her venomous voice now somehow directly connected to my heart rate. I shook my head.

Her hate and hostility swirled within me and mixed with my own fear until I felt woozy.

I latched onto that regret within her, and intuitively knew I had leverage. "I wonder, what did Jessica look like the moment she realized her own mother was about to kill her?" My voice remained even as my heart thrashed against my ribs.

"Shut up!" she screamed, the pain blasting out of her.

"She must have been so surprised that her mother, the same mother who gave birth to her, cared and nurtured her until she was eight years old, would suddenly turn on her."

The woman's eyes darkened, going flat.

"Tell me, Sandra, did you grind her bones, too?"

"You're dead!" she screeched. She lunged at me, her body unfurling like a poisonous snake.

I jumped onto my bed and toppled to the floor alongside it, my foot barely escaping her hand. I scrabbled on hands and knees and launched myself toward the door and out of the hospital room.

I ran down the long corridor, entered another wing, and stopped dead in my tracks. Four people were completely motionless, slumped over in their chairs or flat on the floor, not one appeared alive.

Bang! Sandra crashed through the door behind me and spurred me into action once again. I ran toward the nearest exit, through the back doors that led to a three-story parking structure.

The concrete building was massive around me. One light illuminated the entire thing, leaving specters of shadows everywhere. Two translucent figures, slow and steady as sharks floating through water, came into focus. Skinwalkers in their vaporous forms. Blindly, I began to run flat-out into the shadows, away from them.

That's when I felt them and the deep, unrelenting

pressure. I turned to face the yellow glowing eyes. They were coming at me so fast I lost my footing. My body lurched backward. I landed on the pavement with elbows-first, bits of loose concrete biting into my skin.

I screamed. At once the two creatures plunged into me. I flailed about, trying to unhitch myself from these non-material things. My wiggling was useless.

"No!" I yelled, but the sound reverberated off the concrete walls. "You will not have me."

I kicked and thrashed. Pain shuddered through me, like drowning in an ocean of boiling acid. I tried to scream, but nothing came out, as if my vocal chords had been ripped right out of my throat. Then I knew. They had my life force, and they were pulling it from my material body, sucked by a force stronger than momentum.

I tried to hold on, but my mind closed in on itself, the blackness edging my vision built and eventually cut off all light. This time the assault was stronger, a million times stronger than before, the combined power of the two of them like an enormous electric eel slithering through me, gigantic tentacles filling every square inch of me.

I pushed against the force, and for a second, it relented. Secured by an astral thread to my own body, I pushed again. When the sensation of that thread thinning away registered in me at some deep primitive level, I knew it was nearly over for me.

"Do not kill her until we all have enjoyed the consumption of her power!" A voice bellowed from somewhere in the parking structure. Stefano? The assault abruptly stopped, and the Skinwalkers left my body with an audible pop.

"Sarah, so nice to see you again," said Stefano. He strode up to me, his boots clacking against the concrete. My heart rate ratcheted up with every step until the pounding rang through my skull. Tall. Dark hair. Black suit. I stared in silence, trying desperately to catch my breath.

"Oh, come on, now. Is that how you greet family? I'm practically your brother-in-law now." His liquid voice and glinting white teeth emphasized the evil that emanated from him, like nothing I'd ever felt before. It was pure, unadulterated by any other emotion, and distilled into something so dark it seemed there was no humanity left within him.

"We've worked very hard to get you here, Sarah. The least I would expect is a polite hello." His handsome smile and sinister energy unnerved me.

"Stefano," I said.

"Sarah." His mouth twisted into a sardonic half-smile. "The exalted Indigo Child." He had a fluid grace about him that seemed inhuman. I stared in silence as he stepped toward me, amused. "Indigo Child," he repeated. His voice was silky, but his obsidian eyes looked like they could pierce right through me. There was something about the way he looked that was distinctly vampiric. He made a theatrical gesture toward the three Skinwalkers who waited as if ready to strike at his signal. "They are all here to meet the great Indigo Child."

"Why are you doing this, Stefano?" I whispered.

He ignored my question. "Perhaps I should introduce you to everyone?" I didn't respond. "This is Jared and Violet." He nodded toward the vaporous Skinwalkers. "And of course, you know Sandra." He turned toward the escape exit where she stood in her human form. I shivered.

Stefano smiled again. "Originally, we came to extract your powerful Indigo soul from your body, but now, because of Evandro's betrayal, we are here to torture you as well." He glanced at the nearest two Skinwalkers, who shimmered as if laughing.

"Is there nothing left of your humanity, Stefano?"

"And your boyfriend deserves to be punished for choosing an Indigo Child over his own brother." I stared at him, silent. He continued on, "I'm sure your boyfriend has explained? How we hijack bodies, extracting each and every soul. Your Indigo *élan* will be a wonderful addition to our powers, once we have devoured your soul, of course." Darkness emanated from him, like ever-tightening waves of boiling oil that washed over me.

Then his expression shifted, as if he were seeing me differently, from amusement to curiosity. "Are you afraid?" he asked, his eyes narrowing.

"I'm not afraid of dying, Stefano." I jutted my chin out, but my body was tensed up like an over-tightened drum. His smile returned.

"Good. You can make this easy on yourself, or you can make it hard." His silky voice massaged me but left me far from relaxed. "Either way, we will have your *élan*."

"You've seen my power. You should be the one who's afraid," I said through clenched teeth.

"Oh, yes, the power you have with Evandro?" He glanced around. "But I don't see your precious Evan here now, do you?" He mocked, smiling then, a gruesome, self-satisfied smile. He took another step toward me, and I pressed back further into the rough concrete beneath me.

"But before you die, you need to do me a little favor."

I glared at him in silence.

"Evandro will be returning shortly to save you. The traitor will pay the price for his betrayal."

My stomach tightened around another ball of fear. "What will you do to him?"

Stefano smiled again, this time a dazzling smile. "Oh, we will take Evandro to meet his fate, that's all. And the side benefit is that we get to consume all of his rich, Sapphire Child essence."

Stefano's smile turned to a sneer, and I felt my legs begin to shake and my palms sweat. Sapphire Child? I wasn't about to ask and give Stefano the satisfaction of knowing he had information that I didn't.

"Haven't you even noticed yet? You can't tell me you don't see the truth that our mother hid from father all those years?" Stefano asked.

I didn't answer, my mind reeling. Could it be true? Could Evan be a Sapphire Child? Was he like me?

"Our mama, perhaps the greatest traitor of all, hid her deformed son's secret by placing a spell on him and giving him that talisman to keep it hidden." Stefano stepped toward me and placed his slender fingers on my jaw. His fingertips gouged into my skin, and I batted his hand away.

This caused an eruption of laughter from Stefano. "Evandro, a Sapphire Child, in a *Malandanti* family. How absolutely comical. Can you believe our mama would betray her own husband that way? Betray our *Malandanti* heritage?" Stefano's expression changed, and his eyes shadowed over with something darker than I'd ever seen in him before. Something that chilled me to the core of my bones. "If the *Malandanti* ever knew she was capable of such a thing, she would have surely been burned alive."

Glittering black eyes re-focused on my face and his mouth turned up in a smile. I wasn't sure this expression was any better than the last one. "Of course, I ensured that happened, didn't I?" I stared at him, refusing to respond. "But I digress. Getting back on topic, I have a little favor to ask you." His head tilted to the side.

"No. I'm not doing you any favors."

Stefano laughed. "What choice do you have, little

Indigo?" he mocked as he stepped across the space between us, and lowered himself to me until he was a mere inch from my face. My head hit the concrete behind me with a tooth-chattering thunk.

His face, its prominent planes and angular edges, emanated a thick heat. He gripped my shoulders, not roughly, but with a strength that ensured I was going nowhere.

Black emotions coiled around me, an almost sickly sweet sensation that twined into me like a poisonous vine. I tried to shrug him off, but his fingers gripped even tighter.

"Indigo, you're coming with us, like it or not." I looked up. His pupils enlarged just as a dark, lusting sensation came over me, and I knew he was feeling something else for me, something new.

I lunged sideways from his grip, scrabbled to my feet and kicked him before running for the exit. I toppled into Sandra, the momentum jarring her into the crash bar of the door, so that our bodies were splayed, mine on top of hers, half-in and half-out of the building.

I immediately wrestled her so the door shut behind us, leaving Stefano and the others locked outside. I turned to face her. To my surprise, she shrank away. A strange attack urge overcame me.

Heal her pain. Remind her of her humanity. The thought hit me like a semi-truck from out of nowhere. She looked at me, wild-eyed, her expression no longer predatory, now more fearful.

"It's okay. It won't hurt," I said as I grabbed her by the shoulders and flipped her, holding her around the arms and chest so she couldn't move. She tensed under my grip.

"Stefano!" she screamed, her howl slicing into my eardrums. She attempted to wriggle from my hold, but something had already begun between us. Her fear seemed to trigger some kind of primitive urge within me, an inborn reflex. I thought of Evan saying he felt better after I'd experienced his memory of the traumatic branding.

"I'm going to help you," I said. "Hold still."

A strange squeak erupted from her lips until I penetrated her mind with my own. Then she went silent.

My head was filled with images, none from my own experience, and I instinctively knew they were hers. The scenes played out as if on fast-forward, speeding through my mind as I experienced her entire lifetime. Images of abuse sliced through me: a father molesting her, a mother passed out on the floor, a date-rape on a deserted gravel road, the birth of a child, the product of that rape.

A swelling begin inside me, a powerful sensation that galvanized and gained momentum as the images flashed. A final, horrible image filled me, one of Jessica being drowned in her own bathtub.

A sharp intake of breath and a tortured scream pierced the air of the stairwell as Sandra re-lived the moment she had sacrificed her own daughter. Her body flopped back as the images and emotions screeched to a grinding halt.

The emergency door blasted open behind me. Stefano stood in the doorway, his mouth agape as he surveyed the scene. Then his mouth turned up into a smile.

"Bravo, Indigo!" he said as he stared at Sandra's limp body. "Is she dead?"

"Yes," I said, bluffing.

Stefano watched me with granite eyes as if evaluating my credibility. I was certain the woman was alive, but overcome with the pain of processing her memories, perhaps unable to move. I glanced back at her, silently praying she wouldn't give it away.

"You surprise me with your power, Indigo. You will

be worth more to us than I expected. Perhaps you would consider joining us?"

"What makes you think I won't kill you, too?" I approached Stefano until I was within a very dangerous inch from him. I hoped he wouldn't notice my trembling.

"You may have power, Indigo, but you are just a fledgling, like our failed Sandra here." He nudged her with steel-toed boot. "Don't underestimate me." He stepped forward, grabbing my arms in an iron grasp and yanking me toward the interior of the hospital. "Now, we deal with Evandro."

I launched myself sideways in an attempt to escape, but his hold was too tight. My flailing only caused him to lock me in a bear hug.

He steered me along, his jabbing grip pushing me forward. I had no idea how I was going to get out of this. As we turned the corner into the Admissions area, I stifled the urge to wretch. Those four people were still slumped over in their chairs, desks and the floor. Their bodies were flaccid, their faces blank and staring. Catalepsy.

"You did this?" I asked, doing my best to contain my mounting horror.

Stefano smiled. "Of course. We have extracted and consumed their *élan*." He walked to a nurse who was slumped forward over a desk, picked up her arm, and dropped it theatrically. "This meat suit will eventually rot."

I swallowed hard. Free of his hands, I took the opportunity to turn and run.

"*Indigentia resisto*!" Stefano's booming voice shuddered through me. I felt as if I'd been hit with the same tearing, burning sensation I'd been afflicted with earlier today.

I doubled over, the pain shredding my insides as if I

were being repeatedly stabbed with a knife to the abdomen. I fell to the ground, the pain so all-encompassing that, in that moment, I wished for instant death.

"*Indigentia,*" Stefano whispered, gesturing with dramatic animation. Suddenly the two Skinwalkers were hovering over me in their physical bodies.

Stefano nodded. "*Indigentia a mortis.*"

It happened again. All three plunged into me, Stefano included, my soul under assault. The plucking sensation of having my life force squeezed and pulled from its earthly home was an indescribable agony, my ribs expanding, my skin stretching.

A wet squeak erupted in my ears as reality began to collapse in my mind. Every nerve ending screamed, the sensation like acid had been brushed over every square inch of my skin, a thousand knives were being plunged into my back, my hair ripped out at the roots, my nails torn from my fingers.

The bottom dropped out of my awareness, and I had the vaguest sensation of falling. I didn't stop grasping, clawing at something indescribable, to hold me here, to this body, to this life. I fought to hold on but was losing.

A bellowing snarl rang through the air, along with a glass-shattering bang.

The pressure lifted, just slightly, but enough that I could open my eyes. From my peripheral vision, I could see Evan, Ernie and Paulette enter the room, side by side. In an instant, Evan was at my side and the second our hands connected the energy pulsed from us. The vibration sizzled from him and reverberated around the room in a deafening blast. Everything after that seemed to slow down, as if time itself had gone into slow motion.

All three Skinwalkers burst out of my body, pain shuddering through me. The Skinwalkers' bodies canted toward Evan, Ernie and Paulette, almost graceful in their predatory stance. My breath caught in my throat.

Evan appeared impossibly immense, as if his entire body had engorged, his arm muscles thick and ropy, a matrix of blue veins popping just under his skin. The energy in the room began to crackle as his presence alone changed the atmospheric pressure around him.

Ernie and Paulette both began to chant, the same rapidly changing octave singing as before, in two different tunes, but similar in its pacing. Stefano, Jared and Violet stopped dead in their tracks. Somehow, the chanting seemed to render them immobile.

Evan pulled me upright. "They can only hold them off for a few minutes. Only long enough for us to get out of here."

I glanced over to Ernie and Paulette, who both nodded in unison as their mis-matched singing continued, unbroken.

~ ☾ ~

CHAPTER THIRTY

"Where were you?" I asked pointedly. We cruised along in Evan's Mercedes at an unlawful, sweat-inducing speed, putting as many miles between us and Stefano as fast as humanly possible.

"After you were admitted, they came on so fast I didn't even have time to react. It seemed like I had just gotten you settled and they were there."

I blinked hard on the stinging sensation in my eyes. "This is all my fault. If it wasn't for me, Ernie and Paulette wouldn't be in this mess."

"You can't blame yourself. Ernie and Paulette care about you. They know what you are. And they know you're worth protecting."

We were finally on Evan's street and rapidly approaching his home.

"What about Paulette and Ernie? We can't just leave them there."

Evan looked at me, his gaze intense. "They told me to get you out of there. They can handle that much. If there's anything I learned today, it's not to underestimate their power." He pulled up to the front of his house and put his car in park.

I glanced up at his house. "What are we going to do? They'll find us here."

Evan's voice came out in a garbled, tight note. "We'll kill them."

I reached up and stroked his cheek, the stubble rubbing my fingertips as I gazed into his sapphire eyes. I knew I had to tell him, and now, facing death, I no longer had the luxury of waiting until the right time. He needed to know the truth.

"I have something to tell you first," I said.

"What?"

There was no time to word this thoughtfully, so I jumped into it. "Stefano said something, Evan. He said something that explains everything."

Evan waited, unmoving. It didn't even seem like he was breathing.

"He said your mother put a spell on you, to keep the truth from your family, from the *Malandanti*."

Evan's eyes shadowed. "I know. Because of the *caul*."

I shook my head. "Not just that. He said the talisman kept your secret hidden, kept the spell in place so the truth would never come out. But when he removed it that day, he saw something, Evan. He saw what you really are. A Sapphire Child."

Evan stared at me, his eyes going from focused to unfocused in the blink of an eye. Then he slowly turned his head so he faced the dashboard and his head dropped backward, hitting the leather seat. His mouth gaped open as he stared straight up. The silence seemed palpable.

"Evan?"

He sat forward in his seat. "I don't believe it," he whispered. He stared straight ahead.

"Why not?"

"How could I be a Sapphire Child?" he asked, though I knew it was a rhetorical question. "I don't even know what that means."

"I don't know what it means, either."

Evan shook his head, his brow-line continually moving up and down in contemplation. "He's lying. I know my brother. He wouldn't just say that if it was really true. He made it up, some kind of strategy to gain an advantage. It's a manipulation strategy. It's got to be."

"But your eyes. They're so blue now. And every time we did that connecting thing...they were such a brilliant color. I've never seen anyone with a color of eyes like yours before. They're exactly the color of the purest sapphire."

"That doesn't prove anything."

I went on. "And that day when Stefano destroyed the Lucifer brand and then tore your Valente crest pendant off. That day they looked as bright as Christmas lights. I could have sworn I saw blue flames lighting up each iris."

"I'm not denying the possibility. But I do think we need to be wary of the source of the information, the underlying motive behind his telling you."

He had a point. "True."

He turned to me, his eyes shimmering in the dash lights. Then he placed a hand around the back of my head and knotted his fingers through my hair, pulling me to his lips. He kissed me with urgency, his left hand grasping mine, holding it tight in his palm.

He pulled away and leveled his gaze at me. "Kill him with me. Please."

I had to catch my breath. "Okay," I whispered.

He nestled his face into my neck and let out a long breath of air that tickled my skin. Then he placed his forehead on mine. "Thank you, Sarah."

We went into the house and found the phone was already ringing. Evan jogged over to it and picked it up.

"Hello?"

I watched as Evan's face transformed before me, his eyes hard and imperious, teeth glinting between lips stretched tight.

"Thanks." He hung up. "They got away." He ran to my side and grabbed my hand, pulling me back to the door.

~ ☾ ~

"Hurry. Let's take only what we need."

From within the living room, a strange popping sound emerged. I glanced in but couldn't locate the source of the sound. Then a billow of white powder blew the glass doors of the fireplace open, sending a cloud of floating haze through the room. I immediately started coughing.

"Run!" Evan yelled, grasping at the doorknob.

I turned toward him and as he opened the door. A haze of white exploded from the doorway. I staggered backward, choking on the particulate. Immediately, my tongue began to swell in my mouth. My knees buckled beneath me. I hit the floor, jarring my elbow against the hardwood. I looked up to see three faces emerge through the white cloud. Stefano, Jared and Violet.

Evan squared off with them, his hand over his mouth, blocking their access to me. "Sarah, cover your mouth. It's corpse powder."

Stefano's mouth curled up in a smile of smug amusement. I got back onto my feet, ignoring the throbbing in my elbow.

"Ah, yes. So smart, my little brother. None of our tricks will get past you, will they?" Stefano said with a snarl. "Hello, Evandro. What will you do when her tongue turns black and necrosis sets in?"

My tongue felt dead, like a chunk of meat in my mouth.

"It won't matter," Evan said through gritted teeth. "Together, we have the power to heal. Did you know that?"

Stefano laughed, a sound that rang hollow. "Really? How impressive. So, did your woman tell you the truth? Makes sense, doesn't it? Sapphire Child and Indigo Child, their combined powers beyond that of any known magic. Too bad father had never been able to see you for what you really are. He would have devoured you in an instant."

~ ☾ ~

"Maybe he did know, Stefano. Did you ever think of that?" Evan snapped.

Stefano rolled his eyes. "No. Our mama was very clever. She always had something on you, didn't she? That baby bracelet, an anklet, a tiny ring. She protected you from the moment she saw you and has continued to protect you still. Even from the grave."

Stefano slowly began to step toward us, and I stiffened.

"Why did you cut the seal, Stefano. What purpose could that possibly serve?" Evan asked, pulling me closer to his side as Stefano advanced. The fresh air in the doorway had reduced the thickness of the corpse powder, but my tongue continued to remain swollen and thick in my mouth.

"I wanted you to be free of any possible protection—the sigil, the amulet. I wanted to see you for the freak you really are." Stefano's lips curled back as he continued. "Now, you can give your soul to me, little brother, or I will just take it."

Stefano launched toward us.

At that moment, our hands clasped together. We focused, and instantly, Stefano came to a standstill. Evan's body began to grow and vibrate, as if he was channeling lightning directly through himself.

Walls began to bend and buckle as paint crumbled to the floor. Hissing energy rose to a thunderous roar when a shock wave detonated through the air and a torrent of smashing glass fell from the windows. The lights overhead shook and then burst in an explosion of glass that rained down on us. The ceiling cracked into fissures, the tiny seams crisscrossing through the plaster until the entire ceiling gave way to the pressure and exploded, leaving a haze of fine particulate hanging in the air and chalky residue on everything below. I held my hand over my mouth and nose but the taste of paint lodged in the back of my throat.

Evan continued on, jaw clenched. A wild vibration blasted through me as my tongue felt like it returned to its original size, the throbbing in my elbow, gone.

Our control of the elemental energy in the room blew all three of them backward toward the doorway. Various crashing sounds clattered around me as yelling rang in my ears. The pressure continued to the point where a set of window blinds flashed and burst into flames. A layer of compressed thermal air sent another shock wave of heat blasting through the room of our house, so hot it singed my hair and eyelashes.

Stefano righted his body. He lunged into a cloud of dust as Evan sprang toward him. Evan seized the front of his shirt and lifted him up, Stefano's feet dangling beneath him.

In a move of sudden violence, Evan threw him against the wall. The crushing sound of flesh crashing through splintered wood echoed through the room. Stefano fell to the ground in a crumpled heap. The other two Skinwalkers stood motionless as if frozen in fear. Stefano sat up.

Evan's lips curled up into a smile that was both beautiful and terrifying. "Time to go to hell, big brother." He stalked toward Stefano but only made it half-way before Stefano roared and sprang at Evan, knocking him backward. The two of them hit the floor and slide along the hardwood for several feet. Their bodies were matched in both size and strength.

"*Traitoris, a mortis*!" Stefano bellowed. The other two Skinwalkers bodies immediately lost internal tumescence while simultaneously their shimmering selves were at his side in a flash as their human forms slunk to the floor with a thud. With Stefano in his human form, and the other two in their astral form, they began their assault. Evan screamed.

~ ☾ ~

I scrambled to my feet just as the two Skinwalkers dove headfirst into Evan's corporeal body, Stefano holding him down.

Evan's eyes rolled into the back of his head as a hiss of air was expelled from his mouth, as if his lungs had collapsed within his chest. The air pressure around me changed again as I watched what had been done to me, so many times, now happening to Evan.

I launched myself toward him, but Stefano beat me. His body changed, his physical body falling alongside Evan as his spirit form exited, slinking toward Evan within an inch of my face. Evan's mouth opened and a hissing sound emerged as air expelled from his slack mouth.

An unbearable silence surrounded me as I bent over Evan, his chalky skin in stark contrast to black hair, his body writhing, the skin stretched taut from the Skinwalkers within him. His skin rippled, as if he was filled with something slithering just beneath the surface.

Everything was in slow motion, reality drawing out in an infinite moment of horror. My heart hammered inside my head, my lungs felt devoid of all oxygen as I realized what was happening. Evan was dying.

I screamed.

Reality wrapped around me like a black shroud, strangling me. My breath scraped dryly as I placed both hands on Evan and prayed for a solution. I began to hyperventilate, my breathing erratic and rapid. I loved him. He couldn't die.

I pulled myself together and reached down into that dark part of myself, that part that would do anything for him. A picture-frame series of images flashed through my mind, like an old movie reel of Evan's life, but flickering in and out of focus.

I could see his mother, a paper-thin pathetic creature smoking at a kitchen table, staring out the window. His

~ ☾ ~

father's detached expression as he barked orders, and a young Stefano, who was holding a lit cigarette. Then finally, the remainders of his house a pile of black ash. Then I was forced out, and thrown backward from Evan's body.

It didn't work!

Evan's slack face stared at nothing, his eyes open and taking on a milky quality, as if he had cataracts. I leaned back and closed my eyes. *Please!*

"Sarah." I heard from a voice behind me. I turned around to come face to face with Sandra Crow in human form. I jerked away involuntarily. But her face seemed different now, the twisted grimace replaced with impassive, gentle eyes that shone in the natural lighting.

"I will help you," she said. I looked up, and behind her in the doorway, were Paulette and Ernie. They rushed in and over the vacant Skinwalker bodies toward us.

"It is okay, Sarah. Sandra has returned to us," Ernie said.

Sandra turned toward Evan and reviewed the scene: Stefano's corporeal body alongside Evan's, the other two Skinwalkers flaccid on the floor, and Evan's own body shuddering with the assault that was taking place within his skin. Sandra leapt out of her body, her spirit-self diving into Evan, her human form crumpling to the floor behind her with a soft thud.

The thought of what it felt like for Evan, with all of those souls inside of his body like that... If it had been me, I would have surely died. Would Evan survive Sandra's attempt at saving him? Could I even trust her?

I didn't have a choice.

The air pressure around me changed as all of the souls were violently expelled from Evan, like an internal combustion of volatile gasses. Sandra's form immediately returned to her body, but she lay limp on the floor.

~ ☾ ~

The sound of Evan's sharp intake of breath emerged as the diaphanous forms hovered about him, coiling like venomous snakes. Then Stefano's body reanimated.

Evan's eyes flew open, and immediately, his gaze found my face. "Sarah." He held his hand out to me, for a hand up. "We need to get out of here." He was right, and I knew it.

I knelt down to him and pulled him up, heaving him to standing. Our combined touch created a thin zap of combustible pressure into the air. The spirit forms of the other two Skinwalkers were blown backward and furled in the air like smoke in a strong wind. Stefano stood on the other side of the room, and while he wasn't overly affected by the air pressure, he knew he was next. He inched backward, and then he turned to run.

Evan and I focused our energy. In one sweeping motion, we unleashed a current that crashed around us like grenade combustion. A burst of energy emerged from him, this one like a tightly contained electrical current, and filled the room. The atmosphere changed once more, charged with the radiant, dark energy, the swirling air crackling and snapping around me. Voltage sizzled from our union.

We continued, the energy we were creating crackling and solidifying around me, creating a low rumble that started in my feet, moved up to my torso and then right through to my chest, like a bass guitar being thrummed within my own body. My heart stuttered.

The sound had reached a volume so thunderous that all sound was lost in the roar. Current twisted through me like a thousand volts of lightning, but then it stopped. I lost sensation in my extremities.

The concussion of the blast flung Stefano's body sideways into a sliding mirrored door in the front entrance that simultaneously burst. He hit the floor, his entire right side oozing blood, tiny shards of glass embedded into his arm, blood spreading on his clothing in a slow crimson stain.

One business-card sized fragment was embedded in his neck, and blood trickled between his splayed fingers. The other two Skinwalkers' spirit forms began to etch through the room like slithering snakes, away from Evan and me.

Evan's eyes flashed as he watched their retreat. Rage shadowed his face as the atmosphere began to shimmer, the pressure mounting, spiraling, until the air literally bowed, visible to the naked eye. A series of explosions thundered around us as drywall blasted apart. I ducked, but dust lodged in my throat and scratched my eyes.

The Skinwalkers shimmered, their vaporous form flickering in and out, until they evaporated entirely.

Bleeding profusely, Stefano leapt at Evan, knocking him sideways into the wall. A grinding crunch ripped through the air, followed by a yell. Evan toppled to the floor with Stefano on top of him, the glass shard a grotesque protuberance from his neck. Stefano placed his long, thin hands around Evan's neck, his nails digging into Evan's flesh, making the skin of his neck a livid red under the pressure.

I launched myself onto Stefano, wrapped my arms around his neck, and plunged my mind into his. My thoughts were assaulted with the fast-forwarding of images, foreign landscapes of lush greenery and towering foliage.

An angry father.

A disappointed mother.

Stefano playing with matches.

The fire.

Finally, the image of the charred and blackened corpse of his mother and father.

Afterward, a deep melancholy ripped through me as the image of a teenage Stefano, crying and alone in the forest, tumbled around my mind.

I took it all in. The experiences of his life became an all-encompassing black pain that spread like a malignancy within me, its black threads twining into each and every cell of my body.

I gasped. I had been plunged into an icy sea of tragedy, and the very core of my being trembled at the memory of his tortured life. I absorbed it like a sponge as Stefano lay limp from the experience. I began to shudder uncontrollably as Stefano's wilted form fell sideways, taking me with him.

Evan ran to my side with a horrified look. "Sarah? Are you okay?" He pulled me away from Stefano and up onto my feet.

"I'll be fine," I said. Evan's eyes flashed, but his attention was drawn back to Stefano, who lay unmoving on the floor. Evan stared at Stefano, *focusing*.

"Wait," I said. "Maybe he's healed."

"No, it's not possible. He's part demon now."

"Wait, Evan." I crouched down in front of Stefano.

Horror crept into Evan's voice. "What are you doing?"

"He's almost healed. Let me finish."

"No! He's—"

Stefano's eyes flicked open and he stood up, grabbing me and spinning me so that my arms were folded across my chest, rendering me immobile, like a straightjacket. He immediately sprang across the room, taking me with him, and then dragged me backward. Now I was his human shield.

Evan's eyes flashed as his hands clenched and unclenched at his sides. When I saw his arms rise and then lower, I knew he had no idea what to do.

"Let her go, Stefano," he said in a low growl. "Or you will beg for me to kill you."

"Evandro. Brother," Stefano whispered, his breath hot past my ear. "You're one of them." Acid dripped from the word, as if just uttering them turned his stomach.

Paulette and Ernie, knowing Evan was rendered useless, began their chant behind me, causing Stefano's body to immediately stiffen. I struggled against his arms, hoping I could take advantage of his motionlessness. My heart sank when he started to move once again, pulling me with him.

Stefano tightened his grip and led me, sideways, toward the front door. Evan began to move slowly toward him and kept his eyes locked on mine. Just seeing the way he looked so vulnerable and terrified made my heart turn to ice.

Stefano scuttled around Ernie and Paulette, their chanting loud and unsettling on either side of me. Why wasn't their chant working? Why didn't it stop him cold like at the hospital?

Once at the front door, he opened it and began to back the two of us out. I gave one violent yank, kicking and wrenching, and finally broke free of his hold, stopping him from dragging me through the doorframe. With one solid push to the middle of my back he flung me forward to the floor. My hands instinctively flew out to break my fall, my palms hitting the hardwood with a loud slap. Heat tore through my hands and up my arms. I turned my head to look up.

Stefano grabbed the triangular shard of glass that protruded from his neck and pulled it out, a torrent of gushing blood rushing behind it. Then with a flying leap, he hurtled toward Ernie and Paulette, knocking them to the floor. Their song ended abruptly as air was forcibly knocked out of their lungs. Ernie went tumbling to the side, but Paulette was directly beneath Stefano.

In response to this new threat, Evan lunged forward, but it wasn't fast enough. With an arcing motion, Stefano raised the shard of glass in the air and swiped

Paulette, directly across the throat. Screaming erupted as Paulette's terror rifled through me, like a searing knife.

Stefano jumped to his feet and whirled around just as Evan propelled himself through the air. He side-stepped, missing Evan's rapidly accelerating body. Evan hit the side wall with his shoulder and crumpling to the ground with a groan.

I lurched to my feet, scrambling to grasp at Stefano, but he pivoted on his feet, the motion sweeping me sideways. I staggered, landing beside Paulette. Twisting on the floor, I looked back just in time to see Stefano bolt through the front door and disappear from view.

Evan jumped over me in the doorway and tore out of the house, hot on Stefano's heels. I went to follow, but Ernie grabbed my arm and held me in place.

"No, Sarah. Let Evan go after the bad walker. Evan accepts the outcome of this battle." His wizened gaze cut right into me. Evan and Stefano's footfalls were long gone.

I turned to Paulette, her still, unmoving body on the floor. "Paulette," I moaned. My words came out in a warbled jumble. I started to cry.

Ernie nodded, his black hair flopping over his forehead. "She died with honor. She died protecting you, for the Creator."

"No... I... No!" I choked out. Tears streamed down my face as I pulled out of his grasp. I wriggled free and fell to my knees, leaning over Paulette. Mouth open, she seemed to be looking at me, but her eyes were unseeing. The cinnamon color of those eyes had taken on a murky tone, her skin whitish and waxen. Blood gushed from her neck, creating a brilliant crimson streak that puddled on the floor beneath her.

I felt like I'd lost a part of myself, like a hole had been gouged out in my chest and there was nothing but emptiness in its place.

I glanced up to Ernie and jumped at what I saw. Evan, his shadowed form backlit in the doorway, had returned. He looked down at me, eyes dark and shining.

"Stefano got away," he whispered. Then his eyes seemed to register what was beneath me, Paulette's unmoving form. His skin turned ashen. "Is she...?" He looked up at Ernie, who nodded.

"No," Evan whispered. "Oh God, no." Self-recrimination dripped from his words, his expression like a punctured balloon.

"Let's try to heal her," I said, my face wet with tears.

He ran to me, dropping to his knees alongside Paulette's body. We held hands and galvanized our energy before placing our palms on her chest. We channeled our energy into her body.

The sizzling began in the air around us, but then a strange sound began, like a low bubbling. Paulette's body began to move under our palms as the sound of combustible gases erupted from her corpse. We yanked our hands away.

"Stop," Ernie said. He stood at Paulette's feet, hovering over us and gazing down. "Paulette is gone. She is with the Creator."

The sound of my crying filled the house, the cries of horror, pain and regret. When my breathing finally settled and my diaphragm stopped spasming, I attempted to speak.

"I tried to heal him, Evan," I said. "I thought I could heal Stefano. I was so wrong." I choked on my words.

"I know. I'm sorry, Sarah." His eyes were red-rimmed. "Stefano is already part-demon. He can't be healed. It's too late for him."

"That's where you're wrong," said a female voice from behind Evan. We both turned. It was Sandra Crow, pulling herself to standing, her hand on the wall for stability. Once on her feet, she bent over like an old willow branch ready to snap.

Her expression was impassive; the snarling, feral look from earlier today was gone, replaced with a new, gentle expression. “I’ve been healed. You healed me, Indigo Child.” She began to walk toward us, and from the corner of my eye, I saw Evan stiffen.

“Don't come any closer!” His voice was a low rumble. She stopped dead in her tracks.

“Evan. She saved you from their attack,” I said. He stared at me and then at her. I turned to Sandra who was surveying the scene, regret filling her face.

She looked down at Paulette’s still form. “Another death that could have been prevented,” she whispered in a toneless voice. Then she turned back to face me, her chin quivering. “The curse has been lifted, Sarah. I don’t know how you did it, but it’s over.” She looked partially relieved, but her feelings of horror still bled into me, like a blossoming virus.

“My past, my memories, they don’t hurt me anymore. I’m immune to them now. She restored me to who I really am,” she said. “But I don’t believe my conscience will survive my guilt.” Her lips were pursed, the lines around her mouth heavily creased.

I stepped toward her, but Evan grabbed my arm, his grip tight and hard, squeezing my skin.

“Evan. It’s okay.” He looked at me, long and hard, before he finally let go. I held my hand out to Sandra and she placed her clammy palm in mine. Then, she collapsed at my feet, almost bringing me down with her. Squatting onto one knee, I turned her so she was facing me and held her hand.

“I’m sorry,” she whispered in a frail voice. “Forgive me.”

“I forgive you,” I said. Her warm breath on my cheek stopped and her eyes went instantly blank. Her hand became a dead weight in mine.

"Sandra?" I whispered, leaning over her and pressing my fingers to her neck. There was no pulse. Why did she die now? After helping Evan and fighting Stefano? After all of her work to make things right?

I looked at her face, melancholic even in death.

I inched away, easing Sandra's hand to the floor. I stood, measuring the wreckage around me—the broken glass, the splintered wood, the crumbled drywall.

Arms engulfed me, their strength like a security blanket. I turned to cling to Evan. He folded me into him, and I wrapped my arms around his wide shoulders, nuzzling my face into his chest.

Ernie began to sing, and this time, his song softened the raw edges of my pain. Even though she was no longer here, I could still hear Paulette's voice cut through the veil between the living and dead, clear as day.

When he was finished singing, Ernie stepped toward us. Our home looked like a tornado had just blasted through the middle of it. He looked at Evan intently, hidden truths contained behind those walnut-colored eyes.

"Come with me, young man," Ernie said to Evan, pointing to our living room. Evan nodded hollowly, and followed him, lowering himself onto the leather.

"I see it now. You are the Sapphire," Ernie said in his rich accent. Something flashed through Evan's eyes as he stared straight ahead, his gaze fixed on the shattered inner window panes. Ernie continued, slowly. "What was once hidden is now seen." He gestured toward me with a thin, crooked finger, the nails yellowed.

"I don't understand. How is it possible that all these years, I've been one of the very people I was hunting?" Evan said.

"Old, bad medicine. Your ancestors have been

perfecting their dark magic for many years, and your mother was well versed in it."

Evan cleared his throat repeatedly. "Do you think my mother knew and hid the truth from my father?" he asked. His voice sounded small, weak.

I squeezed his hand and nodded. "That's why she lied about the *caul*, and gave you the amulet. To protect you. To keep the truth hidden, so you would be safe."

Ernie turned to Evan. "Your mother lied to your father?"

Evan nodded, his Adam's apple bobbing in his throat, his mouth a pained frown.

Ernie looked Evan directly in the eye. "A mother's love is very powerful medicine. And love can transcend evil. There was good in her heart."

My chest felt like it just might explode as I watched Evan's reaction. His eyes began to shine, right before he leaned forward at the waist and his head dropped to his hands. His shoulders began to shake, his back heaving.

~ ☾ ~

CHAPTER THIRTY-ONE

Twenty minutes after Ernie called Amber and Noreen to give them the bad news about Paulette's death, Amber and Kate arrived at the house.

When she first arrived, Amber saw her mother's still form under a sheet, and she'd stared straight ahead, her back ram-rod straight, silent. Then tears began to form in her eyes, shimmering at first, and then trickling out. Now, her face was streaked red and black from mascara and rubbing away her tears.

"How can I live without her, Sarah? How?" Amber's voice closed off with tears.

"Amber," Ernie said, standing over us with drooping eyes. "Your mother fought for her people. She fought for Sarah. She fought for what was right." His words brought on a fresh wave of tears, her back wracking with sobs.

I placed my arm around her shoulders and pulled her into me.

"Why did this have to happen? Why?" She looked directly into my eyes then, her hazel gaze piercing. Accusation seeped from her into me, and I cringed at the sensation. Then she abruptly jerked her head toward Evan and glared.

"If it hadn't been for you! You and your *Malandanti* brother. If it hadn't been for you, she would still be here!"

Evan jumped, his eyes blinking as if he'd been slapped across the face. The tension in the air became nearly palpable.

~ ☾ ~

Evan's eyes cast downward. "I'm sorry, Amber. I'm so sorry."

Amber's eyes flashed, and a savage look came across them. "You're the one who should be dead. Not my mother."

Evan nodded in silence, gaze fixed on the floor. Every bone in his body emanated self-disgust.

Did she really think that? That Evan deserved to die? I imagined myself in her place, at the horror of losing my own mother, and my heart twisted at the thought.

Ernie stepped forward and lowered himself to one knee. He gathered Amber's hands into his own and set them atop his knee. "Evan is one of us now, Amber. He is as much a victim in this as your mother."

Her eyes narrowed. "What?"

Ernie went on to tell Amber about how Evan had been a Sapphire Child all along, and how his upbringing had kept it hidden from everyone, including him. "Your mother knew he was good, Amber. She knew he was worth fighting for. She always did what was right in the Creator's eyes. She stayed true to her beliefs until the end."

Amber's eyes shone as she listened, her expression wilting.

"I'm sorry Amber," Evan said, his eyes also shining. "I wish... I wish things were different. I wish I'd been able to protect her."

Amber looked down and bowed her head. Her knees rose back up, and she turned herself into a little ball, her arms obscuring her face. Kate stroked her back as I stroked her hair. She looked back up at Evan, her shoulders hunched, and then she looked directly at me.

Amber's gaze seemed to go right through me. "She gave up her life for you," she said.

My heart sped up as my ears pulsed. "I know."

*****

~ ☾ ~

Nothing would ever be the same again. I would never be the same again.

In the immediate aftermath, police were called, and we had to explain the scene within normal parameters of human abilities. With four people dead, one murdered, the others dead of unknown causes, and all of the blood and broken glass in Evan's house, we were immediately suspects. We were all transported to the police station and interviewed for over four hours, a camera recording our every word.

We found out later that while we were at the police station, Evan's house was a crime scene, where the Forensic unit took pictures and acquired samples of evidence, the Homicide unit there as well. Eventually, Jared, Violet, Sandra and Paulette's bodies were removed and taken to the morgue for autopsy to determine the cause of death.

Ernie's statement undoubtedly solidified our alibi, which we had rehearsed well before police were called. Both Ernie and I had witnessed the physical altercation between Evan and Stefano, our stories exactly the same, describing how the physical fight explained why the house was a mess. All three of us told police how Paulette had been trying to help Evan against Stefano's attack, and that it put her in harm's way, which resulted in Stefano retaliating and killing her.

None of us knew why Sandra died, other than the weight of her own guilt combined with witnessing Paulette's murder, which could have possibly caused her own major health incident.

More concerning was the death of Violet and Jared. With that final blast of compressed energy, their spirit forms had disappeared, their corporeal bodies left behind, uninhabited. Did this count as a murder? Would Evan's soul be in jeopardy?

Then there was the whole hospital situation; four

people in comas, their vitals rapidly worsening, and a patient missing. Me. I told them I left because I felt better, and that was the end of it. They didn't mention Stefano, Sandra, or the other Skinwalkers, and I didn't bring it up.

Fortunately for me, a coma isn't something the police investigate, especially since they couldn't link the comas to anything suspicious at the scene. As far as I was concerned, the less supernatural explanation needed the better. I certainly didn't want to end up in a straightjacket.

The interview process was painful. They grilled me about the two situations for hours, asking the same question in as many different ways as possible.

"You never saw the people who had collapsed?"

"Why wouldn't you go through the official process of discharge?"

By the end, I had a headache with the effort of trying to keep my story consistent.

Evan was questioned longer than the rest of us, but with Ernie's and my witness statements corroborating Evan's, there wasn't enough evidence to hold him. They let Evan go with explicit instructions to not leave town.

We didn't listen. Instead, we fled Evan's home, living in hotel rooms and only having contact with Amber and Kate through cellular phones, living a nomadic life out of our suitcases, homeless and anchorless.

We weren't about to risk being found easily and couldn't risk staying with my family or friends in Slave Lake for fear of leading Skinwalkers directly to them. And despite all of the evidence that would lead us to think Stefano had likely bled to death, I would never really relax until I saw a body. And that probably wasn't going to happen.

Finally, we came to settle in Washington State. A lovely small city called Oak Harbor that was completely surrounded by water. Why Oak Harbor? I couldn't really say. All I know is that the day I arrived in that town, I couldn't run anymore. So we didn't.

In the last few hours before we left, Amber had said she'd forgiven me, but I could feel the coolness emanate from every fiber of her being, the way she stiffened when I was around, the way she averted her gaze whenever she saw Evan, and the way I was overcome with a shroud of dark melancholy every time I allowed her feelings to wash over me.

Not that I could blame her. It made my own heart ache whenever I thought of Paulette, so brave and vibrant, even in those last moments before her death. I loved her like my own mother, and just the image of her smiling face, her russet-colored eyes was enough to make my own eyes sting.

The scent of that day haunted my nightmares, and I would wake up screaming with the smell of pain and drywall dust lingering at the edge of my consciousness. I would never be able to forgive myself for having been responsible for her involvement.

Because in the end, the entire mess had centered on me, me and my Indigo aura. My own survival had meant her death, and forever, that burden would weigh on me.

I had Evan now. Evan, my love, my Indigo counterpart, but with his love came the ever-present threat that lurked in the background.

Would Stefano or the other Skinwalkers find us again? Would we ever be free?

Evan was worried about me. He could see in my eyes and in my expression that I was in pain, and he did whatever he could think of to ease my burden. He kissed me often, listened when I needed to cry, and always, always held me when I just couldn't hold it together any longer. He was my rock.

At night, I clung to him. Too many nights I'd woken

~ ☾ ~

up screaming, with the vision of Paulette, bleeding and staring at me, blank-eyed. He did his best to reassure me, but I wondered if deep down, he really believed his own words.

One evening, we lay together in the bedroom of our tiny, one-bedroom apartment, arms and legs entwined, holding onto each other. It was only when the tears finally stopped flowing that I found my voice again.

I nuzzled into him even further. Evan was looking up at the ceiling, his eyes unfocused. "I bet you healed me. I bet you did it before you even knew what you were doing," he said with a hitch in his voice.

He had a point. In the beginning, he had wanted to consume my Indigo soul as much as Stefano, but very early on, he'd abandoned his original goal, side-tracked. Maybe it hadn't been just love. I wasn't sure whether this was a good realization or bad.

"Remember the day, at the lake? The first time we saw each other after the Skinwalker incident in the old house?" he asked. I nodded. "I'll never forget that day. That day, my real life started. I felt like I'd never truly seen another human being before that moment, like I'd only ever seen fuzzy, indistinct faces behind a lens of detachment. Up until that point, I'd lost everything, my parents to the fire, and my brother to his all-consuming desire for power. All I knew was the power-hungry evil, the greed. But the moment I saw you, touched you, it was like you were crystal clear in my vision. It was that moment that I knew."

"Knew what?" I asked, my chest heavy.

"I knew I'd met the woman I was meant to be with. Forever," he said, his eyes leveled on mine.

At that moment, I felt like my mind finally solidified once again after weeks of being scattered, as if I'd finally had confirmation that the world really was round.

Evan continued. "I remember my mind racing, my

thoughts desperately searching for a way out of my miserable existence with Stefano, destroying people, using them." He paused. "I wanted out. And God, how I wanted you." He spoke with a finality that made my heart sing and every cell in my body soften. "I still remember, plain as day, something happening to me that day at your store." He looked at me with an expression of complete openness. "Something inside me changed. Like a switch was flipped."

I was immediately hit with the recollection of that moment when I'd touched the brand on the back of his hand, when Evan's eyes rolled back in his head and that strange click emerged from his mouth. Was it possible? Did I heal him that day, without even knowing what I was doing?

"The more I think about it, the more I'm convinced it's true," he said, his fingers stroking my back. "I think you healed me that day."

"Are you sure you want to give me all the credit for the change? Maybe you had something to do with it," I said. I gazed up into his brilliant blue eyes, and for a moment, felt completely at ease.

"I doubt it. I don't remember anything but pain and anger before." He paused to kiss my nose. "And now everything has changed." Next, he kissed my chin.

I smiled. "Okay. You're welcome, I guess?" Then I kissed him back, this time on the lips.

"I have the girl of my dreams and a hope for a normal life." He stroked a stray hair from across my face and tucked it behind my ear, looking at me with such reverence my heart rattled against my ribs and my chest tightened.

"The girl of your dreams? Really?" I asked, nearly breathless.

His face scrunched up and he quirked his brow. "Are you kidding? Every time I look at you I feel like I have to pinch myself. But I don't want to, because I'm afraid that when I wake up, my life will be back to that awful time, and it will all have been a dream, a beautiful dream, never to be realized."

The tightening sensation spread within my chest. "Shh. You're going to make me start crying."

"I love you more than life itself, Sarah Ross," he said with the most heartbreaking crack in his voice. "Every time I thought I'd lost you—that moment you jumped off the bridge, the Skinwalker attack at the house—I wanted to die, too. Because without you, I don't think I could survive."

Just looking at him caused hectic tears to spring to my eyes and my breath to catch in my throat. "I don't know what to say." A single tear slid down my cheek.

"Tell me you love me, too," Evan said, wiping away my tear and blinking back his own.

"I love you, too."

He kissed me then, a kiss so deep and so intense it took my breath away. I felt like I was floating, and I never wanted to come down.

"As long as I have you, Sarah, I have everything I've ever wanted."

~ ☾ ~

ACKNOWLEDGEMENTS

I would like to thank the following individuals:
My husband, Darren, for his encouragement, patience and steadfast support; Elizabeth and Alec for their unwavering confidence in me; my parents, Lyle and Lynne, for a lifetime of guidance; Wanita, for sharing her Skinwalker experience; and Hayley E. Lavik, Karyn Good and Kat Aubrey, for helping to pull this manuscript out of the slush pile.

A special thank you to:
my editor, Nancy S. Brandt, whose brilliant editing and dauntless dedication to making this the best story possible, was invaluable; Lin Browne, whose attention to detail is unsurpassed; Sherry Soule, for turning my dream into a reality; and the fabulous people at Crescent Moon Press for their willingness to take a leap of faith.

Joanne Brothwell

JOANNE BROTHWELL lives in the country on the Canadian prairie with her family where her stories are inspired by the dead things that appear at her doorstep on a daily basis. You can find her online at www.joannebrothwell.com

CPSIA information can be obtained at www.ICGtesting.com
Printed in the USA
BVOW071242060812

297167BV00001B/57/P

9 781937 254315